Praise

"Powerful yet sensiti...
– **Sunita Khaund Bhuyan, Violinist
and Leadership Practitioner**

"A fresh, exceptional and very moving perspective....
absolutely fabulous ... totally gripping"
– **Sanjeev Srivastav, Journalist and Book Professional**

"Brings alive a forgotten piece of history and entwines it superbly with the turbulence of the times that unsettles ordinary people's lives"
– **Govind Bhattacharjee, author, academic
and former civil servant**

"Extraordinary .... original in its conceptualization, powerful in its characterization, this is a novel that touches the innermost recesses of one's heart"
– **Dhruba Hazarika, author and former Civil Service Officer**

"A gripping account, a moving story of human identity and dignity"
– **Professor Srikanth Kondapalli,
Professor, Jawaharlal Nehru University, New Delhi**

"On the meanings of home and belonging. ... everyone's timeless story .... with great insight and finesse, leaves an indelible mark as a testament of our times"
– **Professor Malashri Lal, doyenne of Indian literary critics,
and member of General Council of the Sahitya Akademi,
the Indian National Academy of Letters**

"A heart wrenching story which keeps the reader interested and absorbed throughout"
– **Jishnu Baruah IAS, Chief Secretary, Assam**

An
UNFINISHED
SEARCH

*One Lineage,
in One Village,
through Three Nations*

Rashmi Narzary

Pippa Rann
books & media

An imprint of
Salt Desert Media Group Limited,
7 Mulgrave Chambers, 26 Mulgrave Rd,
Sutton SM2 6LE, England, UK.
Email: publisher@pipparannbooks.com
Website: www.pipparannbooks.com

Copyright © Rashmi Narzary 2023

The moral right of the author has been asserted. The views and opinions expressed in this book are the author's own and the facts are as reported by her, which have been verified to the extent possible, but the publishers are not in any way liable for the same.

All rights reserved. No part of this book may be reproduced by any mechanical, photographic, or electronic process, or in the form of a phonographic recording; nor may it be stored in a retrieval system, transmitted or otherwise be copied for public or private use – other than for 'fair use' as brief quotations embodied in articles and reviews, without prior written permission of the publisher.

ISBN 978-1-913738-06-8

Designed by Raghav Khattar

Printed and bound in India by Replika Press Pvt. Ltd.

To

All whom war
or national partition
has left rootless, separated, or identityless

Contents

Glossary — 9
Prologue — 11

1. The Year Twenty Seventeen — 15
2. The Year Eighteen Fifty-Seven — 29
3. The Year Eighteen Sixty-Three — 39
4. The Late Eighteen Sixties — 57
5. The Year Eighteen Seventy-Three — 71
6. The Year Eighteen Seventy-Four — 87
7. The Year Eighteen Seventy-Seven — 99
8. The Year Eighteen Eighty — 117
9. The Year Eighteen Ninety-Seven — 137
10. The Year Nineteen Fourteen — 155
11. The Year Nineteen Sixteen — 171
12. The Year Nineteen Thirty-Two — 203
13. The Year Nineteen Forty-Three — 227
14. The Year Nineteen Forty-Seven — 245
15. The Year Nineteen Fifty — 259
16. The Year Nineteen Seventy-One — 271
17. The Year Two Thousand — 289
18. The Year Twenty Seventeen — 305

Epilogue — 311

Glossary

*P*lease note that the expression "**La ilaha Illallah Muhammadur Rasulullah**" is usually interpreted as "I bear witness that there is no deity but Allah, and I bear witness that Muhammad is the messenger of Allah"

1. **Bhai phota**: A ritual that celebrates the bond between brothers and sisters
2. **Gosht**: Meat
3. **Haat**: Market held in rural areas, generally on a regular basis
4. **Hakim**: Physician practicing traditional means of treatment
5. **Huzur**: A title of respect
6. **Jhumar tikka**: Jewellery worn on either side of the head, on the hair
7. **Jumuah**: Friday Prayer or Congregational prayer of Moslems
8. **Khuda na Khwasta**: God forbid

9. **Maafi/Mwaafi:** Pardon
10. **Mashi-ma:** Aunt
11. **Nikaah:** Marriage, in Islam
12. **Qazi:** Islamic Judge/Legal Scholar
13. **Rehem:** Mercy
14. **Shehzada:** Prince
15. **Touba:** A strong exclamation to shun a sin, from which the word "taboo" is derived.

Prologue

For all those who have never been to Malegarh, now in Karimganj, Assam, India, the Border Security Force and the Bangladesh Border Guards had agreed to bend the fence there just about so much as to not let the actual site of the Malegarh battle lie on a no man's land.

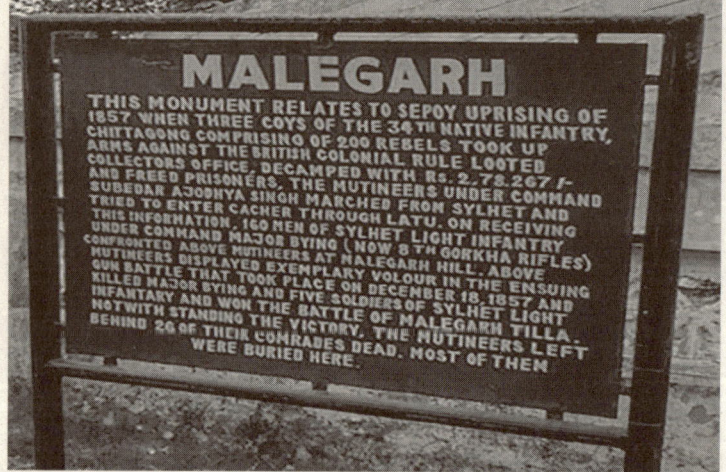

. . . Up those steps, inside the Malegarh War Memorial

... and somewhere here rests a martyr who was said to be known only as Aryaan. No surname, no family name. Somewhere here he rests, if at all ...

1
The Year Twenty Seventeen

Malegarh War Memorial

'No, Asman, not today. Not now!'

A shadow fell on Asman Hazratkandi's wrinkled face as the Border Security Force soldier stopped him at a distance from the dusty, ungravelled approach path that led to the hillock ahead. Asman Hazratkandi got off his bicycle and adjusted the long white kurta that he wore over a blue and yellow chequered lungi.

'But I had tended to those graves, huzur, I planted the flowers around them, and I pulled out the weed and grass along the sidewalks. So that the martyrs there may lie in peace. I tended to each one of those graves, like each had my grandfather's abbajaan resting there, I don't know in which. So, I tended to each. Please, huzur, let me in!' he pleaded.

It pained the soldier to see the eighty-five-year-old man begging him thus to let him in. Asman

Hazratkandi would be about his grandfather's age. Or even older.

'Please, Asman,' the soldier said, placing an apologetic hand on Asman's stooping shoulder, 'not today. The ministers will be here any moment.'

'Yes, I know,' Asman replied, 'and it is them, at least one of them, that I need to please ask...'

'But they won't be alone. They will be surrounded by lots of people, Asman, all very important people. Senior officials, bureaucrats, police, political leaders, so many of them. From both India and Bangladesh. You won't even be allowed anywhere near the ministers, let alone speak to them or ask something,' the soldier tried to dissuade Asman.

Asman Hazratkandi thought for a while and then asked again, 'Then can't I even be allowed to speak to anyone of those big officers, huzur? Someone? Anyone, please?' Asman looked at the hillock ahead. The otherwise tranquil Malegarh hillock, that gave those lying there in eternal slumber all the solitude they ever needed, wore a festive look today. The place was teeming with Border Security Force personnel, State police officers of Assam and personnel from all ranks of the Indian Army. Because the hillock was on the outskirts of the town of Karimganj, lots of people from the nearby villages too had gathered to see what was unfolding. These were people from both sides of the Indo-Bangladesh International Border at Sutarkandi. Some came to have a look at the ministers;

some came all dressed up and ready to appear on television because they heard that the media would be there to ask random questions to random people about the Malegarh Monument. Some stopped just as they were passing that way. For whatever reason, the place was crowded, and the lone narrow road was getting congested. Up on the hillock, where Asman Hazratkandi's grandfather's father lay, organizers had put up garlands of fresh, bright yellow marigold on the black granite plaque that read,

> **In the memory of those who sacrificed their lives**
> **In the great Mutiny of 1857,**
> **For the freedom of the Country**

Asman Hazratkandi, however, could only read the Bengali translation of these words, written above the English words. He forgot count of how many times he read those words, the ones written in Bengali, running his fingers over them. On those occasions, he had unrestrained entry into the site of the monument. He had guarded the monument from stray goats and miscreants, had warded off boys and men who came in with boards of dice and bottles of rum to sit in the solitude there. He had guarded this monument like it was his family's heritage. But today, guards stopped him from entering.

Asman Hazratkandi pushed his cycle slowly across the road towards the narrow patch of grass that grew all alongside the road. His cycle didn't have a stand. So he put it gently down on the grass as if putting a child to sleep. Because his were hands that tended to graves, and grew flowers around them, they were always gentle with everything, living or not. He sat down on the grass next to his cycle and watched the preparations for the celebrations at the Malegarh hillock. The hillock which had the answer to the one question that stayed with him, unanswered till today, since that first time when his grandfather Anjaan Hazratkandi brought him to see the graveyard. Asman was then around fifteen years of age. But he remembered well. All that his grandfather had said. He recollected his grandfather's eyes and the way his voice choked often during their conversation that day at the hillock.

The soldier from the Border Security Force too had been slowly walking up and down the road keeping a watch. He now walked up to Asman and stood near him.

'You know, huzur,' Asman Hazratkandi found courage to talk, 'it was in the year 1947 that I first came here. With my dadajaan. My grandfather. See that plaque there?' he said, gesturing towards the garlanded plaque. The soldier turned to look but the view was obstructed by all the people around it. 'That plaque was not there at that time,' Asman went on, 'the grave slabs too were not here. But the memorial was. There was no boundary wall, no, nothing much of a monument. Even that blue board, you see huzur? With the story of the valiant Malegarh martyrs? No, even that wasn't there. Very few people knew about the significance of this place then. Even I didn't think much of it those days. But my dadajaan did. Because he was in search of his father. His father's name. He was in search of freedom of a different kind, huzur, he was in search of freedom from being without an identity.' Asman ran a hand down his grey beard as he looked up at the skies. 'You know what dadajaan had said to me that day, huzur, standing there on the hillock?'

'What did he say?' the soldier asked.

'He said,

Asman, now on, where we have been living is no longer India. It is now Pakistan.

And, huzur, I asked him if we would have to move away to some other place, if we were shifting house. Then dadajaan had said,

No Asman, we will remain where we are. It is only the nations that have come and gone by us. Our address has changed. Not by a street, a village, or a district. But by a country! By a country, Asman, by a whole country, even though we remain just where we are. The same skies above us, the same ground we walk on, the same Dooni streamlet that shall continue to flow into the Sonai river that meanders through the land, Asman, the same village of Hazratkandi, the same district of Sylhet. Yet, it will be a different land. A different country....'

Asman Hazratkandi thought for a while before speaking again, 'I remember my dadajaan's voice choking when he said all of that, huzur, he had a lump in his throat which he didn't want me to see and had a bigger burden on his chest. But I saw both the lump and the burden. As the nations changed again and again, that lump, and that burden started to grow on me.'

'How old was your grandfather then, Asman?' the soldier asked.

Asman looked at the far horizon and stared at it for a while. As if recollecting. Or calculating the years. Then looking up at the soldier, he said, 'How many years would that be, huzur, if he was born in the year of the mutiny?'

The soldier thought and said, 'Mutiny...eighteen fifty-seven ...Wow! That would be ninety years! He lived well, Asman, your grandfather lived well!'

'But not long after that visit to these graves. He passed away soon after,' Asman replied.

'Oh! And did you come to these graves again soon after he passed away? After your grandfather?' the soldier asked. He was starting to find it all very intriguing.

'I did. With my abbajaan a couple of times. We would just walk around here and rake in the fallen leaves in winter and pile them in a corner and burn them. ammajaan had once sent a few saplings of the gulmohar with us, and we planted them among the graves and along the periphery of the site.' He paused. As if wondering if the soldier still had any interest in listening. It seemed he had.

'Didn't stray goats and cows eat up the saplings?' the soldier asked, curious.

Encouraged, Asman Hazratkandi went on, 'Abbajaan brought fine, thin sticks of bamboo from home with him and made fences with them around the saplings. Then he started to visit this place once every day because the saplings had to be watered. He brought a bucket with him and in it fetched water from the ponds over there to water the plants. Once the roots grew steady, they no longer needed watering everyday. But it had become a habit with abbajaan to tend to them. He sometimes collected cowdung from the fields nearby and sprinkled them around the base of the plants.'

A child was running towards the approach lane and the soldier hurried across the road to turn him away. He stood near the lane for a while and then once more crossed over to Asman.

'So, your father too used to tend to the graves?' he asked Asman.

'It started from those saplings ammajaan had sent. Yes. Once the plants were on their own, abbajaan, by habit, started pulling out the weeds. Then one thing led to another, and he started to plant flowers in the whole graveyard. Huzur, actually, it was my dadajaan who used to tend to these graves. Then when age caught up and his fingers started shaking and his hands no longer obeyed him, he stopped coming here. He had to. Because even if he wished to, he couldn't. No, no more.'

'So, it was then that you took over? He asked you to?'

Only then, faced with that question, did Asman Hazratkandi realize that nobody had asked him to tend to these graves of the martyrs. He was simply drawn to them. To tend them. Very lovingly. Very possessively. As one would his identity.

'No, huzur, nobody asked me to. It just came to me,' Asman replied.

The soldier suddenly heard a commotion and had to walk away, towards a group of young men and women alighting from a van equipped for livetelecast of the proceedings at the function. Their equipments were the cause of some fuss with the security personnel and the reporters had some issues walking through the metal detector placed at the bottom of the steps, at the entrance to the monument. The soldier from the Border Security Force walked in to help his fellow guards. Once the matter was settled, the soldier looked for an opportunity and slowly, though alert and never neglecting his duty, walked up once more to Asman.

'When will they arrive, huzur? The ministers?' Asman Hazratkandi asked him.

'I don't know, Asman, I wasn't informed about that. I am only to guard the place and see that everything is safe for the VIPs and the people gathering here. This place, the Sutarkandi border area, has always been a matter of immense security concern, being an international border area. There has been a lot of illegal border crossing, of both human and cattle,' the soldier took pride in his superiority of knowledge about international affairs, even though it was confined to the Indo-Bangladesh International border at Sutarkandi. But he wondered how the old, grave-tending Asman Hazratkandi would find that out.

'I have known Sutarkandi since the times when it was just one land, huzur,' Asman said, 'then I saw the land being split from one to two, and now here I am, living long enough to see one part of that split land,' Asman raised a hand motioning towards Sylhet in Bangladesh, 'first made a part of one nation, then detaching itself to be on its own. Huzur, I was born on that land. Since then I have been staying on the same land which was once known as India, then came to be called Pakistan. East Pakistan. And now it is Bangladesh. But it remains the same land. Isn't that strange, huzur?' And Asman Hazratkandi himself answered that question, 'Yes. It truly is. That some stretch of land should go through such phenomenal change of address, despite being rooted just where it had always been. And here I am, one man who has lived through it all and seen all of it change. By just remaining there, at that same place, growing old where I was born. Being rooted, yet I know not about my own roots, huzur. Earlier when I used to come here with my dadajaan and then with my abbajaan, I didn't have to write my name on the register at the Sutarkandi Border Security Outpost. I didn't have to write anything while crossing back as well. But now I have to. At the crossing, under that imposing, green board made to stand tall enough to cut into the skies, to separate it into the Indian sky and the sky of Bangladesh.'

He stopped and looked at the chaotic activity that was increasing around him all this while. The reporters were done fixing up their cameras and microphones and were taking test shots. Frantic, last-minute arrangements and orders were barked into mobile phones. A red carpet was rolled out from the gate right upto where the granite plaque was. Candles and earthen lamps were being readied to be lit along the boundary walls, the steps and on the tombstones after sundown. Asman Hazratkandi sat on the grass and watched. Then he suddenly asked the soldier, 'Do you know who might have a list of all the martyrs lying there?' He didn't expect an answer though. Both Asman Hazratkandi and the soldier fell silent. But their silence was drowned in the din around them.

'Come now, Asman, get up,' the soldier at last said, very gently. 'Pick up your cycle and go watch the celebrations from a distance.'

Asman took his gaze towards the hillock but remained sitting on the grass. The officials and people around the plaque were getting the Indian Tricolour ready to be hoisted. A group of children, neatly dressed in their school uniform, were standing in a row next to the plaque. Maybe, Asman Hazratkandi thought, they would sing the Indian national anthem. He too knew it. On the blue board that stood just outside the monument, was written in white letters, about the twenty-six Indian sepoys of the 34th. Regiment Bengal Native Infantry, more popularly called 34 BNI, who lay their lives at the village of Latu in the district of Karimganj, Assam, giving a tough battle to the British under Major R.P.V.Byng, who was then the commander of the 11th. Sylhet Local Battalion. Major Byng and five members of his troop had also lost their lives in that battle. Thus was written on the blue board, but Asman couldn't read it. It was written in English. But he anyway knew the story all too well.

'Asman,' the soldier asked, 'Then you surely know of the Sepoy Mutiny of 1857. Today they are observing here the one hundred and sixtieth anniversary of that first war of India's Independence. It seems it was the martyrs lying there who brought the war of independence to these parts of the country. You must be feeling so proud, Asman, that your grandfather's abba was one of those bravehearts.'

Asman suddenly turned towards the soldier and asked abruptly, 'What is your name, huzur?' And then as an embarrassed afterthought, added, 'Mwaafi, huzur, forgive my audacity to ask, but...'

'Come on, Asman, no problem,' he said, 'Jaising Hmar. I am Jaising Hmar.'

'Hmar,' Asman repeated softly under his breath.

Then he again looked at the soldier whom he only now came to know as Jaising Hmar after talking to him for all this while, and asked, 'Hmar...that is your family name?'

'Yes, Asman, my family name. It is the name of the clan to which I belong. My father, my grandfather, his father and forefathers, we all are Hmars. We hail from Mizoram.'

Asman Hazratkandi gave a sad, heart wrenching smile that further deepened the furrows between his wrinkles.

'But I don't know mine, huzur, I don't know my family name. I don't know what clan I belong to. Nor did my abbajaan and my dadajaan know.'

Jaising Hmar felt a pang of sadness and compassion fill his heart for the old man squatting on the grass in front of him, alone even in the midst of a gathering crowd from two nations, not knowing where he belonged. Fate and decisions of people in higher echelons, who didn't even know of Asman's existence, had made a mockery of his identity.

'So you are Asman......?' Jaising Hmar let his question trail away.

'I am Asman Hazratkandi,' he replied unfeelingly, 'Hazratkandi is the name of the village where I live.'

He paused.

'But huzur,' he resumed, my grandfather had said that he didn't even know if we even belonged to Hazratkandi.'

A flurry of activities began along the road. Sniffer dogs were once more hurriedly led up the steps towards the monument. Police sirens shrieked at a distance and dazzling, large MUVs with beacons glowing atop them appeared at the horizon, chaperoned between pilot and escort vehicles. This carcade itself was the centre of attraction for so many villagers who had gathered there.

'Asman!' Jaising Hmar's voice suddenly had an urgency in it, 'you'll have to go now!'

Asman Hazratkandi picked his cycle and stood up. He didn't leave though.

'But huzur, I need to just ask someone this one thing. Just one. If they can help me find out the names of the martyrs lying there. Please, huzur, please. I seek to know my family name...'

'I'm sorry Asman,' and out of compulsion Jaising Hmar had to almost shove the old man aside.

Frail and old that he was, Asman Hazratkandi felt his limbs giving way and he staggered to one side and dropped on the grass. He felt as if a cloak of mist had suddenly enveloped the whole hillock. Through that mist he faintly heard someone's voice, a voice that seemed to have come from a great distance away, saying again and again, 'No Asman, not today! Not now!' But as the voice receded into the mist, it also took away with it Asman's senses.

2
The Year Eighteen Fifty-Seven

The hour before sunrise during mid December is a cold one in the small village of Hazratkandi, in Sylhet, East Bengal, India.

A thick fog hung over the Dooni whose waters had now dried down to a mere trickle. Wide patches of white saccharum rose like candy floss on the sandbanks near the waters but the fog hid them from view. Some distance away in the middle of the fields, now harvested and with the stumps of paddy pricking out from the earth like witchs' claws, in a small thatch hut, Najma woke up earlier than usual. It was still dark inside, so she lit the kerosene lantern. Pulling the free end of her saree over her shoulders like a shawl, she woke her husband Habib as quietly as she could.

'Get up!' she whispered. She took care not to wake Rafiq in that same room. Her tone was hushed but there was urgency in it. And strangely, no panic.

Najma had always been thus - quick and steady of decision. She didn't know how to read or write, yet there was wisdom in her decisions. Habib always respected them. Despite her small stature, she was big in her confidence. Najma softly walked up to Rafiq's bed and looked at him through the mosquito net to make sure he wasn't disturbed. Rafiq was the son of a poor, distant relative. Najma and Habib took him in since he was about six years old, in the hope of having someone to take care of them in their old age. 'This girl will give birth any moment now,' she told her husband, motioning with her head towards the adjoining room.

'So, uh...?' Habib was still in a daze.

'So, hurry!' Najma held him by the arm and rushed him towards the door, handing him a shawl as they went, 'Go!' she said, 'Go fetch Sahina and her mother-in-law!'

'But it's dark outside,' Habib said, opening the door and looking out into the foggy, pre-dawn darkness. The chill wind from the open fields rushed into the house through the door as soon as it was thrown open and Habib shivered.

'It's cold too,' he said halting at the doorway, turning to look at his bed.

'Drape that shawl. Quick. Don't waste time. As for the darkness, it won't remain for too long,' she replied sharply.

Habib turned and looked at the lantern inside the house.

'I'll need that. There's only one in the house,' she said, almost pushing Habib out. 'Now go! Hurry!' she said as she shut the door and went about making necessary arrangements before Sahina and her mother-in-law arrived. Starting a fire that early in the morning took time during the cold months when the firewood was always damp from dew on them. But she had to start one now to put the pot of water on the fire. She would need hot water. She readied old, clean clothes and a piece of sharp straw carefully picked from among the paddy stumps in the evening before. This, Sahina's mother-in-law would need to cut the umbilical cord. Because Najma was getting ready for the birth of a child in her house. She and Habib had none. And all along, the moans and groans from the girl in the other room punctuated the silence of the house.

Soon the groans started getting louder. Rafiq, all of thirteen years now, turned on the bed. The moans were reaching him.

Back in the girl's room, Najma asked her, 'At least tell me your name.'

Since Habib and Najma brought the girl home the day before, she had neither spoken a word nor eaten a morsel. Habib and Najma were returning from the weekly market at Sutarkandi late that afternoon when they saw this girl, about to drop herself into the Sonai river, in an attempt to drown herself. She was heavy with child. The very instant Najma saw the distraught girl, she understood that it was a pregnancy gone all wrong. There she was, Najma Rahman, married to a doting husband for more than two decades now, still waiting and longing to bear a child of her own. And here was this youthful girl, carrying a love child she was loathe to give birth to. A crowd had gathered around the girl. Some tried to pull her down from the rickety bamboo railing of the narrow bridge but the girl scratched and tore at their clothes as she kept pulling herself away to drop into the waters below. Some pleaded with her, others shouted. But the girl seemed oblivious to her surrounding, so hollow that she felt about everything around her and within her, despite the heaviness in her womb. Najma elbowed her way through the people and startling everyone there, gave a sharp slap to the girl. She swayed and fell back towards the people but Najma quickly and lovingly cradled her in her arms. Then searching for Habib in that crowd, said, 'I'm taking her home.'

And now, lying in the small house of the childless couple Najma and Habib, writhing in an agony that wrapped her entire being, that very girl was about to give birth. Her moans were rising.

Najma wiped away the drops of perspiration on her forehead.

'What made you take this step?' she asked her.

The girl only turned her head the other way, towards the wall. Her moans came in more rapidly and now there were small spurts of cries as well in between the moans.

'Let me at least know your name,' Najma paused, then added, 'before the other women arrive.'

The girl now turned to look at Najma with a trace of suspicion in her eyes.

Thinking that the girl got alarmed at the mention of other women, Najma added as an afterthought, '.... to assist me in delivering the child. Your child.' Najma turned to look once towards the door.

'What will I tell your child when it grows up and asks me?' Najma persisted, to try and know something, whatever, from her. About her.

A fresh trickle of tear ran down the outer corner of her eye and flowed into her dishevelled hair. In the soft light of the lantern, Najma noticed how pale the girl looked. As if the last bit of colour from her face had drained out with that tear. Her limbs were otherwise lissom, and she seemed tall as compared with Najma's own smallness. She wouldn't be more than twenty-two, Najma thought. Najma's assumptions were usually right. But this once, she was never to know whether she was right.

'Well then, I promise that your secret will stay with me,' Najma said, clasping the girl's hand. And Najma meant it. 'Not even your child shall know your name, if that should be so.' She felt the girl's feeble fingers clasping back in response.

'Karishma,' she replied softly, her lips barely parting.

Both women fell silent.

The thought that came to Najma's mind was that the name gave away neither her faith, nor her village.

'What else am I to know if someone from your family, or the child's father's family come looking for it?' Najma asked.

Karishma looked up at the roof, but she didn't see the bamboo rafters that supported the thatched roof of the house. A pale glow was starting to grope its way through the small breaks in the thatch. The girl looked at all of that. But she didn't see any of it. Her gaze went out through the thatch. She would say no more. Time was running out, and Najma turned to look towards the door. Habib should have arrived by then with Sahina and her mother-in-law. It was also time for his namaz. Just then she heard a knock at the door. Najma walked with hurried steps to open the door and was relieved to see the women. Sahina's husband Aslam too had accompanied them to Najma and Habib's house. Najma left the menfolk in the outer room where Habib and Rafiq slept and hurriedly ushered the women to Karishma. They knew the urgency of a moment such as this. Sahina and her mother-in-law had together assisted almost all the births around there for some time now.

'It's time for the birth alright, but the baby is not yet of full term. This is premature,' the old lady said the moment she laid a hand on Karishma.

In the next room, the men sat silent for a while.

'You heard about the battle at Malegarh?' Aslam asked Habib to distract himself from the noises coming from the inner room.

'Oh? Malegarh, at Latu? When was that?' Habib asked.

'Some four days back. On the eighteenth.'

Habib nodded.

'Which regiment?' he asked after a pause. Every conscious, adult Indian was now taking more and more interest in the war of independence.

'Bradshaw ka Paltan, so Qazi said. Some 200 rebels, or so he heard.'

Around those times, names that sepoys used more commonly for regiments, after their founders, had also spread among the local villagers, and thus the 34 BNI came to be popularly known as Bradshaw Ka Paltan.

'Our loss?' Habib asked.

'About twenty-six.'

'Their's?' Habib's whispers were growing louder in his excitement.

'Maybe around five. And the Commander too. Someone called Byng.'

'Aamin!' Habib said looking up, his voice once again a soft whisper.

In the other room, fatigue of both body and mind was overpowering Karishma.

'One thrust, child, come! You'll be able to. For the sake of your love,' the old lady egged her on, 'one more heave, dear!' Karishma's hands gripped the sides of the bed and her nails dug into the mattress with all the strength left in her. The hands and forehead broke into a sweat while her feet were getting cold. She was trying… but would not be able to try for too long. She was totally exhausted.

'Yes, child, yes,' Sahina's mother-in-law said as she gently pressed the baby downwards. Then with one final thrust, Karishma screamed, 'Aryaan!'

Just then they heard the muezzin's call floating out from the mosque at their village, at Najma and Habib's village. Hazratkandi. And that December dawn, the muezzin's call absorbed in it the wails of a newborn in the house of Najma and Habib Rahman, in Hazratkandi village of Sylhet, India. In one room of that house, Habib and Aslam bowed towards the west in prayer while in the other, Sahina and her mother-in-law cut the infant's umbilical cord with the straw in one neat sweep, bathed and wrapped the child in an old, clean saree and handed it not to Karishma but to Najma. Najma's eyes glistened with tears as she hugged both the baby and its mother, Karishma.

'Aryaan, the father?' Najma asked her.

Karishma's strength was fast failing. She could only blink a 'yes' to Najma's question.

'Fate!' Najma thought, 'once again, even this name doesn't give away where he could be from or what his faith may be!'

'Where is he now?' Najma asked.

Karishma's breathing was getting faint and slow. Najma took her ear close to Karishma's lips to hear her.

'Malegarh,' she managed to gasp, '....battle.'

'Aryaan is a sepoy?' Najma asked, still holding on to the baby.

'Was,' Karishma replied, her eyes suddenly getting flooded with light from inside her being.

'Was? He is no more?' she asked Karishma. Now it dawned upon Najma why the girl wanted to drown herself.

Karishma remained staring at Najma without replying, the light in her eyes still there.

'He is no more?' Najma repeated, bringing her mouth closer to the girl's ear.

'She too is no more, Najma, she's gone,' Sahina said standing behind Najma, putting a comforting hand on her shoulder. Then she slowly sat down on the cold, hard earthen floor beside the bed next to Karishma's head and gently putting a hand on the girl's forehead, as gently brought it down, closing as she did so with her palm the open lids of those eyes that gave out all the light left in the girl into Najma and Habib's house. 'Rahimaha Allah!' the old lady whispered into the girl's ears, 'Have mercy on her, Allah!' And Karishma was no more. She passed away, giving birth to a love child she bore for a soldier she knew as Aryaan. Giving birth as if for Najma.

'This is how the Almighty gives, Najma, as and when he wishes to. And he will also take as he wished,'

Habib said. Not knowing anything about her faith, Najma and Habib gave Karishma a Moslem burial. And to them, Karishma gave her child. Najma knew that this was one child who would have no one coming to take it away from her. With Rafiq, she always had this apprehension that someday his parents might take him back.

Najma and Habib named the child Anjaan. The Unknown. Because they knew nothing about him. They gave him their family name, Rahman. They gave him place in their home and hearts. He became their son Anjaan Rahman.

Anjaan. Of Hazratkandi village.
Born in the year 1857.
In Sylhet Province, East Bengal, India.

3
The Year Eighteen Sixty-Three

Anjaan had started going to the mosque at Hazratkandi village with Habib and Rafiq. All the men folk from the fifty or so households in the village went to that same mosque. Anjaan had also started learning his alphabet in Arabic and getting the initial lessons of the Qoran. Sometimes when Habib had to attend to other household chores, Anjaan went with Rafiq. How he loved those trips across vast, endless sprawls of open fields that rolled on and on till they reached out far from Anjaan to meet the skies. The only fences that broke the flow of the fields were those put up around paddy and vegetable patches to keep away cattle. Like him, even those cattle gathered around the Dooni when the sun was bright. Anjaan wasn't scared of the cattle. And they in turn were oblivious to Anjaan's presence on the sloping banks of the stream. Anjaan also loved the feel of the lazy warmth of the sun on his bare arms, of the sun that shone down from the azure, open sky above him.

'But Anjaan,' Rafiq told him one day when it was just the two of them walking to the mosque, 'these fields and the skies that you think are open and free, are not so.'

Anjaan looked up at the sky. 'Not free? If they are not free, where are the fences and the chains?'

'No Anjaan, not fenced and chained in that manner,' Rafiq tried to explain.

Anjaan looked back over his shoulder and then ahead of him. No, the fields too were not chained in any way. Then he looked at Rafiq. Rafiq was tall and well built for a nineteen-year-old. Unlike the small statured Habib. He had started growing a beard too. And he never forgot to put on the taqiyah on his oiled and combed hair unlike Anjaan. Amma always had to remind Anjaan and put it on his head. Whenever she did this, she always planted a kiss on his head over the taqiyah. Anjaan sometimes pretended to forget the taqiyah just so he received this kiss. He never saw Rafiq seeking a kiss from amma. But then he thought, big strong boys could do even without a kiss. For Anjaan, Rafiq was the strongest man ever. He was so much in awe of Rafiq.

'But Rafiq, you can break any chain, can't you? If you wish, you can beat up anyone!' he said, looking up at Rafiq with the confidence of being under his protection. Rafiq only smiled. 'These are not chains that you can see, Anjaan,' he tried to explain, 'these are invisible chains, shackles that make you slaves of other people. We are slaves of other people now.'

'We are slaves?' Anjaan asked, 'even you, Rafiq?' he asked, stunned.

'Yes, even I. All Indians are.'

'Slaves of?'

'The British.'

Anjaan didn't know who the British were. 'Can't you beat him up? This man called British?' he asked cheerfully. Because Rafiq, he thought, was strong enough to show his might to just anyone. 'You are stronger and bigger than abba too!' and he laughed, looking up with admiration at Rafiq.

'That isn't your abba,' Rafiq wanted to tell Anjaan. But he stopped himself. The little boy held on to his hand as they walked, till they reached the mosque. Once inside, Anjaan ran to take the place right opposite Laila. She smiled indulgently at him, her dimples stealing his little heart. Laila's father Ijaaz Miya had a cycle and umbrella repair shop and Anjaan had gone there a couple of times with his abba. Whenever Laila was at the shop with her father, they played under the wide canopied gulmohar in front of the shop under the watchful eyes of Ijaaz Miya. Now at the mosque, all the little girls sat in one row and the boys sat opposite them to take their lessons. Whenever Laila arrived earlier than Anjaan at the mosque for their lessons, she made sure that the seat right in front of her was left waiting for Anjaan. And when Anjaan arrived early, he did the same for her on the other row. While the little children sat for their lessons, Rafiq walked towards the well to wash before his own prayers. At a distance he saw Faizul walking towards the well.

'Rafiq! So, how's life?' Faizul waved and walked up to Rafiq. Faizul was a relative of one of Rafiq's parents in some way, though Rafiq didn't know exactly how. Not that he had any intention of knowing either.

'Good,' Rafiq replied.

'Good,' Faizul repeated, 'but it won't be for too long.'

Rafiq placed the bucket, in which he was drawing water from the well, on the ground and still holding on to the rope of the bucket, looked up at Faizul. The mosque was slowly filling in. Faizul was a devout Moslem, said his prayers five times each day and fasted every day during every ramzan. Rafiq remembered that his parents held Faizul in good esteem and looked up to him for advice. Ofcourse, that was when Rafiq was really young, and still lived with his parents.

'Well? Why so?' Rafiq asked him.

'And why not so?' Faizul said, 'it'll be so because of that little boy who has started calling Habib his abba. Do you even know whose blood or what sort of blood runs in his veins?' Faizul walked even closer to Rafiq, looked this way and that to see if anyone else was within earshot and then lowered his voice almost to a whisper. 'Rafiq,' he said, 'look to the future, my boy, there is much more at stake than just giving a home to an orphan.' All along, Faizul continued his act of washing up, just in case others got suspicious. 'Don't you see, Rafiq, that he may lay claim to Habib's land and house? Don't you? Well, let's assume he doesn't. Don't you think Habib may feel it only right to divide that property in half between you two?' He paused to see how Rafiq took it all. Faizul didn't know that a few others too had been hinting upon this for some time now to Rafiq. Rafiq hadn't said anything or reacted in any way though. But he hadn't disagreed either.

'Let's assume, even Habib won't think of it that way,' Faizul went on, 'but don't you think Najma would convince Habib to do so? Biased, and crazily in love with that child that she is? That child born out of wedlock of some...some... whore, maybe? You, she has brought up since you were six years. But this child was born into her lap. And has nowhere and no one to go to. Don't you think she will definitely be prejudiced towards him over you?' Rafiq felt chains crawling up his spine. Iron chains. Shackles. Invisible ones. He didn't look up at Faizul. Instead, he continued to rub the soles of his feet, one at a time, on the rough concrete floor at the washing area. Unmindfully.

Encouraged, Faizul continued, 'At six years he is a charming little boy, yes I can see that. But he won't remain six all his life. And he won't remain little, Rafiq, in size too. Who knows, he may grow taller and stronger than you. And who knows, he may overpower you and lay claim to Habib's lands.' Having said all he had so carefully prepared, Faizul felt like his message went well and hard to Rafiq. 'Oh, by the way,' he said while leaving the well, 'Rashida asked me to convey her wishes to you.' Only now did Rafiq look up at Faizul. He smiled absent-mindedly as a response. Faizul had always wondered if he could marry his daughter Rashida to Rafiq. 'I guess Faizul, after all, is right,' Rafiq thought. He finished washing and sat inside the mosque for his prayers, at a corner far from Faizul.

On their walk back from the mosque, Rafiq's thoughts were no more on the invisible chains that bound India. They were on the chains that would be around him soon if he didn't heed to what Faizul, and many before him, had been casually letting him in to. For quite some time now. If Anjaan did grow up to be big, strong, and dominating, with Najma always taking his side and Habib taking Najma's side, Rafiq knew he would have to leave Habib's house and go back to his own parents. To be among five other brothers and two sisters, one yet to be married. And with no land from which to inherit even one sixth. His parents worked in other people's fields. He remembered his days before Najma and Habib took him in, how they sometimes went to sleep without food. And now when he had food and the prospects of inheriting some land, however little, it would be foolish to not look to the future when there had been well meaning people showing him what the future might as well turn to, if the little boy they called Anjaan of Hazratkandi stayed on. 'Life will no longer be good,' he thought. Meanwhile, the little Anjaan of Hazratkandi held on to his hand and hopped, skipped, chatted, and hummed as they walked back home, feeling safe against the most brutal of chains, as long as he was with Rafiq.

Najma was at the door when they reached home.

'So, there you are, my little Nawab!' she said, coming a few steps forward to take Anjaan's hand, 'So did you see cows on the Dooni today?'

Rafiq didn't remember having been received by her this way at the door.

'Why yes, amma!' the little boy replied with glee.

The word *amma* hit Rafiq. Anjaan was making inroads to their hearts, he thought, and into their land. Rafiq didn't remember being called her *little nawab*.

With Anjaan's arrival, Najma started sleeping with him in one room and Rafiq and Habib slept in the other. Early one morning after their prayers, as both men were folding their mats, Rafiq broached the topic. Ever so unsuspectingly.

'Kaka,' he said gently, 'don't you ever wish to know about Anjaan?'

'Well? What is there to know about him?' Habib replied.

It was awkward for Rafiq to start the conversation. But the seeds of a split had been sown.

'I mean, in the sense that, you don't know whose

blood runs through those veins. What decent people would engage in such sinful, immorality to give birth before a nikaah?'

'Now stop this nonsense! Rafiq!' Habib shouted, his body suddenly shivering with rage.

But Rafiq went on, 'You don't know what faith runs in that blood, kaka, don't you feel, well, what he is born with will surely show up someday? Sooner or later? What might you expect of a...a...' Rafiq gulped before saying it, but he did, '...a bastard?'

'Rafiq!' Habib yelled at him.

Najma rushed into the room and came to stand as close to Rafiq as she could, facing him. He was so much taller and stronger than her. Yet, she looked up at him and without saying a word, raised her hand high and far and swung it back with full might to slap him hard across his face. Despite her small stature, her slap made Rafiq stagger. The slap stung not just his face but his pride and his hopes of inheriting Habib's land. Fury swirled like a hurricane inside him and he flung the prayer mat on the bed with all the force that he would have probably used up to return that slap. And stomped out of the house, banging the door hard behind him. It remained swinging to and fro for a long time. Habib's hand immediately went for his chest and his thin, bony fingers clasped over it as a sudden, excruciating pain pierced his heart. A sinister wince distorted his face, and he reeled back towards the bed, gasping for breath as he did so. Still holding on to his chest, he dropped on the bed.

Habib Rahman would never get up from that bed. He survived the stroke but became a paralytic. In a few months' time, he even stopped being able to speak. But he still could recognize people and hear them talk. He wished he couldn't.

Anjaan continued to walk with Rafiq to the mosque, but he no longer felt safe, assured, and confident of Rafiq's strength as he used to. Rather, he was beginning to get intimidated by that strength. With Habib crippled and wasting away and Anjaan still only eight, Najma no longer held the command she used to in her little household. Even her own health was failing. Partly due to age but mostly because of the way things had come to be in her household, in a way she was never prepared for. She no longer had the energy or the inclination to pace about the home and hearth taking care of every chore herself. And when they walked to the mosque, Anjaan no more chatted away as he used to. He no more held on to Rafiq's hand either. He merely walked along side Rafiq. And Rafiq ignored the boy like a cow would a crow trailing it.

Soon Anjaan was at an age where girls and boys received their lessons separately at the mosque. The boys started theirs when the girls finished. One such day when the girls were leaving the mosque, Laila's friend Tahira asked her, 'You heard about Anjaan, haven't you, Laila?'

'Heard what?' Laila asked back.

'Hush, Tahira, not so loud,' said another.

'But everyone seems to know already,' Tahira went on.

'But knows what?' Laila was getting impatient, 'what is it about Anjaan that everyone seems to know but me?'

The other girls giggled. Laila blushed. When she realized that she was giving away her feelings, she said, 'No, I mean, how is it that we all are here together and all of you know something that I don't know?' But her feelings didn't go unnoticed.

'Well then, Tahira, go on, tell her,' Fatima said.

'So, you see, Laila,' Tahira was carefully placing her words because she knew Laila was a girl who knew her mind and spoke it out. They all were sometimes even scared of her courage.

'So, I see what, Tahira?' Laila persisted.

'Anjaan, you know, is not Rafiq's brother. Not his true brother. I mean, not his brother at all.'

'He doesn't even belong to that family,' Fatima added.

'My amma was saying he doesn't belong to Hazratkand,' Tahira said.

'My abba too was saying so,' Fatima quipped, 'he said he belonged nowhere.'

'Yeah, no roots and no family name either, that's what my abba too was saying, I overheard,' Tahira said, lowering her voice.

Laila listened to all of it quietly. She just walked on. The dupatta that covered her head slipped off, but she wasn't aware of it. She and the rest of the girls were also not aware of the fact that Anjaan was walking up behind them. He had heard the whole of their conversation.

And back by the well at the mosque, Faizul caught up with Rafiq, feeding him with more and more disdain for the little boy with each passing day.

'Rafiq, now is the right time to think of what you wish to do with Anjaan,' Faizul had said one afternoon. It was at the Sutarkandi market. 'Why does this boy need to read and learn? Feel pity for Najma instead, Rafiq, feel pity for her old bones. This woman may not live long. Why need she do all the house-hold chore when this well muscled, orphan boy is around? He anyway is not a *Rahman*. It isn't a sin to have as a slave someone who is not from your family.' Faizul once again succeeded in driving his point home. He turned to go and then again walked back, 'Oh! How forgetful I am. Yes, Rashida was asking if your throat feels better.' Rashida had no inkling that Rafiq had a sore throat.

'Tell her I am better,' Rafiq smiled as he waved and walked away.

For Anjaan however, life only got worse.

Rafiq made him stop coming to the mosque to take lessons. And in that while, he was made to chop wood for fire, sweep the yard and feed the cows and milk one of them. Soon, callus began to harden his palms. Once when fatigue and hunger made him doze in the kitchen, Rafiq stormed in, pulled out a burning piece of firewood and struck the boy with it across his arm. Anjaan was to live with that scar on his left forearm all his life.

Najma mostly had to sit by Habib's side, nursing him and massaging his head as she kept talking to him. He heard them all but failed to reply, neither with eyes, nor with lips. He had bedsores all over his back and they were getting infected with pus and faeces. So Rafiq made Anjaan take those soiled bed clothes to the Dooni and wash and dry them there. The scrubbing led to rashes in his hands and the constantly wet fingers peeled away the edges of his nails, making them bleed. And he was not to come back home till all the clothes were dry. He then had to gather the dried clothes in a neat pile and carry them back home.

'Why does Anjaan remain so long away from the house now-a-days, Rafiq?' Najma had asked one day.

'His true colours are showing, kaki,' Rafiq replied.

'But my heart doesn't want to believe this,' she answered. And at the same time, she feared it might as well be true. For even she didn't know anything about Anjaan, nor about Karishma.

'So sometimes you should think with your head instead of our heart,' Rafiq snubbed.

And while Anjaan waited for the bed clothes to dry by the Dooni, he fell asleep with hunger gnawing at his insides. He lost count of how many days he went thus without meals. His stomach hurt from being empty while his chest hurt from being heavy. Weariness always bore down on him.

Even on the day Habib coughed his last, fatigue and hunger held Anjaan down with sleep at the banks of the Dooni. He didn't get to see the last of the man he came to call abba. Father. As the months passed, Najma became more subdued while Rafiq became more and more emboldened to inflict his might. There was no one in the house anymore who could impose on him, whether emotional or physical. He began to hold sway in that house. At the same time, he also saw that Anjaan too was growing, a growth shaped more out of hard labor than out of love.

'This boy has to be taken care of before it is too late, Rafiq,' Faizul often told him, 'however hard you make him work, he has to take it. Slaves ought to. But mind! When love makes a man grow, he is vulnerable and breakable. But when pain of mind and body does so, he grows strong beyond breaking. Mind, Rafiq, mind! Get rid of the boy before he grows beyond breaking.'

So, the more he was made to work, that much more his limbs became taut and sturdy. And as that was the way that Anjaan was growing up, it added to Rafiq's anxieties.

Back at home, when Najma tried to resist Rafiq from treating Anjaan in a manner that tormented even her, Rafiq shot back, 'Then how else does one treat a slave?'

'Slave?' Najma asked back, shocked.

'Slave! Yes! That's what he is, kaki, a slave!'

Najma came and stood before Rafiq. As she had done some long years back. Once more, she stood looking up at him that day.

'So, you wish to slap me one more time, eh?' Rafiq laughed. There was such malice in that laughter. 'But you no longer have the guts. I shall drag you by the hand that you raise to slap me and throw you out of this house, get it, dear kaki? Along with that bastard you picked up from the streets. That fellow from nowhere, son of a whore!'

Having spewed out what he had been wishing to and having established his might over Najma, when Rafiq turned around, he saw that Anjaan was standing at the door.

'And it's time you knew it too, Anjaan!' Rafiq shook a finger angrily at him and yelled, 'this,' he paused, took a deep breath, and said, 'is not your family!'

'Rafiq stop!' Najma shouted, 'No! Don't!'

'And why not?' Rafiq was getting more and more indignant, for he knew there was no one strong enough to restrain him any more. Not in that house at least. 'The old man who died for good was not your abba, Anjaan, no, he wasn't. And she,' he said pointing at Najma, 'is not your amma.'

Najma slowly stepped back and sat down on the bed. Like her husband once did.

'Anjaan walked up to her and sat by her feet, 'Amma?' he looked up imploringly at her. As if asking if what Rafiq was saying is true. Even if it was, it didn't matter to him. He loved this woman.

'You are not a Rahman, Anjaan, that is not your family name,' Rafiq told Anjaan with a sneer, 'you have no family name. Because you have no family! You have no identity! You hear that? You are no one!'

'Enough Rafiq You have said more than enough!' Najma's eyes were getting red with fury and pain.

'Then what is my name, amma?'

'Amma? Stop calling her amma!' Rafiq shouted with rage, 'She is not your amma, don't you understand? You don't belong here. You don't belong anywhere!'

Najma knew it was all coming to an end. Her love, her nurturing, everything was falling apart. She didn't see herself living long. She feared for Anjaan. And this time round, it was Anjaan who slowly stepped out of the house. But as he went, he didn't bang the door behind him. For it was the door of a house to which, he had been made to realize, he didn't belong. He felt he had no right to bang a door that was never his to enter.

'No, Anjaan, don't go!' Najma ran after him.

'Hah! Let him go, kaki, let him,' Rafiq said, a sigh of relief settling upon his heart. 'He anyway belongs nowhere.'

But Najma ran after him. It was difficult for her to catch up with a boy almost ten years old by now. And as she ran, she knew it was time to tell Anjaan what she hadn't shared with anyone till then, not even with Habib. Habib died without knowing that Najma knew Anjaan's father's name. Even though just partly. But that, Najma thought, may yet give the boy a clue to start searching for his identity, for the land he belonged to, if ever he so wished. Had situations not come to this, she would not have told Anjaan either. Anjaan would have grown to be a Rahman. And remained a Rahman. But now that he had been told he had no family name, Najma's conscience allowed her to give in his father's name to Anjaan. As for the name of his mother, since Najma gave her word to the dying girl that it would remain with her, she kept it with her.

'Anjaan!' Najma shouted across the fields. Anjaan ran even faster. The afternoon sun scorched down on his skin and singed it, while pebbles and razor sharp blades of grass nicked the soles of his bare feet. He was running towards the Dooni. After having spent so many afternoons sleeping by it, Anjaan began to find a kind of solace by the waters there. Its banks felt like a cradle that waited for him, to gently rock him to sleep. And hence it was to those banks that he was heading now.

'Anjaan! Child, stop! For my sake!' Najma shouted after him.

Anjaan paused and looked back. He halted, waiting for Najma to catch up. Meanwhile Rafiq too had started following Najma to take her back home. He was scared that if she got too much time with Anjaan she might convince him to return with her. Najma was out of breath when she reached Anjaan's side. She held his arm and in between short, quick breaths, said, 'Your father. Aryaan. At Malegarh. He's a martyr.' She spoke hurriedly because she saw Rafiq coming after her and she didn't want him to hear any of this. And when Anjaan saw Rafiq, he pulled away from Najma and ran as fast as he could towards the horizon. *To the Dooni?* He didn't know where. He just ran. Away.

For he had a name to find.

His family name.

He had an identity to look for.

His father's identity.

And so began Anjaan of Hazratkandi's search for his family name and identity.

4
The Late Eighteen Sixties

*A*njaan woke up to the flutter of white, homebound egrets against a darkening sky above him. Still lying on the sloping banks of the Dooni, he watched them form their airplane-like pattern as they flew across the skies. How effortlessly they fell into the pattern. They too had a home to which they could return. Near his bare arm on the grass, a troop of ants was carrying a dead grasshopper to its nest. They had food. Seeing them, he realized he was hungry. A few ants took a detour and crawled up his hand. Anjaan sat up to shake them off, otherwise he would have remained thus lying on the grass. For unlike the egrets and the ants, he had neither home nor food to return to. Hunger made him walk down to the river and cupping his hands, he lowered them into the water. It was cold. 'This water, Anjaan, is for cattle. Don't drink it,' his abba had said. But now Anjaan quenched his thirst with it.

It was getting dark. The last of the egrets too had become smaller and smaller till they disappeared into the far horizon. As darkness closed in, a fear of it began to slowly creep into his young heart. He got up and started running along the Dooni, because that was the only path he knew, wherever it might take him to. He didn't know how far or how fast he ran, but he slowed down and stopped when the shadow of a long, narrow house loomed at a distance. It had square windows at equal intervals all along the side facing Anjaan and light blinked out from a few of them. He started walking towards the house first slowly, then fast, then faster, before he turned to look over his shoulder and broke into a run. He was scared of the dark. And the dark was chasing him. He wanted to cry.

He thought of amma.

As Anjaan neared the house, he slowed down and cautiously crept into a shed just outside it. He could hear men's voices inside the house, in a language he didn't understand. When his eyes got used to the darkness, he could make out that he was sharing the shed with two carts, probably horse-drawn, for there were a few horses too, the kind on which men in uniform, helmets and guns once rode through their village roads and who stopped by at their mosque to enquire and talk with great authority to the maulvi. There were a couple of bicycles too. Meanwhile, hunger ate into his stomach. He drew his knees close to his chin and tightly wrapped his arms round his legs to hold them that way, lest any noise from his stomach gave him away. It was, however, his sobbing that gave him away.

Anjaan raised a hand to screen his eyes from the light of a kerosene lantern that moved closer and closer to his face.

'Hoi! There!' a man called out, still holding up the lantern at Anjaan. His voice was gruff and his words boomed through the stillness of the night. It heightened Anjaan's terror.

'Thief or beggar, you!' the voice bellowed.

Anjaan didn't see the man, for the light blinded him. But he heard more than one voice now outside the shed.

'You alone?' the voice asked.

Anjaan nodded.

'For whom are you spying?'

Anjaan stood up and retreated further into the back of the shed.

'No, Mahib, he looks plain scared to me,' said a new voice, 'looks like a runaway. Nevertheless, just look at his size. Won't be able to take us on. Come on, call him out.'

'Boy!' it was the first voice again, 'here, come out!'

Anjaan stepped farther back.

'Come out, will you? If you're just scared and hiding, you'll be fine in the kitchen over there. Come on out now!'

Slowly, with a pounding heart, he stepped out of the shed.

'Hungry?' the man asked Anjaan.

Anjaan started sobbing and nodding at the same time.

'You honest, eh? When you say you don't have another mugger holed in there?' one of the men threatened. 'Here, Sujit,' he said to another, holding out the lantern, 'go look up.' Sujit took the lantern and went into the shed. 'Nobody here!' he called back in a while. The men, big and youthful, led Anjaan into the kitchen.

While Anjaan hungrily ate the rice, dal, and pumpkin curry, one of the men walked in hauling a coir-matted cot on his back and dumped it in the corner of the kitchen. He then threw in a pillow and a sheet. 'There, lie down over there for the night and in the morning, don't try to run away. Well, you can't run away from an army camp anyway.' Anjaan looked up, his hand with a fistful of rice in it, paused midway between mouth and plate. Only now did he notice that the man was in khaki trousers and a khaki full-sleeved shirt. Most of these men were. Some were in khaki pullovers too, but now their sleeves were carelessly rolled up and their untucked shirts peeped out from underneath the pullovers. Anjaan would come to know only much later that the camp the soldier mentioned was the 9 Periphery Supply Camp, the camp at which

Anjaan had arrived.

'What's the name, boy?'

'Anjaan.'

'Hmm, Anjaan. Anjaan what?' the man who brought in the cot asked, as he walked about in the kitchen cleaning up after the day's last meal.

'Anjaan...' *Rahman* almost came to his lips, but he immediately clenched his teeth and held it from escaping. His knuckles made a mash of the rice on his plate. He feared that the army men might let Rafiq loose on him.

'So? Anjaan what?' the man barked.

'Of Hazratkandi!' Anjaan said in one quick gasp, almost coughing out the words.

'Well?' the man looked curiously at Anjaan.

'Yes, er..Hazratkandi!'

'But that's the name of the neighbouring village. Are you cheating on us?' he barked louder.

Anjaan began to sob. And in between sobs he said, 'Anjaan, huzur, is all I have for a name.'

'Well, well,' the man's voice softened, 'wipe out that sob and whimper. The camp is no place for a mouse. Be a man, boy, bulge up that chest! Now go to that cot before I put out the lantern. And no tricks, no mischief. Mind you. Even if you're up to any, you can't get away with it, just remember that. We'll see what we can do with you in the morning.' Anjaan would later come to know this man as Balraj. Once on the cot, Anjaan curled up into the foetal position and immediately fell asleep.

My little Nawab! Did you see cows in the Dooni today?
No, amma, but there was a grasshopper......it was dead.

In the morning, Anjaan was made to help out in the cart shed. As the days went by, he became good at washing the mud off the wheels and brushing and grooming the horses too. And sometimes when Sujit would repair and mend the carts, he made Anjaan hand him this tool or that hammer. On such occasions, Anjaan watched keenly and even picked up a little of the work. He also learnt, in the course of time, to mend and repair the couple of cycles in the camp whenever they required mending and repair. He was no longer intimidated by the khaki shorts and trousers because now he too owned a pair of each. They were someone's leftover, altered by the camp's tailor Dinbandhu to just about fit Anjaan. Sometimes when the cart went out to the Central Supply Depot at Narikuli by the river Koshiara, Sujit and Balraj would ask Anjaan to hop in. During those rides he preferred to sit at the back of the cart looking towards the fields and the roads as they seemed to move away behind him. Sometimes when the road came close to the Dooni, he got a glimpse of the waters there too. The men at the camp were loud and rough in their demeanour but Anjaan could feel that they no more eyed him with suspicion. It was just their way to be thus boisterous. Soon, his cot was moved from the kitchen to a corner of the dormitory where the rest of the soldiers stayed. He learned to replace the wick in the lanterns and when the men played chess with the board perched atop an empty fuel container, Anjaan would stand on his toes till his nose reached the edge of the board, and watched intently. On those occasions when the soldiers played, they talked about how the movement for independence was growing. He heard them discuss how the British discreetly watched over activities of priests, teachers and maulvis. Anjaan often wondered if he would someday hear the men talk of the martyrs' hillock at Malegarh. That was also the reason why he preferred the open back of the cart, hoping to come across the hillock during one of those rides. But the day he did come across it, it was totally unexpected. Balraj and Mahib had gone to the bazar at Latu. 'Hop in, my boy!' Balraj said with a wave of his hand.

Having picked small knick-knacks in the market, they rode towards Malegarh.

'This is what that started most camps and regiments this side of Bengal, Anjaan,' Balraj said as Mahib slowed the horses by the foot track at the base of the hillock. Anjaan looked enquiringly at Balraj.

'It's quiet out here, isn't it?' he asked, as Balraj walked him up to the hillock.

'Well,' Balraj replied, putting one arm on Anjaan'sshoulder, and pointing at the hillock with the other, 'It is. The dead don't make noise.'

'Is this where the dead from the village get buried?' Anjaan asked.

'No, boy, this is the martyrs' grave,' Balraj told Anjaan.

'Oh!' he replied, remembering the word amma had said.

'This is the Malegarh crematorium,' Balraj added.

Anjaan stopped in his tracks. That which he was wishing and preparing to visit for all these years had happened just so suddenly that he forgot to ask all that he had been planning and hoping to ask, to whoever took him there. He instead found himself asking Balraj, 'Who are martyrs?'

'Those who die for their country and their people, Anjaan,' Balraj explained, 'these here died fighting the British. To free India from her shackles.'

Anjaan lost count of the summers that he stayed on in the camp. Three, maybe four, maybe more. The camp, however, was not a battle regiment. The camp's task was to collect supplies of food, medicine, ammunition, fuel, and other provisions from the Central Supply Depot at Narikuli and distribute these to regiments in the more interior areas, sometimes even by bicycle and on foot to areas that had but just a foot track leading up to bases there. Yet, in the event of an emergency, soldiers from Anjaan's camp too were called out for patrolling. Anjaan wondered whether during such times, the patrolling took Balraj and all to Hazratkandi. He wanted to ask them, but he could not muster the courage. He wondered if they might have stomped into the mosque in his village to raid it. He wondered if Laila was there at that moment. If she was, he hoped she was safe. Might she also be thinking of him sometimes, he wondered.

Soon Anjaan no longer had to stand on his toes for his nose to reach the chess board perched on the empty fuel container. Now, when he walked alongside Balraj, he reached upto the breast pocket of Balraj's khaki shirt. The men sometimes made him ride on horseback along with them and on those occasions, Anjaan loved to watch how they lightly nudged the horse at its side with their heels to get it moving. He also watched how they pulled the reins to make it stop. It fascinated Anjaan to see how a majestic beast like the horse too could be brought under control and made to obey commands. He watched all of these with such keenness that even without his realizing, he soon learnt to ride them on his own. As the days passed, he also learnt how to change the wheels of a cart and how to grease their creaking joints and how to saddle a horse.

'Too much grease in the joint will make the dirt stick in a thick layer, Anjaan, making the wheel slow down and hard for the horse to pull. And too little will make the iron creak and wear off. So, the trick is to know just how much grease is the right amount.' It didn't take Anjaan long to learn just how much that was. He observed well and learnt fast.

Once during one of their rides to deliver provision, Balraj had told him that he belonged to Lahore. Anjaan didn't know where that was. He just knew that Balraj belonged to some place, had a homeland and a family back there, and a family name too. Sandhu it was. Balraj Sandhu. Everyone at the 9 Periphery Supply Camp belonged somewhere, and they all had a family name. Anjaan often contemplated asking Balraj about the martyrs at Malegarh. And yet, the same insecurities that made him want to ask about the martyrs also kept him from asking about them. He also feared that Balraj might grow suspicious of him. But wasn't Balraj also an Indian like himself? During their hours at the chess board, Anjaan came to know from their talks what kind of shackles and chains bound the free skies and open fields that Rafiq had mentioned. He was now old enough to understand all of it.

Running small errands for the men in the camp, Anjaan sometimes cycled to the village market. On those occasions he often thought of cycling out to Hazratkandi. And maybe, just maybe, look up amma. Might she still be there in that house? But Hazratkandi was far from the camp, and he feared he might lose his way. He wanted to see Laila too. If, he thought, he ever returned to Hazratkandi, it would be for her. But he also wondered whether she still remembered him.

During his almost four years in the 9 Periphery Supply Camp, Anjaan had seen many men move in and move out. Some were sent away because they could not adapt to conditions in these parts of India and fell sick. Others abandoned the khaki uniform to lend their support to those rallying for freedom, while some stood loyal to the British because they were their employers. Here too, Anjaan didn't know where he belonged.

Then one bright, sunny morning Sujit was checking the carts' wheels and bathing the horses. Most men were away from the camp. The few that were left were unusually preoccupied. Some were cleaning their rifles, and a few were polishing their boots. Mahib was putting a part of the pots and pans to one side, a few others were helping Sujit with the horses.

'Anjaan!' Sujit called.

Anjaan looked around but didn't see him.

'Here boy, under the cart!' Sujit replied from below.

Anjaan looked down and saw Sujit's legs peering out from underneath one of the carts.

'Oh! There you are,' he grinned. Anjaan had almost ceased to smile, though his smile was now returning.

'Now stop that grin and pass me that rag by the oil can. Quick,' Sujit said.

With one hand Anjaan picked the rag and with the other he covered his grin. Carefully, he bent his head low under the cart to hand the rag. 'Readying for a long patrol?' he asked Sujit.

'The whole camp is moving, Anjaan,' Sujit replied, eyes still fixed on the floor of the cart.

'Where to, this time?' Anjaan asked. A couple of times earlier when the camp moved, Anjaan too went with them. But those times the camp moved within East Bengal.

'Madras,' Sujit replied.

In his travels across camps and bazars this side of the river Koshiara, Anjaan had never heard of Madras. Yet, since he began listening to their talks, he thought he heard something like it. Madras.

'How far from here? Along the Dooni?' Anjaan asked.

Sujit pulled himself out and wiped his hands on the rag.

'Many, many days from the Dooni, Anjaan, that far Madras is from here.'

'Oh....,' Anjaan exclaimed, not knowing what to say or do next.

'So far that we cannot ride the horses or make them pull the carts. Balraj will put these and everything in the camp onto train wagons. We too will go by train. Or maybe by ship,' Sujit said.

Anjaan sat quietly on the ground beside Sujit for a long while and let all that Sujit said sink into him.

He then asked, 'And I?'

'If you want to come, I can speak about it to the Subedar, to let you join us.'

'When are you moving?'

'In two days, from here. Maybe we'll go to the port at Narikuli and get aboard the ship at the ghat there on the Koshiara. It will be a small ship, for Koshiara's is a small port. It'll take days from there to reach Madras.'

The whole of that night Anjaan lay in bed awake, thinking. If he wished to go, they'd surely take him. But if he wished to stay, where would he stay? And yet, he wished to stay. He had a few things left to be done and one thing to search for.

He had to visit the Malegarh hillock one more time. Perhaps many more times. Till he found his answer.

He had to visit Hazratkandi. To look up amma.

He had to see Laila.

He would stay on.

Early next morning, Anjaan walked up to Balraj and stood there a while, wondering how to start, what words to use. Then he just blurted out, 'Can you please put in a word for me at the Central Supply Depot at Narikuli before you leave? So that they take me in? I will be handy there like I was here. I will be sincere...' his voice broke off.

Balraj stood up, gently placed his hands on Anjaan's shoulders and looked into his eyes. For the first time in all these years, he didn't know how many, Anjaan saw tears welling up in the eyes of the burly Sikh. Balraj nodded. 'I will, child, I will,' he said and sobbed.

'Wipe out that sob and whimper, Balraj kaka, the camp is no place for a mouse,' Anjaan said, borrowing Balraj's words from all those years ago. 'Be a man, bulge up that chest!' And the two laughed and cried together in each other's arms.

5
The Year Eighteen Seventy-Three

The Central Supply Depot at Narikuli by the river Koshiara was much busier than Anjaan's earlier camp of thirty men. Cargo vessels pulled into the depot's dock every week, bringing in supplies from Calcutta. These vessels would unload large gunny sacks and boxes on to the small wooden pier that ran out into the water from the bank. There would always be gulls, terns and the red wattled lapwing on the pier and they didn't seem to mind the people or the vessels, nor the goods they unloaded. When someone passed by close enough, they would just hop some distance away, only to come back. And so they flit about from pier to water and back again because they could peck at the grains that escaped from the gunny sacks and fell on the planks of the pier. Their callsfilled the waterfront and vied to be heard over the noise of the vessels and ferries, their honks and men shouting as they maneuvered goods from the vessel to the pier. From there, they carried the goods to the warehouse at the depot. The depot and its office were close to the Koshiara, but the warehouse was closer. A smaller channel was dug out for small row boats to reach the warehouse from the cargo vessel to ferry goods too large or heavy for men to carry on their heads and backs. Some of the provisions were reloaded into smaller ferries and boats to be taken to camps across the Koshiara. Anjaan had seen much of the river since he had come here, and the Koshiara was so much wider than the Dooni back at Hazratkandi that Anjaan wondered if even Rafiq would be able to swim across it as he did across the Dooni.

On the day he arrived, Edward Fidley, the superintendent of the depot, asked him as he turned the pages of the work register, 'Name?' Anjaan was taken aback by the boom in the voice of the small statured, thin, almost fragile, and feminine man.

'Anjaan,' he replied.

Edward Fidley looked up from the register, 'Anjaan what? Surname please!'

Anjaan gulped, 'of Hazratkandi.'

'Not village, lad, surname! Title!' Edward Fidley emphasized.

'Ji, Hazratkandi!' Anjaan forced his voice not to quiver.

'Like the village?' Edward Fidley asked.

'Yes huzur,' Anjaan replied. He hadn't understood what he was asked.

Edward Fidley shook his head as he started writing, 'Indians never cease to amaze me!' So the boy's name came to be formally recorded as Anjaan Hazratkandi.

'Age?' Edward Fidley asked next.

Anjaan shook his head.

'Age!' Fidley repeated, 'umarr!'

Anjaan once more shook his head.

'Hmm...seventeen?' Edward Fidley helped him with a guess. Anjaan stared. He didn't know.

'Those limbs don't look less than seventeen,' Edward Fidley said to himself. Indeed, for a sixteen-year-old, Anjaan was tall and well built. And thus, Edward Fidley wrote down in the register:

Name: Anjaan Hazratkandi
Age: Seventeen years
Address: Hazratkandi village, Sylhet division, East Bengal, India.
Year of Enrolment: 1873

Anjaan was thereby officially given a surname that wasn't his, and he was allocated an age that he wasn't. Besides, he was given one anna every week as wage. Not that he had much use even for that. Because he received his meals from the depot's kitchen, and a certain amount of bath soap and clothing was given for no charge to depot workers as it was to the sepoys in the camps. Once every month, all registered depot workers were lined up for a haircut and shave. That too was for free. So, most of the wage remained with him just the way it was handed to him. While receiving that one anna, Anjaan had to ink his left thumb and press down its imprint against '*Anjaan Hazratkandi*' on the register because he didn't know how to write his name.

Anjaan wasn't entrusted with any specific job. However, he was the errand boy who did every odd job around the depot. Everything that he learnt with Balraj, Sujit, Mahib, the cook, the cleaner, Dinbandhu and everyone else at the camp helped him raise his position at the depot. Soon he became indispensable to Edward Fidley. Anjaan started liking it here too though he knew this wasn't where he wanted to be for life. What, however, he loved most was, like he used to with Balraj, Sujit and Mahib during his stay at the 9 Periphery Supply Camp, the rides that took him to the inner camps to deliver supplies through the vast open fields, sometimes green with paddy and sometimes golden brown with ripe grains, yet sometimes fallow after the harvest. During such times the fields were dotted with cows and goats. He loved the rides along the Koshiara for it reminded him of the Dooni. Though Anjaan had already picked up how to rein a horse at the 9 Periphery Supply Camp, Edward Fidley had now polished his raw knowledge and taught him the subtleties of the skill for a smoother, more enjoyable ride. Soon, he began letting Anjaan go by himself on a horse for errands. At other times Anjaan was permitted the use of the bicycle too. That was a privilege usually reserved for the more efficient and favoured among the depot workers. And on those evenings when there was no work at the depot and no rides either, Anjaan would walk down to the banks of the Koshiara and sit on the edge of the pier letting his legs lazily hang down above the waters while he watched the boats sail by. Some of them had large sails that looked like kites floating on the water, yet some had arched bamboo canopies on them that served as a house for the boatmen. Sometimes, a boatman would sing a soulful song as he rowed past and it made Anjaan imagine that he too must be missing some place he belonged to, some place that was his home. Or was it a beloved one that he missed? These boats, he felt, were so similar to the thoughts in his mind. Both would just come and pass by. Yet, it was during those moments that he could see what he wanted to do, where he wanted to take his life to. As if he read his destiny in the blankness of the sails in those passing boats. It was also during one such moment that he thought he should visit Ijaaz Miya. Thus, sitting by the river one evening, he tried to count the summers he lived at the 9 Periphery Supply Camp. Another summer had already gone by at the Central Supply Depot too. Much had changed in him during these five or so summers but Ijaaz kaka, he thought, probably remained the same. Laila, however, must have changed. He himself had too. He hoped Ijaaz kaka would recognize him.

Once when he and Manik Roy, the driver of the depot's horse-cart, drove past Hazratkandi towards Biyanibazar, Anjaan's heart pounded when he saw the dome of their mosque from the road, far away towards where the makeshift sheds of the weekly haat were sticking to one another. It was afternoon and as they drove past, he heard the muezzin's call float through the fields to reach him. But the horses moved on with Anjaan Hazratkandi at the back of the cart they were pulling, leaving the prayers behind. As if he was running away from the prayers, from the huts, fields and the haat, and from everything else that was associated with Hazratkandi.

Or was he though? Anjaan wondered, as he lay in bed that night. That day's trip past Hazratkandi made him long all the more to go back there, even if just once. He longed to see amma, to ask her more about the martyrs at Malegarh. Now that he had seen the hillock and his supply delivery trips took him around Sutarkandi, Malegarh, Biyanibazar, Kakordhia and places he was yet to get familiar with, knowing some more about that one martyr at Malegarh that his amma had said was his father, would probably help him in his search for his name, his family and the home where he belonged. He turned over to the other side and the wrought iron posts of the bed clanked. Rafiq, however, would not let him in, he thought. But now Anjaan was no more the little boy in awe of Rafiq, no more the boy who hadn't seen beyond Hazratkandi. He had grown. He was big and strong and rode around in a horse-drawn cart. That in itself gave him the confidence he never had all those years ago when he left the only place that he had thought was home. He decided he would go to Hazratkandi. He would get off the cart and walk along the Dooni. Still lying in bed, he slowly shut his eyes but his mind continued to reminisce. He would count the cows drinking from the Dooni standing with their hind legs on its sloping banks and with the front legs just about touching the water. He would visit the mosque too. Anjaan didn't know when the trail of thoughts lulled him to sleep. In his sleep, however, he dreamt of none of these. He dreamt instead of Ijaaz Miya's umbrella and cycle repair shop. He dreamt of himself and Laila sitting at the shop. He saw Laila no more as the little girl sitting across him at the mosque taking lessons from the Qoran but as a young girl. He dreamt he was at Hazratkandi.

Soon, the size of the camps and regiments were increased because the freedom movement was gaining momentum around the Sylhet province and East Bengal, as it was elsewhere in India. Bigger camps and regiments called for more supplies, and more supplies meant that, on a single day, Anjaan and Manik Roy had to reach more bases. And when they delivered the supplies, Anjaan had to get the signature of the camp-in-charge in a record book which he had to hand over to Edward Fidley back at the depot. Even without knowing to read and write, Anjaan knew the signatures from their flow and pattern, just as he would have known a design. The trips too got more frequent. But with Manik Roy, Anjaan started to look forward to these supply delivery trips because he was so full of stories of the English sahibs, and he was always abreast of events. Sometimes when they rode through village tracks, little children coated with merry layers of red dust and running noses would run after the horse-cart, holding up a slipping lower garment at the waist with one hand and waving at them with the other. Some would shout at them.

'Give us a ride!'

'What are the names of the horses?'

Anjaan would smile and wave back with a sense of primacy. They remined him of his own childhood.

'Are you from around these parts, Manik kaka? Sylhet?' Anjaan asked during one of the trips.

'West Bengal,' Manik replied, 'Poriduar.'

'But you know your way so well around here,' Anjaan was amazed by Manik's knowledge of the shorter routes and the tracks crisscrossing the province.

'Because, son, I have been here for long. I came here along with Fidley Sahib and have been here since the depot was set up. Earlier it used to be a small supply centre. But after the incident at Latu...'

'The one about Malegarh?' Anjaan interrupted, suddenly getting keener than usual.

'Yes, that,' Manik Roy resumed, 'so after that incident, camps were reinforced and we had to have more fuel, more provisions...'

'What exactly happened at Latu, Manik kaka?' Anjaan interrupted once more. He wasn't interested in the details he already knew but he still asked because Manik Roy might come up with something significant, something he hadn't known earlier. So, he had to let him talk on. Manik slowed down the cart and pulled the horses to the side to let two rickshaws pass by. These were almost the same as the cart Anjaan and Manik Roy were riding, just that these were pulled by men in place of horses. He stopped his conversation to concentrate on manoeuvring the cart past the uneven and slush filled road. 'I could have just driven past,' he explained, lest Anjaan underestimated his horse-riding skills, 'but for the provisions at the back.' Though Anjaan thought he was in truth evading the question on Latu. He tried once more. 'So, kaka, was there a battle at Malegarh?'

'There was,' he replied, after a pause, 'many of our men died. Men from the Bengal Army. Indians.'

'How many?' Anjaan asked.

'Hmm...between twenty-five and thirty maybe?' Manik Roy put the answer as a question.

'You knew any of them, kaka?' Anjaan was slowly veering towards his search.

Manik Roy laughed and bent his head to spit out the red juice of betelnut, 'You are intrigued, eh?' he said, 'well then, you and I will drive round to Malegarh one of these days during our trips, okay, son?' Anjaan remained quiet. He still hadn't come any closer to the answer he was hoping to.

Manik Roy guided the horses to a sharp turn to take a track towards Kakordhia, away from the main road. This was a shorter route, he said. This would take them past Hazratkandi and Biyanibazar and, would follow a bendy route before arriving at Narikuli. Off the road at Hazratkandi, Anjaan looked out for the umbrella and cycle repair shop. It had been a long time, and he had been young when he had been there last with his abba, so it took him a while to figure out the place. Though Hazratkandi didn't seem to have changed much in all the years that he had been away.

'There used to be a cycle repair shop somewhere here,' Anjaan remarked, looking out intently.

'There was? You'd been there?' Manik Roy asked.

'A couple of times, yes. Don't know if Ijaaz kaka, the owner, would recognize me.'

'Want to look him up?' Manik Roy offered.

Anjaan's heart missed a beat.

'If it's on our way, no harm,' Manik Roy suggested.

As they took another turn and came upon a narrower road, familiarity slowly crept into the far corridors of his memory. His eyes widened and he strained his neck to look out farther and better.

'If it's still there, then it should be along here somewhere, Manik kaka, because I remember that pond. I used to fling pebbles into it to make them bounce and hop in the waters like a frog. But the pond seems smaller now.'

'That's because you have grown big,' Manik Roy explained. 'When you are small, the world and everything in it surpasses your smallness, your size. As does happiness. But then when you begin to grow, it is then your size that begins to surpass everything, even happiness. It is, son, only worry that grows side by side with you.' Anjaan only partly understood the words. But soon someday he would wholly know what Manik Roy meant.

Soon they saw it at a distance. Ijaaz Miya's cycle and umbrella repair shop.

'There! There!' Anjaan couldn't hold back his excitement, 'Yes! It is that shop, Manik kaka!' The shop was just the way he remembered it, with those same walls of woven bamboo and flat, thatched roof. 'You want to stop by?' Manik Roy asked, amused at the boy's enthusiasm.

'If only Ijaaz kaka is there. Yes, please,' he replied, almost shivering.

As his eyes fondly glanced inside the shop, he found it just the way as he remembered seeing it the last time, with tools and pliers scattered about its earthen floor. Ijaaz Miya was there in the shop, sitting on a morha with a cycle lying next to him. He was tightening something near the brakes of the cycle with a wrench. The gulmohar tree in front of the shop too was just the way Anjaan had remembered it. The lowest branch still had rickshaw tyres hanging upon it. For a moment, Anjaan even thought they were the same tyres that he remembered seeing as a little boy, still hanging the way they used to all those years ago. Suddenly, it all came back to him, and he felt for a brief while like he had never been away at all. He remembered sitting in the shade of the gulmohar and playing with Laila while abba got the cloth of his umbrella stitched where it gave way, or sometimes got repaired the spokes and shaft of the umbrella. The same long wooden bench still stood in the shades there for customers to sit while their umbrellas, cycles and rickshaws were getting repaired. Anjaan started to sweat despite the cool breeze from the open fields all around.

'Want to stop by, son?' Manik Roy broke his reverie.

'Can we?' Anjaan looked at Manik Roy.

Manik Roy slowed down.

'Well, kaka, please let's stop a little distance away and then walk in. I don't want to alarm Ijaaz kaka with a horse-drawn cart pulling up to his shop,' Anjaan said.

'Aha, true! True! Considerate boy, Anjaan,' Manik Roy said, patting him on the back with one hand while the other held on to the reins.

Ijaaz Miya looked up from the cycle when Anjaan walked into the shop.

'Salaam waleikum, Ijaaz kaka!' Anjaan greeted the old man, his breath getting faster.

'Walaikum assalaam,' Ijaaz Miya greeted back, adjusting his foggy glasses, 'what is it that you might want, young man? I see you're accompanied neither by bicycle nor by rickshaw. Nor do you carry an umbrella.'

'I came for no repairs, kaka. Look well. Do you recognize me?' and Anjaan went closer to Ijaaz Miya, stepping through the spread-out paraphernalia that he was working with, and sat in front of him. Ijaaz Miya stared into the face for long. Then he held Anjaan by the arms and stood up.

'I've seen you earlier,' he tried hard to recollect, 'around here...I guess at the mosque...why! Of course!' His eyes lit up, 'you are...' and suddenly the light faded, '...but you were only about ten and you had run away....'

So that's how the word was let out, Anjaan thought, dismay once again filling his heart when he was just beginning to look forward to seeking out life. 'I was thrown out,' he wanted to tell Ijaaz Miya. To everyone. But he didn't. It didn't matter anymore. It wouldn't change anything.

'I wish to come back, kaka,' he said instead.

'You are...,' Ijaaz Miya thought hard while still looking at Anjaan.

'Yes, kaka, I am...,'

'Najma and Habib's adopted son, aren't you!' Ijaaz Miya said at last.

The old man put an arm lovingly around the boy and led him to the bench.

'While you were away and growing tall, son, much has happened here,' Ijaaz Miya took it upon himself to fill the missing chapters in Anjaan's childhood.

'Amma...?' Anjaan couldn't wait to hear about her.

'Najma is no more.'

Anjaan's fist clenched, and a lump crawled up to his throat. Ijaaz Miya went into the shop to bring the morha near the bench and sat on it. 'The year before last, malaria was bad in Hazratkandi,' he said, 'and poor Najma was not taken care of.' Anjaan felt his ears getting hot.

'The house? And .... others in it?' Anjaan asked.

'Well,' Ijaaz Miya said, stretching out his legs in front of him, 'for others, there was only Rafiq. That boy! He made the wretched woman work even when the fever raged. After Najma, he sold the land and the cow, feasted on the lone hen, and left Hazratkandi. Don't know where for. Nobody from here has seen or heard anything of him since. Some say he took with him a Sylheti, a Hindu girl, and so disappeared for fear of being beaten to death.'

Anjaan looked up to see behind the shop. Ijaaz Miya's house was there. He wondered why Ijaaz Miya hadn't mentioned Laila till now. He felt anxious. Might she have been married off? Manik Roy was by then done tying the horses to a tree and relieving himself of a bursting bladder by the wayside. He had also taken out from the back of the cart his little box of betelnut and made himself a betel nut and leaf coated with lime and kattha and was shoving it into the tender groove between his cheek and gum as he walked upto the bench.

'Ijaaz kaka,' Anjaan introduced, 'This is Manik kaka. Manik Roy. It's he who brought me here.'

Ijaaz Miya took his right hand close to his forehead as a gesture of greetings, while Manik Roy brought his palms together into a namaste.

'Allow me to offer you some black tea, Manik babu, my daughter Laila brews it just right, not strong, not weak.' Anjaan's heart felt as if it had just been given some more space to breathe freely. He now knew she was home, hence yet unmarried, he assumed.

'Thank you, Ijaaz Miya, that is kind of you,' Manik Roy said, 'but maybe we shall keep that for another time. We must be at the depot before dark. The horses will have to be fed. But I promise, we'll come back for the tea soon. What say, Anjaan?'

'Yes, yes!' Anjaan smiled and nodded as he stood up. He sure would, even if Manik Roy didn't.

'Ijaaz kaka, do give my regards to all at home,' Anjaan said, 'tell them I was here,' he added, though he actually wished to say, 'Tell Laila I was here.'

Ijaaz Miya stood up and watched the two walk up to the horses and drive away before returning to the brakes of the bicycle. Being a young girl's father and the age that he was of, he understood that which was said as well as that which went unsaid.

The young boy accompanied neither by bicycle nor by rickshaw, not even with an umbrella, was to make many more visits to the cycle shop.

6
The Year Eighteen Seventy-Four

Ijaaz Miya closed his shop early that evening. As it was, there were not too many people that day. He pulled the wide bamboo shutters of the shop together and looped the iron chain hanging from one part of the shutter through a hole in the other and fastening the padlock through the chain, he inserted the key, turned it with his ear close to the lock to hear the *click* and then pulled out the key. Out of habit, he clasped the padlock and gave it a tug to ensure that the key had done its job properly. Also out of habit, he dropped the key into the pocket of the long kurta that he was wearing over his green and yellow chequered lungi and then walked not towards his house at the back of the shop but towards the bench under the gulmohar tree. He sat down on the bench and looked out onto the road, letting his mind wander far away along that road somewhere. Laila heard him drag the bamboo shutters over the dry, uneven red earth and she started the fire in the kitchen. Theirs was a modest, thatch house with walls of long, flattened bamboo and an earthen floor. It had two rooms, with windows that opened towards the river at the back of the house, beyond the fallow land. There was plenty of light and breeze during autumn but, during the monsoons, they had to keep the windows tightly shut, for the winds washed the rains into the rooms, making the earthen floor all soggy and slippery. Laila used to sleep with her amma in one room and her abba slept in the other. Sometimes, however, when she turned in her sleep and sought out her amma to snuggle close to her, she found that amma wasn't there. And on those moments, she heard muffling noises in her abba's room. She would be too sleepy to go and look for amma or to find out what the noise was all about, so she just turned and went back to sleep. Just outside those two rooms, there were two more rooms, even smaller and with their roof lower than the other two rooms. One was the cow shed and the other was their kitchen. Laila now started the fire there just as her amma used to. She was very small those days. Those were also the days when Anjaan sat opposite her at the mosque. In her thoughts, he was her best friend. And at home, she sat next to amma when she put in dried leaves into the small earthen fireplace on the floor of the kitchen. Amma then lit the dried leaves and when the fire leapt up, she put in the firewood. Sometimes, when the cooking was over, but the fire was still leaping, amma would pull the piece of firewood out from the fire and sprinkle water on it. Amma didn't teach Laila any of it. But she picked it all up. She watched and learnt. At home, she followed amma everywhere she went and watched whatever amma did. As if Laila knew amma wouldn't be around for long. It was the year when many cyclonic storms, big and small, whipped through Hazratkandi. Abba was at the cycle repair shop, and their cow and her calf were grazing by the river at the back of their house. When the skies began to darken rapidly and the winds got worse, amma did not wait for abba. She hurried out to bring in the cows before the rains lashed. She managed to pull out of the ground the small bamboo wedge to which the cows' ropes were tied and was pulling them home as fast as she could. But before she reached home, the rains started to pour in sheets. The wind tore through the rains, twisting leaves off the boughs and hurtling them across her face. She had to push her way against the force of the wet wind, her feet stumbling on the edges of her wet saree that clung to her feet, as if they were trying to tie them up. Yet she managed to bring the cows home through the rains and tying them to the post in the shed, hurried to start a fire to dry the cows and keep them warm. All along, however, she herself was still in her wet clothes, drenched to the skin and cold to the bones. That very night, she started to shiver with raging fever. She never got well. Ijaaz Miya got little pellets of herbs and roots from the hakim for her, but the pneumonia didn't leave her. When it at last did, and amma came out of the house, it was on a bier. Laila was always scared of cyclones and storms, and Sylhet had many of these. Whenever the winds started rushing in and out from the sea, she had always clung on to amma. She had always been scared of cyclones, though never of a loss it might cause. But after her amma was gone, the onset of every cyclone made her panic not for the cyclone itself but for the loss it might leave her in.

Now though, she was starting the fire like her amma used to. She had been doing it for the last two years since amma had left home in the bier never to return. Then, having poured the salted black tea into abba's glass and with some jaggery on a plate, she waited for her abba to come in. When he didn't come long after she heard the bamboo shutters of the shop drag over the rough, sun-baked ground, she went out towards the shop to find out. The sun had long set but there was still some feeble light left that gave everything an orange tinge. Ijaaz Miya was sitting on the bench, deep in thought, still looking towards the road. Laila went and sat near him on the bench.

'Abbajaan?' she said softly, not to startle him, 'I thought I heard you close the shop and so made you your tea. Aren't you coming home?'

Ijaaz Miya slowly turned towards her and gently placed a hand on her head.

'I want to sit here for a while longer, child,' he said.

'Then do you want me to bring your tea here?' she offered.

'Ah! That'd be wonderful!' he smiled.

Laila walked towards the kitchen to fetch his tea and jaggery. Everytime the boughs of the gulmohar swayed even the slightest, there was a gentle fall of tiny leaves. Some of them green but most of them yellow. Every morning Ijaaz Miya swept the front of the shop but by afternoon, the leaves were all over it once more. Somehow, Ijaaz Miya came to find soothing company in them. He never felt alone while working at his repair shop, for there would always be atleast a few of them in fall, looking up on Ijaaz Miya before they came to rest on the ground. Laila soon arrived with the tea.

'Come, sit here a while, Laila,' Ijaaz Miya said, taking the tea and jaggery from her. He dusted the fallen leaves off the bench with a couple of sweeps of his free hand for Laila to sit on.

'Some six years or so ago, I'm not sure how many exactly, there was this boy from our village who ran away from home. Do you remember?'

Laila looked at her father. She remembered him every moment, every day.

'Habib and Najma's adopted son,' he helped her recollect, 'do you remember?'

'Oh yes,' she replied after a moment's thought, 'he used to come for lessons at the mosque but then, all of a sudden, he stopped coming.'

'Anjaan, wasn't he?' Ijaaz Miya asked just to be sure.

'Anjaan, yes,' she nodded. 'So, what of him?'

'Anjaan visited today,' Ijaaz Miya told her very calmly.

It took some time for Laila to absorb the news. She wanted to ask so many things about Anjaan. She wanted to ask if he remembered her, she wanted to ask how he was to look at now, she wanted to ask how he arrived. She also wanted to ask if he would visit again. Instead, she just listened and waited for her abba to talk. She breathed deep to calm her heart. Occasionally, a red gulmohar flower fell from the tree. Ijaaz Miya looked at his daughter as she bent to pick up the few flowers on the ground to avoid her abba's eyes.

'He said he would come again,' he told her.

The next time that Anjaan visited was many months later. This time too he visited with Manik Roy. But this time Manik Roy drove the cart right upto Ijaaz Miya's repair shop and cheerfully called out even before he alighted from the horsecart, 'Salaam Waleiqum, Ijaaz Miya!' Seeing the horses, Ijaaz Miya had already come out of his shop to receive Manik Roy and Anjaan. 'Namashkar, Manik babu!' he greeted, 'Come! Come!' Anjaan demurely followed Manik Roy into the shop yard and remained standing while Manik Roy helped himself to the bench.

'And today you will have to take tea,' Ijaaz Miya insisted, 'my Laila brews it just right, not strong, not weak.'

Manik Roy laughed heartily, pulled out a foot from its sandal and tucked it under the other thigh on the bench and said, 'For exactly that I have been wanting to come.'

'Wonderful!' Ijaaz Miya exclaimed, 'so while you make yourselves comfortable, let me just go and inform Laila.'

Those few moments seemed to be longer than all the years Anjaan was away from Hazratkandi. He didn't know if he should just sit on the bench and wait or do something else with himself to hide his anxiety. He walked into the shop and sat down on Ijaaz Miya's morha that was placed next to a standing bicycle. Its pedal needed fixing, and it looked like Ijaaz Miya had been halfway through it when they arrived. Anjaan had fixed pedals at the 9 Periphery Supply Camp, he even remembered being appreciated once by Sujit for doing a good job of it. So he pulled the morha closer to the cycle and set about fixing it to distract his thudding heart. Ijaaz Miya came out soon after and sat on the bench. Laila followed, after a while. Anjaan couldn't see her face when she walked into the yard because she headed straight to the bench towards her father and stood near him. He only saw her bare feet and ankles peeking from below the legs of her dark purple salwar. A little of her lower arm was showing from where the sleeves of her pink kameez ended. She was holding a big, round, brass plate with three small glasses on it. Anjaan could see the tea through the glass. Appetizingly translucent, not strong, not weak. There was a saucer too next to the glasses but from where Anjaan was sitting, he didn't see what was in it. Or maybe he didn't notice. For his gaze now gently searched Laila's face. He saw it only from the side, through the pink muslin dupatta that covered her head. From underneath the dupatta her braid rested lightly on her back. He tried to remain looking at the bicycle's pedal though he was done fixing it. Ijaaz Miya picked a glass from the plate and offered it to Manik Roy.

'Manik babu, this is my daughter, my precious Laila.'

'Adab-arz-hai,' Laila greeted, delicately bowing her head.

'Bless you, child!' Manik Roy replied, her smile warming his heart.

'Anjaan, looking up something in there?' Ijaaz Miya asked, motioning towards the shop.'

'Nothing, kaka, just saw that the mending of the pedal was half-way through. So instead of just sitting, I completed the work,' Anjaan replied wringing his fingers, suddenly feeling awkward.

'Come now,' Ijaaz Miya called him, 'come have some tea.'

Laila turned towards him and walked a few paces forward, holding the plate out to Anjaan. He looked at her and smiled, a gush of hot air moving underneath the skin on his face. She smiled back. It was the same dimpled smile, those same eyes. He would have recognized her had he seen her any where else. Only, she was taller and seemed more mature. Through those eyes that looked back at him, Anjaan could see that she was still the same outspoken, strong headed, fearless person that she had always been during her childhood.

'You look different,' she said, smiling at Anjaan, 'I wouldn't recognize you elsewhere.'

Anjaan looked at her fingers that trembled in their grip around the edge of the plate as he picked up the glass. He had an urge to touch them and calm them, but he didn't.

'Jaggery?' she asked.

Only now did Anjaan see what was there in the saucer. He picked up a small piece.

'Come sit here, Anjaan,' Ijaaz Miya called him to the bench, 'so you picked up some bicycle repair work at Manik babu's depot?' he asked.

'Actually kaka, I picked up a little bit at the 9 Periphery Supply Camp where I used to be before I came to the Central Supply Depot at Narikuli. Manik kaka's camp, that is.'

'I see,' Ijaaz Miya nodded.

'And a little bit of cart and carriage repair work too, though not as much that I may call myself a fine hand,' he said, taking the glass to his lips. Laila stood there watching him.

'This, our Anjaan here, is an asset at the depot, Ijaaz Miya,' Manik Roy explained, not without some pride, 'he is indispensable to our superintendent Edward Fidley sahib. And he definitely knows so much that I may call him a fine hand!'

Laila noticed Anjaan blushing. She could also see that her abba was impressed to hear that.

'Some more jaggery, Manik kaka?' she asked.

Manik Roy patted his robust belly and said, 'Look here, child, this already looks like one of those sacks of potatoes slumped at the back of the cart,' and he laughed heartily at his own humour. Anjaan always felt that Manik Roy had a way of making situations easy and lively. Laila lingered around, waiting for the men to finish their tea. She then picked up the glasses and went in to leave the plate.

'Abbajaan,' she called back over her shoulder, but looking at Anjaan, 'I'll be back in a moment.'

That day both Laila and Ijaaz Miya saw Manik Roy and Anjaan off. While Ijaaz Miya walked them to the cart, Laila stood under the gulmohar tree, taking in as much of Anjaan as she could till the horse drawn cart disappeared into the distance.

That night Laila heard her father toss and turn in the adjacent room till late at night. Sleep didn't come to her either, but she lay still on her side. These days, everytime she heard her abba toss and turn at night, she knew what he would broach the next morning.

'Lailajaan,' he would say, 'age is catching up with me and my health is failing.'

'So, I'm there to take care of you,' she would say.

He would then pause before asking, 'And who will take care of you?'

'You ofcourse, abbajaan,' she would say.

'And after me?' he would invariably ask back.

'I'm big enough to take care of myself,' she would say. She also knew Ijaaz Miya would at that point mention her friends.

'Fatima and Tahira have long got married,' he would say.

'Good for them,' she would always shoot back.

'When will you?' he would ask, exasperation slowly creeping in.

'I will, when my shehzada comes looking for me,' she would giggle.

What Ijaaz Miya didn't share with her on all those occasions was his anxieties about the shop as well. He was no longer able to work as much as he used to earlier. He didn't have the resources to hire someone who knew the work and whom he could trust, with both the shop and with a young girl at home. He couldn't close shop either, for without the shop their homefire would cease to burn.

That night too as Laila heard him toss and turn in bed, she knew exactly what thoughts were passing through his mind. What she didn't know was that tonight he was thinking of Anjaan as a likely answer Allah had sent for all his questions.

But would Anjaan come and stay with them? To work with him? Ijaaz Miya wondered. He sat up on bed. Hadn't Anjaan said that he wanted to come back to Hazratkandi?

Only, Ijaaz Miya didn't know whether Anjaan would be his Laila's shehzada.

7
The Year Eighteen Seventy-Seven

In the months that followed, Anjaan sat by the banks of the Koshiara more often than ever before, quietly by himself. Sometimes he slowly paced the length of the pier, pensive, wondering where to go from there. That pier, that led him only halfway across the river and abandoned him in the middle of nowhere, was so similar to his life. At other times though, he just sat there, looking down at the rippling waters, searching in its depths the answers to all the questions that flowed aimlessly through his mind. Earlier he would walk down towards the river with Manik Roy who regaled him with stories from West Bengal and his native village Poriduar. And sometimes, to emphasize his tales, he sang songs too. Anjaan particularly enjoyed the way Manik Roy sang baul songs. Anjaan had heard these songs in the villages around Hazratkandi, in the villages of Bhowmik kaka and Dey kaka. But when

Manik Roy sang them, there was a slightly different pitch to the same songs, as if they belonged to a different land. It was a pitch that Manik kaka said was unique to Poriduar, making them sound somewhat differently charming. Because songs too, it seemed, had their own lands to belong, their own identity to hold on to. At other times, Edward Fidley would take him out on a stroll with himself. And during those walks he would tell Anjaan about people, places and legends from his homeland, England.

But these days Anjaan liked to be by himself. One night, at the dormitory that he shared with a few other registered workers of the depot, he dragged out his steel trunk from underneath his bed after the rest of them had fallen asleep. Whatever worldly possession he gathered from the time he arrived at the 9 Periphery Supply Camp, was locked in there. He unlocked it as quietly as he could so that he did not disturb the others, but more than that, it was he who did not wish to be disturbed. Then he as quietly lifted the lid of the trunk. It was heavy, for it was supposed to be an army trunk. Buried deep inside his few articles and clothing of a few pairs of shorts and shirts and one pair of full trousers, a pair of shoes that he hardly wore and that still looked as good as new, two pairs of socks, a knife, a comb and a few other knick knacks was a cloth bag with drawstrings. Dinbandhu, the tailor at the 9 Periphery Supply Camp, had stitched the bag for Anjaan with leftover cloth brought to stitch curtains for the lone, large window in the camp's small office. The bag was round at the base and Dinbandhu had attached fancy pompoms at the end of the drawstrings. Anjaan didn't have anything much to keep in it those days while he was at the 9 Periphery Supply Camp. But once he began to receive his wage at the Central Supply Depot, the bag was just the right place for him to put his annas into.   And now, while the rest in the dormitory slept, he loosened the drawstrings and emptied the bag on his bed. The contents poured out with a languorous clink, breaking the silence of the night. He quickly put his hands over them to hush their clinking. He then began counting them. During the nights when Anjaan couldn't sleep, he found the dormitory too quiet for comfort. Except for the occasional snore of a workeror a stray mouse scampering along the wall, the dark, high roofed dormitory felt menacing. The wind on the Koshiara made eerie sounds and, if a river dolphin or a fish plonked and splashed, the sound travelled right across the sand banks through the open windows into the dormitory. The depot mess, where they had their meals, was way across the back of the dormitory. Long after Anjaan and his fellow workers retired into their beds, sounds of pots and pans being scrubbed and washed at the river and being brought back would permeate through the silence and eddy around their wrought iron beds. During cloudless summer nights, swarms of glowing fireflies made the riverfront appear as if the star-studded sky had come down to earth. And sometimes, when Anjaan looked out, he saw a flickering light at the window of Edward Fidley's residential quarters. A couple of times when he saw his silhouette at the window, it scared him. Maybe it was the presence of the river, and the sounds that came from it, that often made the nights intimidating. Bhagirath Basak, the worker who now slept soundly on the bed next to his, said there were spirits that swam the river at night to catch both fish and fishermen. And yet, he had to stay awake that night because this was the only time he could be awake and alone at the dormitory. So he emptied his small cloth bag on his bed and began to count the annas. His earnings of these years at the depot. With it, he probably would be able to start something in Hazratkandi. Or maybe he could purchase a small holding of land. He could not make up his mind. But with the amount he had, he assumed he would only get barren land. He looked at the coins, ran his hand over them and slowly, one by one, started picking them and putting them back into the cloth bag. He then tightened the drawstrings. He remembered how lovingly Dinbandhu made the pompoms for him. 'So where would you like to hang these in the bag, my boy?' He had asked. It had made Anjaan feel very happy. The way Dinbandhu asked made him feel he belonged. The way he respected Anjaan's decision, however insignificant it might have been to him, when Anjaan came to think of it now. 'Here, at the end of the strings!' Anjaan had suggested. The delight he felt that moment all those years ago came back to fill his heart now in the stillness of the night, though only briefly. 'There they go then!' Dinbandhu had said, deftly attaching the pompoms to the end of the strings and handing him the bag. Had it not been for all those people at the 9 Periphery Supply Camp, Anjaan thought now as he sat on his bed at the depot, he would have been dead like a certain grasshopper he often thought he saw, but couldn't recollect where, a grasshopper that was being pulled away by ants. He picked up the bag and put it back into the steel trunk. And having locked it, pushed it back underneath his bed as noiselessly as he could manage.

It was only after many more months that he could go to Hazratkandi to see Ijaaz Miya. And Laila. The day he went, he stayed for more than an hour. And while he was there, he helped out Ijaaz Miya at his work even as they chatted.

'My back and shoulders hurt, Anjaan, they no longer allow me to stay bent for long hours over the repairs,' Ijaaz Miya said. Anjaan noticed the stoop on his back and the way groans escaped the elderly man every time he got up or sat down.

'This is the only place for umbrellas and cycles in the next three villages,' he went on, 'so they all come here, my boy, customers are many. But I am no longer able to keep pace with the work that comes by.' He looked up from his work and pointed to something behind Anjaan. 'There, son,' he said, still pointing that way, 'in that small box over there, there are needles.' Anjaan turned to look towards where he pointed and found it. 'This?' he asked.

'Yes, pass that over here please,' Ijaaz Miya said stretching out his hand for the needle box.

After Anjaan passed it over, he watched how the old man then struggled to thread the needle to mend the umbrella he was bending over.

'Allow me, kaka,' Anjaan offered, taking the needle from him, and threading it.

'This is how it is nowadays, Anjaan, this is why I need someone to help me out in the shop,' Ijaaz Miya said sadly, 'someone I can trust. It terrifies me to think of what will be after I am gone.'

'Khuda na khwasta! Ijaaz kaka, you'll live long,' Anjaan said, pity for the helpless old man in front of him filling his heart.

'Assuming even that, son, after having lived long, I'll still be gone one day. Who will then look after my Laila? What will come upon the shop? And without the shop, what will we eat? How I wish I could entrust the shop to someone I can rely on, someone honest and sincere.' And then he added as an afterthought, 'and caring too.'

Both sat in silence for some time. The only noise that passed between them was the *doof doof* of the long needle that went in and out of the thick black canvas of the umbrella Ijaaz Miya was putting together.

Anjaan watched the movement of the needle and still looking at it, asked very hesistantly, 'Ijaaz kaka, have you ever considered me?'

The needle in Ijaaz Miya's hand abruptly halted midway through the canvas as Ijaaz Miya stopped and looked up at Anjaan. 'Well, Anjaan?' he asked, as if to be sure of what he heard. So he asked it with a slight bend of his head, turning an ear towards Anjaan. He couldn't believe that Anjaan himself proposed what he had been wishing for since Anjaan's first visit with Manik Roy. But seeing Ijaaz Miya exclaim thus, Anjaan thought he offended Laila's father, that he overstepped his position. He was, after all, a bastard, as Rafiq had said. It pained him then, it pained him now, but that was the truth of his identity. Nobody had ever asked him about it at the 9 Periphery Supply Camp, nor at the Central Supply Depot at Narikuli because they didn't need to know, it didn't matter to them. Nobody asked him at Hazratkandi either, especially not Ijaaz Miya. That was because here they already knew. And yet, he couldn't erase that truth from his own conscience. With every breath he lived, he couldn't stop asking himself who he was.

Anjaan bent his head and lowered his eyes, 'Mwaafi, Ijaaz kaka,' he stammered, for the first time in his life, 'forgive me for stepping over my limits....I should've known...'

Ijaaz Miya pulled out the remaining part of the needle through the canvas and then paused his work.

'And what if I am relieved to hear you ask that?' he said, looking at Anjaan.

'You are, kaka?' Anjaan raised his head and looked at Ijaaz Miya. Through the foggy glasses of his old spectacles, glasses that were full of stains and scratches, Ijaaz Miya saw light in Anjaan's eyes.

In his subsequent visits, Anjaan and Ijaaz Miya together put up a room in the open space between the shop and the house. The room had bamboo walls plastered with mud and a thatch roof like the rest of Ijaaz Miya's house. The room was airy and well lit. Laila stitched up a curtain from a dupatta and hung it on the window. With his savings from the depot, Anjaan bought a cot, a mattress and a mosquito net, a few pots and pans and a mat for his prayers. For some time now, Anjaan had started growing a beard too. During haircutting and shaving routines at the depot, if the barber saw that the head and the face belonged to an Indian, he asked, 'Darhi?' Meaning whether he should trim the beard or not, according to whether he was a Hindu, a Sikh, a Christian, a Buddhist, or whatever. Anjaan used to let the barber give him a shave because he didn't know to which faith he belonged. But of late he had stopped the barber from giving him a shave. He also bought a taqiyah, for he hoped to accompany Ijaaz Miya to the mosque for jumuah once he came to stay with him at Hazratkandi. Going back to the mosque of his childhood would bring back many a memory, Anjaan knew, some painful, some achingly sweet. But he braced himself for all of that. He also braced himself for many a question. How his heart had pounded when he had seen the dome of the mosque once from the road as he passed by Hazratkandi with Manik Roy on their way towards Biyanibazar! But that was a long time ago. He was more stable now, more mature. He understood that if he had to stay at Hazratkandi, he would have to shake his inhibitions about going back once more to the mosque where he heard Fatima and Tahira speak to Laila about him. He would have to face it all once more. Maybe for just one more time. He had thought hard and well and had decided. He braced himself. Now there was no looking back.

And then finally one afternoon, Anjaan decided to leave the Central Supply Depot at Narikuli to go back to where he thought he belonged, or atleast to where he thought he could begin his search of himself. He decided to go back to Hazratkandi. On that last day at the depot, Anjaan could see that Edward Fidley was saddened. He called Anjaan into his office. It was a small but meticulously kept place, well dusted despite the sand that blew in from the river. It had a clean floor with a neat square rug under Edward Fidley's desk. There was a small figurine of the Virgin Mary on the desk, placed on a slightly raised platform. In all his years at the depot, Anjaan had observed that, every Sunday, Edward Fidley dressed up in his special suits in winter, and his best trousers and shirts in summer, and rode the best horse to the chapel at the far end of the depot's large, open yard. Many more fair-skinned people like Edward Fidley gathered there from far across Sylhet. It was their jumuah, Anjaan thought. Anjaan also noticed, in all these years at the depot, that Edward Fidley wore those particular clothes only to particular and special occasions, occasions that Edward Fidley considered important. After the prayers, the church-goers sat at the long table that was specially laid out under the shade of the large mango tree, not too close to the river. Early on Sunday mornings, Edward Fidley would himself see to the laying of the table, with fine, porcelain cups and saucers, and tall glasses that came all the way from England by ship, Anjaan was told, and flowers of the season in painted, ceramic vases. But he only laid the table. The snacks ofcourse were brought by the visiting church-goers, things that Anjaan didn't know were called cakes, cookies, marmalade and pies. Initally, it had amused Anjaan to see that their womenfolk had dresses on their hands too. 'They are gloves, Anjaan, not kameez for hands!' Manik Roy had laughed. And as they sat over tea, they discussed news from home and the menfolk sometimes also discussed matters that ought not to reach Indians, so it seemed to Anjaan. The women would in that while, read from the Bible and tell stories from it to the children. Anjaan understood the book to be their Qoran. And sometimes they sang songs too, songs that belonged to lands far across the seas and oceans, but echoed with equal love in an alien land like India. For Anjaan though, these songs were the lifeline of those who sang them. Because floating with the winds and the waves, they brought back pictures of home. Home. For they too belonged somewhere.

That day too, as Anjaan stood in Edward Fidley's office looking at the figurine of the Virgin Mary, he saw that Fidley Sahib was in his special clothes. His wide brimmed hat hung from a coat and hat stand near the door, like it always did when Edward Fidley was indoors.

'Here, Anjaan Hazratkandi,' he said, opening the register in which Anjaan had put his thumb and registered himself into the depot, in the year 1873. 'Put your thumb once more.'

Anjaan didn't ask to what he was putting his thumb. He trusted Edward Fidley just as much as Edward Fidley trusted and loved Anjaan. In fact, sometimes Anjaan found it hard to even believe that Edward Fidley was English, just like those who shackled his free skies and open fields. Had Anjaan known to read, he would've read to what he was putting his thumb now.

Anjaan Hazratkandi, aged twenty-one years, of village Hazratkandi, Sylhet division, East Bengal, India, is no longer a registered worker of the Central Supply Depot, Narikuli, Sylhet Division, East Bengal, India, from this first day of April, year 1877.

But he needn't know.

Anjaan's last day at the depot was a Sunday. Edward Fidley was dressed to go to church.

'It's Easter today, my boy, it is the day of resurrection, the day of renewed life. Well, isn't it symbolic, that it is on this day of renewed life that you too are setting out to start life afresh! You will be missed here, though,' he said, 'remember me if you ever need anything.'

For the first time in his years at the depot, Anjaan raised his right palm to his forehead as he bowed his head.

'Adab-arz-hai, Fidley sahib, thank you!' he said, his heart overwhelmed with respect for this particular English gentleman. He stepped back from the desk, still facing Edward Fidley, with his head still bowed. As Anjaan walked past the large French windows of Edward Fidley's office towards the door, a gust of wind blew in from the Koshiara and turned the pages of the enrolment register in a flutter, as if reflecting his days that had flown by at the depot.

'Goodbye, Anjaan! I have asked Manik Roy to drop you off at Hazratkandi,' Fidley sahib said as he saw Anjaan off till the door of his office.

'My depot won't be the same any more, Anjaan, but I'll come to see you sometime,' he added.

Anjaan bowed once more before he stepped out of the office into the yard. A loaded vessel had just cast anchor at the depot's dock and there was a flurry of activity by the pier. The gulls and terns flocked to the planks and the waters, raising a farewell cacophony that sat lovingly in his heart for long years to come. Anjaan watched it all from a distance, for a while, for one last time. Bhagirath Basak helped him carry his trunk to the cart and Manik Roy was already seated and set to take Anjaan to what he thought was home, on an Easter Sunday, to start life afresh. That was Anjaan's last trip on Manik Roy's horse cart. Before hopping on to the cart, Anjaan patted the horses. They recognized him.

And Anjaan Hazratkandi left the Central Supply Depot at Narikuli to go back to Hazratkandi, for he hoped to search for and find his roots.

At Hazratkandi, Ijaaz Miya began to entrust Anjaan with more and more responsibilities and work at his shop as the months passed by. Business at the shop was once more picking up because Anjaan used the knowledge he gathered with Sujit and Balraj at the 9 Periphery Supply Camp and started repairing horse and mule carts and carriages as well. There were carriages which were brought in from the homes of zamindars and rich merchants for repair works and for greasing of the cartwheels. The zamindars and the merchants paid well too. Anjaan, with his knack of learning on the job, impressed the new customers just the way he impressed Ijaaz Miya. Ijaaz Miya's cycle and umbrella repair shop was elevated to a karkhana of sorts. A workshop. The shop was gradually stepping out of its hard days. Anjaan kept a few bicycle bells and bicycle seats too that he had purchased at wholesale rates from Shubhroto Pal at the Latu bazar. Pal was a trader who stocked various such things that he brought from Dhaka and Noabazar. Anjaan also noticed that the legs of the wooden bench under the gulmohar tree were beginning to rot, partly because of age and partly because of withstanding many a noontime monsoon shower. So, he replaced them with new, sturdier ones. Also, when Niloy Bhowmik, Haragopal Dey, Mansoor, Abdul, Tarinimohan and all his old friends dropped by, Ijaaz Miya loved to sit on the bench instead of the morha. To make it comfortable for him, Anjaan fixed horizontal wooden bars as a back support on the bench. Anyone walking into the shop after long could make out that the shop was doing well, that Anjaan put his best into it. Ijaaz Miya worked less now though he continued to just be around the shop, either sitting on his morha or on the bench. Because he looked forward to meeting and chatting up with the people who dropped by, to catch up with happenings and gossip from around the neighbouring villages. Those moments on the bench with his friends sustained him, and all those who dropped by as well. That bench, and the tree below which it stood, too were an intrinsic part of that brotherhood, privy to all the joys, sorrows, worries and the secrets of their nights that they shared.

Ijaaz Miya sometimes asked Anjaan to have his noon meal together with him. And sometimes, when there was too much work at the shop, which usually happened just before Durga Puja, Diwali and Idd when zamindars and merchants wanted their carriages and carts to look festive and new, Ijaaz Miya asked Laila to carry Anjaan's noon meal to the shop itself. It was during one such time that Sirajullah, the hakim from the neighbouring village of Bouderbeel, dropped by. For many villages across, people knew Sirajullah more as someone who talked in a roundabout way than as a hakim. On that day he had no repair work to be done. He just came walking all along the road looking for a particular variety of small bush whose roots he needed to make some medicine. Because that bush grew only on raised ground, he was looking for it along the highway. He had already uprooted those closer to his own home and new ones would spring forth only next monsoon. He came looking for it all the way towards Hazratkandi and when he came by Ijaaz Miya's shop, he thought of sitting a while to rest and stretch his exhausted limbs and update Ijaaz Miya with happenings from around.

'Isn't that Laila?' Sirajullah asked Ijaaz Miya when he saw her in the shop.

Ijaaz Miya nodded.

'It's been long since I saw her last. She has grown! Hasn't she?' Sirajullah remarked.

Ijaaz Miya smiled indulgently.

Anjaan was sitting on the morha and was eating, with his plate of rice placed on a small stool slightly higher than the morha. While he ate, Laila hovered around the shop, picking things from the hard earthen floor, and organizing them into cane baskets lined along the wall of the shop. Every now and then she asked Anjaan where to put something when she couldn't figure out where it ought to go. Anjaan responded each time, either through words or through a hand gesture when his mouth was full. Sirajullah observed all of it. When Anjaan was done with his meal, Laila took the plate and returned to the house. After she was gone and Anjaan resumed work, Sirajullah slid himself closer to Ijaaz Miya on the bench and said in hushed tones, 'Miya, it is neither wise nor safe to put ghee and fire close to one another.' He paused as Ijaaz Miya looked at him, not exactly understanding what he hinted at. Sirajullah raised his eyebrows and motioned with his hand towards Anjaan inside the shop, 'Each stokes the other.' Ijaaz Miya looked towards the shop but remained quiet. Not that he hadn't thought of it. 'I have no medicines in my kit for wagging tongues, Ijaaz Miya, don't tell me later that I hadn't warned.' While leaving, Sirajullah added, 'Get the two married, Ijaaz Miya, your shop and daughter both will be taken care of. Moreover, he'll be an umbrella during rain and sun over your ageing head too.'

Since the moment Sirajullah left, Ijaaz Miya thought and rethought and dwelled upon every word he had said. All of it was true. He would have even broached the matter long ago to Anjaan. There would not have been a better shehzada for Laila, he thought. The only hitch, and a big one at that, was Ijaaz Miya knew absolutely nothing of Anjaan's antecedents, and it was just this that had held him back from asking Anjaan all these years. After all, it was his daughter's life - and not the brakes of a cycle that could be mended if broken.

Might he have been a Christian or a Hindu by birth?
Might he have been born into wedlock or out of it?
What might be his family name?
Where might he have belonged to?

All these questions perturbed Ijaaz Miya as they swirled in his head like one of the cyclones in Sylhet.

Next day, when he asked Laila the same questions that disturbed him about Anjaan, she said without giving them as much of a moment's thought, 'Anjaan is a Moslem, we are his family, he belongs to Hazratkandi. As for wedlock, abbajaan, isn't it enough that he is born out of love? Would you rather have someone born into wedlock out of torture?'

Ijaaz Miya stood stunned and speechless. How simple she made it all appear!

'Then may I ask Anjaan?' he asked Laila, seeking her consent.

Laila only smiled and looked down.

8
The Year Eighteen Eighty

It was Laila Begum and Anjaan Hazratkandi's nikaah.

People began arriving at Ijaaz Miya's house to ask how arrangements were going. He and Laila then sent word with them to others they knew. Only then did Anjaan realize that he had no one to send word to. He just looked on from a distance or from the shop, feigning to bend over work. He, however, kept thinking of Manik Roy. Had Manik Roy not brought him over to Hazratkandi that first time after years of having stayed away, he wouldn't have met his Laila again, he wouldn't have had a chance in Hazratkandi and a chance at seeking his roots, nor would this nikaah come to be, he thought.

And so, some days earlier, he had decided to send word to Manik Roy at the Central Supply Depot at Narikuli about his nikaah. And a day before the ceremonies, Anjaan and Ijaaz Miya neatly stacked up all the tools and tyres, nails and needles, spoke and shaft, brush and blade and every tin can of oil and paint against the wall on one side of the shop. The ground of the yard in front of the shop too was evened out and the bench was set against the outer wall of the shop. Anjaan would pronounce his 'Qabool' three times over from the cleared out and decorated centre of the shop. He had given his best to rejuvenate the shop that was falling apart, and now the shop would be witness as Anjaan would begin life afresh.

Anjaan bought a saree from the Sutarkandi bazar for Laila. This was the first time he ever bought one all by himself. He remembered going to the Sutarkandi bazar once with his amma when she had bought a saree for herself. He tried to recollect what conversations she had with the vendor, how she chose the saree and how she bargained. But he could remember absolutely nothing. He only remembered having gone to the bazar and that next to the saree vendor, there was an old man who sold roasted grams from a large wicker basket. Anjaan remembered amma buying him some. But he didn't remember anything besides that, nothing about how to purchase a saree. So now as he sat in front of the saree vendor, he asked the vendor to unfold every saree that he showed him. Anjaan then held a length of it in his hands and raised his hands above his head, infront of his eyes. He imagined the fabric around Laila's head, caressing her dimpled cheeks and draping her body all the way down to her ankles. He envied how the saree would gently caress her skin and how she would keep pulling it closer over her breasts every now and then. He could almost see her through the saree as he held it against the sunlight now. He looked up quite a few sarees this way and disapproved of them all till the vendor showed him a pink one. He liked the glittering purple flowers on its pink base, the exact combination that was on Laila's salwar kameez that she was wearing when he arrived that second day at the shop from the Central Supply Depot with Manik kaka and when he saw Laila for the first time after she grew out of her childhood days, after all his years away from Hazratkandi. Anjaan also bought a pair of bangles and a pair of earrings. He wanted to buy a pair of sandals too, but he didn't know what size might fit her. That, he thought, he would buy for her after the nikaah, when he would bring her to the bazar. He would let her buy whatever she wished. He would from now on, try to give her all that she ever wished for. For himself he bought a pair of white pyjamas, the kind that Narayan kaka wore during Durga Puja, a white embroidered kurta, and a white taqiyah. He bought a handkerchief and a bottle of attar as well. He also bought a beautiful, cream-coloured laced taqiyah for Ijaaz Miya. He thought of abba. Had he been around, he would have been by his side at the nikaah, as his guardian. A sudden sense of having been rejected and abandoned, pierced his heart. His thoughts slipped back to Balraj Sandhu and Sujit, Mahib and Dinbandhu. He didn't know where they might be. He paid for the stuff he'd bought, put everything in the cloth bag slung on his shoulder, and cycled back to what he began calling home, his lone room behind Ijaaz Miya's cycle shop.

Fatima and Tahira arrived the day before the nikaah. They prepared henna to apply on Laila's hands and feet. Her aunts and uncles too arrived on the day of the nikaah to help Ijaaz Miya make the arrangements. Anjaan's room was swept clean, and its earthen floor was plastered with freshly mixed clay, water and cowdung. He spread a new sheet on the cot and placed a second pillow on it. He had washed the curtain, dried it, and hung it up once more on the window. Only, this time he touched it lightly with a dab of attar. For he wanted the room to fill with fragrance every time the wind blew in through that window, sensuously swaying the curtain that had been Laila's dupatta. He didn't know if Laila ever draped that dupatta around her head. But many a night after he came to stay in that room, he himself surely did. He stood by the window and let the breeze softly tease his face with the dupatta. Today however, he would be able to let Laila herself tease him. The cot, he assumed, would be small for two, but they will have to do with it for now. Moreover, the smaller the cot, the closer they would have to lie to each other. He lightly touched the pillows too with the stick attached to the inside of the lid of the bottle of attar.

Outside, Ijaaz Miya spread a new bedsheet on the backrest of the bench and let the sheet flow down to cover the seat and part of the legs too. After the rituals and pronouncement of 'Qabool', Ijaaz Miya wanted the groom to sit there to receive guests. He would ask someone to carry the bench inside the shop. Laila ofcourse would be sitting in an inner room, along with her friends and aunts. Ijaaz Miya did not plan on having too many guests however, because he didn't want to have around him too many people to answer to, about why there wasn't anyone attending the nikaah from among Anjaan's family and friends, who he was, and many other such awkward questions to which he had no answer. Though these did not matter to him at all after what Laila said she felt about Anjaan's antecedents. What mattered was that Laila had found her shehzada, and that Anjaan promised to be sincere to her. It was just that Ijaaz Miya didn't want any untoward, embarrassing situation during the nikaah.

However, all of those questions still continued to haunt Anjaan.

Early morning on the day of the nikaah, a rider arrived at the shop on horseback. No one had seen him before in Hazratkandi. He got off the horse and still holding on to the reins, asked for Anjaan Hazratkandi and said he was from the Central

Supply Depot at Narikuli and was sent by the depot's superintendent, Edward Fidley. Immediately a commotion started to brew among the few people who had already gathered at the shop yard, though it was yet early in the day for the ceremonies to begin. They were in awe of the horse, the rider, and the very fact that someone of such authority should come asking for Laila's groom. A few started murmuring about the likelihood of Anjaan's arrest, while some children darted across the yard to give the news to Laila. She got alarmed. Suddenly tense, Anjaan came out of his room with brisk steps, but when he saw the rider, his drawn face eased, and a smile spread across it. For he recognized the rider. It was Bhagirath Basak, whose bed was next to his in the dormitory of the depot. With one hand still holding on to the reins, he pulled down a bag from the back of the horse with the other.

'Fidley sahib sent this for you, Anjaan,' he said as he came forward to as far as the length of the reins allowed him. Anjaan walked up to him.

'What might it be?' Anjaan asked, receiving the bag but looking at Bhagirath Basak.

Bhagirath Basak smiled, 'Mutton. Halaal mutton, ten kilos of it.'

'Oh!' was all Anjaan could mutter. His heart went out toEdward Fidley.

'Fidley sahib's wedding gift to you!' Bhagirath Basak said with a smile.

'Come on in, Bhagirath, stay for the ceremonies,' Anjaan said.

'I wish I could,' Bhagirath Basak replied, taking in the happy commotion in the yard, 'but I have to reach the depot, a vessel is due to moor this afternoon and I have to be there. You know how it is during unloading, Anjaan!' Anjaan nodded. He knew it well. 'But it would have been wonderful if you could,' he hoped aloud, genuinely wishing he could. Bhagirath Basak stepped forward and held him in a warm embrace, the first ever despite all those years of sleeping side by side at the camp's dormitory, before riding away. The same little children once more sped across the yard to Laila to give her the news of the superintendent's wedding gift to Anjaan. She blushed. Her kohl lined eyes sparkled.

Maulvi Imdadur Ali arrived on time, carrying in his sling bag the Qoran. Because he would read verses from there at the ceremony. Ijaaz Miya had delegated the work responsibilities well ahead of the big day so that he himself would be free to receive and take care of guests. Laila's aunts volunteered to take care of the cooking. It was to be a simple meal of a fish curry, a mixed vegetable curry of brinjals, pumpkin and potatoes, a dal and steamed rice. One of the aunts made some vermicelli with jaggery and dates. But after Edward Fidley's gift arrived, the wedding feast had halaal mutton too. The tireless feet of laughing and screaming children running without purpose among the people, raised merry dust upon the dry, sun-baked mud yard, but nobody seemed to mind. It overwhelmed Ijaaz Miya to think of Anjaan's position at the Central Supply Depot and his affinity with its superintendent. He also noticed that the arrival of Bhagirath Basak as a messenger of the superintendent quietened many a rising question about Anjaan. Despite the rebellion against the British, Ijaaz Miya wondered, their fair skin and seemingly superior lineage still held sway over a part of the Indians. At that moment, it was precisely that which laid to rest many a rising apprehension about Anjaan, only because he was in the good books of such a nobleman of fair skin and superior lineage, from the ruling echelons.

While maulvi Imdadur Ali got the place at the centre of the shop ready to sit and read verses from the Qoran, Anjaan sat inside the shop with his back to the road and watched him. Just then there was sudden excitement under the gulmohar tree. A buzz rose along with the dust among the crowd as children and men started running towards the road. The maulvi paused in his work and Anjaan walked out to see what might be the reason for even more excitement in one morning, after the excitement of the arrival of Bhagirath Basak. This time he saw more horses on the road in front of the shop.

It was Edward Fidley himself!

'We have come, Anjaan, to stand by you as your guardians,' Edward Fidley said, dismounting the horse and smiling as he handed Anjaan a paper parcel. Later that night Anjaan would open the parcel to find a green kurta of jamdani silk, woven in the looms of the famed weavers of Rupshi village in Narayanganj. Walking a few paces behind Edward Fidley was Manik Roy, grinning and showing his betelnut stained teeth between happily overflowing cheeks. He handed Anjaan, as a gift, an umbrella all nicely packed inside a cloth bag.

'Had it brought all the way from Calcutta, son,' Manik Roy said, with the grin still on.

'Oh!' Anjaan exclaimed, at a loss for words.

'Yes, in the vessel with the containers and gunny sacks,' Edward Fidley added laughing.

Soon the rituals started. When Anjaan pronounced, 'Qabool! Qabool! Qabool!' Edward Fidley and Manik Roy stood on either side as his guardians. Edward Fidley had arrived in a pair of black breeches and a white silk shirt. Anjaan had seen him wearing this shirt many times earlier, but only when he went to church. So, he knew this was a special shirt that he wore only to special occasions. It moved Anjaan to think that Edward Fidley considered his wedding to be a special occasion for him, an occasion worthy of that silk shirt. Manik Roy too had discarded his uniform for Anjaan's wedding. He wore a crisp dhoti and topped it with a white, embroidered kurta. This kurta too Anjaan had seen before. Not on Manik Roy's body, but because Manik Roy had showed it to Anjaan the day it arrived by ship from Calcutta. His wife had sent it. How the carefree Manik kaka had blushed that day when he told Anjaan that she had dotingly done the embroidery herself. That Manik Roy chose to wear such a priceless kurta to Anjaan's wedding meant the world to Anjaan. He could feel a lump in his throat at the way Edward Fidley and Manik Roy had come to be by his side. His heart, that had always been meagre in expressing its abundant feelings, ached with gratitude and joy. For years to come, and as far as many villages across, people talked of Ijaaz Miya's new social standing and how lucky Laila was to get a husband who was regarded with such warmth and love by an Englishman. But while maulvi Imdadur Ali began reading from the Qoran, Anjaan's thoughts drifted away. He thought of his amma. He remembered now as he was getting married, how she used to call him her nawab. She would have been the happiest person of his nikaah, Anjaan was sure of that. He thought of abba, by whose side he had not been able to be as he breathed his last. Maybe it was only because of him that abba had gone through all that he did. For the first time, guilt simmered through Anjaan. He thought of Balraj Sandhu, Sujit, Mahib, and Dinbandhu of the 9 Periphery Supply Camp. He thought of Edward Fidley and Manik Roy sitting next to him at that very moment. How inexpressibly indebted he was to them. And yet, his thoughts also hovered around how different all this would have been had he only known who his father was, and what the full and real name was of the martyr at the Malegarh grave.

It was Ijaaz Miya's voice that broke his reverie.

'Ameen!' Ijaaz Miya said, along with most everyone else, who were listening to the maulvi.

'Anjaan Hazratkandi,' the maulvi asked, 'what mahr do you wish to give to your bride?'

Anjaan blushed and drew out an old but very precious pouch with drawstrings running along the edges of its round mouth, and with childlike pompoms attached to the ends of the drawstrings. The coins inside jingled today, like they did on a particular night that helped him decide which way to walk along the foggy, obscure path of his rootless life. While the pouch itself was his memento of the 9 Periphery Supply Camp, what was inside it was his memories of home from the time that he had been at the Central Supply Depot. These were what had sustained him all along, and these were what he handed to Laila as her mahr. Her wedding gift from her groom. Both the coins and the memories. Because these were his everything, and so was Laila.

'This, here, has all my savings in it,' he said handing it over to Laila, 'this is all I have,' he looked down, a sense of unworthiness suddenly overpowering him. He would add later in the night, in the privacy of his room when just the two of them would be by the dupatta curtain, 'The pouch is all I have, Lailajaan, it is all yours. And so am I!'

There were as many Hindu guests earlier that day as there were Moslem ones. No one asked about Anjaan Hazratkandi's parents, not yet. Ijaaz Miya's heart filled with a kind of peace that he had never known since Laila's mother left them. He desperately longed for her today. She always used to tell him that she would prepare a curry of dried fish, shutki as they called it, for her daughter's nikaah. Because Ijaaz Miya relished the way she cooked it, and he would lick his fingers like a child till the last morsel. But she didn't stay on long enough to watch her Laila get married, to cook shutki for her nikaah. So, without her, there was no shutki curry either for Laila's wedding feast. Ijaaz Miya closed his eyes for a fleeting moment and visions of Laila's mother floated through them. She was smiling and nodding, to let him know that what was happening would bring happiness to their Laila. When he opened his eyes, there were tears of gratitude in them.

It was almost evening when the last of the guests left. Laila's aunt lit the lanterns and placed one in Anjaan's room. Laila was then taken across the threshold of her father's house to that of her husband. Though there were less than twenty steps between the two places, yet she was accompanied by a whole lot of aunts, cousins, and little children. Days later, Anjaan put up a kind of bamboo awning, joining the thatch roofs of his room and Ijaaz Miya's house. Linking the two houses and making them one. This was Laila and

Anjaan Hazratkandi's new home. Though the room remained as his and Laila's, the house came to belong to all three of them with Laila now taking total charge of the kitchen for everyone. So even as she stayed with her husband, she could hear her father cough or groan or call her. And then she would run to her abba along the passage that had just a roof but no walls.

'Good, Miya,' Sirajullah had said one day soon after the wedding, 'wagging tongues have retreated into shut mouths.'

In the years after the wedding, from the outside everything remained just as it was before in Ijaaz Miya's little household. Laila continued to stay in her father's house, Anjaan continued to work at the shop, and Ijaaz Miya continued to spend leisurely moments on the bench under the gulmohar, meeting friends and catching up with stories from them about neighbouring villages. Anjaan seemed to have found some kind of social acceptance in what he had been made to run away from, years ago. He began attending social gatherings too, along with Laila. And that is how it was that he too was at Shankar Bhowmik's daughter's wedding.

The women sat and ate in an area screened off with brightly coloured sheets, away from the men. Singing, laughter and tinkling of anklet bells from dancing feet emanated from behind those screens, and Anjaan strained his ears to hear Laila's voice in that merry group. But his straining caught voices other than Laila's.

'Isn't that Ijaaz Miya's daughter's husband?' An elderly woman remarked, as she walked past Anjaan towards the screened area.

The woman walking alongside nudged her. 'Hush!'

'Living off his woman!' the older woman sneered.

Anjaan clenched his teeth.

The two women took the conversation into the ladies' sitting area.

'I heard he is a bastard?'

'I did too. Who knows! Must have tasted swine and snail while in the womb. What do you expect, when you don't know his roots!'

'Yeah, why would anyone be called a Hazratkandi, otherwise? Hah! The man is so poor, he doesn't have any family name!'

And the women giggled under their dupattas. The conversation drew Laila's attention.

'Had nowhere to go after he was thrown out, so sneaked back after Najma passed away, to feed on his wife's bits.'

'Habib's was an untimely death, only because of this leech they picked from filth.'

The burning anguish that flooded Anjaan now didn't feel any different or less excruciating than that day in his childhood, when he had overheard Fatima and Tahira speak of his rootlessness, for the first time, outside the mosque. Now as he stood feeling lost and alone in a marquee filled with people out to feast and make merry, his eyes reddened with shame and defeat. Anjaan wished for Laila to emerge, so that he could go back home. *Home.* He wanted to run away once again, from the crowd and the wedding. He wanted to be alone at home. *Home*, was it? Just then he heard Laila's voice. Squaring up, yet unraised and composed.

'And so, my man lives in my father's house, he does!' She was saying. The elderly woman's voice tried to say something, but Laila overruled her. 'He cares for me and my abbajaan, and he loves me. He doesn't bash me up, Mashi-ma, like your son-in-law does to your daughter. And you don't, or rather can't, open your mouth at that time to stop him!'

The singing and dancing stopped.

'Your men won't have decent cycles and umbrellas without my husband living where he does. He works hard and feeds his wife and her aged father through honest means. At your age, blessing him suits you, Mashi-ma, not cursing him!'

'Covering up for him, aren't you?' the woman stammered, taken aback by the unexpected confrontation. 'Do you even know what faith his sinful parents might have followed? Know, dear girl, he has no faith. He too must be sleeping around, returning to the cycle shop only to feed like a parasite. Hah!'

Some women tried to hush her. More went and stood near Laila, as if lending their tacit support. But even if alone, Laila would stand and speak for what she believed in.

Anjaan seethed and his palms began to sweat. He felt the stab of a hundred daggers in a corner of his soul which he didn't know existed. 'Lailajaan!' he called out, 'come let's leave!'

Laila gathered her hijaab and as she walked out, she stopped near the woman and said, 'I respect your age, Mashi-ma, but don't make up stories of swine and snail. Instead, accept the truth that your married son often gets sloshed and sleeps with..... Touba! The whole of Hazratkandi knows that. My husband's faith, if you wish to know, is his truthful heart. And the love and respect he holds in that heart. Not just for me but for abbajaan too. Anyone like him need not follow any other faith, Mashi-ma, and he is not identityless. His integrity is his identity.' She stormed past but retraced her steps and spoke on her face, 'It is people like you who need the pretence of a faith to cover the infidelity in your dark heart!' And then she strode out of the wedding, composed as ever, walking side by side with Anjaan.

It was exactly this which too hadn't changed at all over the years. Anjaan was constantly reminded that his acceptance in society was only a shallow pretence, his lack of identity continued to haunt him as it always had.

And so, his quest to know who he was remained, and his visits to the graves at Malegarh continued, just as before.

On days when Laila noticed that Anjaan was unusually quiet and dejected after returning from the graves at Malegarh, she would ask him to sit by her at the kitchen as she prepared the meal.

'But there will come a time, Anjaan,' she often said, 'when the silence of the graves will lead you to some place. Or some person. You're not alone.' And then she would come very close to him and put her hand on his, 'am I not with you?'

Laila, in her own way, took it upon herself to keep Anjaan going in his quest. Her aunts insisted that she convince Anjaan to take up her family name, for the sake of the children that would be born of them someday. But she desisted. Rather, she encouraged him in his search. She stood by him in all those moments when he felt lost. And when he wept, she held his head and said, 'It's alright to weep, Anjaan, the tears only wash your soul so that you have a clearer picture of whatever there is in it, what path it has to show you. Look into your soul for that path after you have lightened your soul from weeping. It's alright, Anjaan, weep.' In those words, and those moments, Anjaan saw in the woman who tenderly held his head, the same headstrong little girl who sat across him in the mosque taking lessons from the Qoran. Inside their closed room, he kissed her dimples.

It was many years later that Laila was able to bear a child. Ijaaz Miya's joy knew no bounds when he was given the news. For he had almost given up hope of seeing his Laila's child. He even heard people talk behind him that it was a punishment Allah inflicted on him for bringing a bastard into the family. It pained him when he heard thus, but he kept all of it away from Laila. This emotional pain had begun to keep Ijaaz Miya mostly unwell. But when Laila came to be with child, Ijaaz Miya once more started to get up and sit sometimes on the morha and sometimes out on the bench under the gulmohar tree. He had himself gone up to the Sutarkandi bazar to buy a small lamb for Laila's child's aqiqah. For on the seventh day of the child's birth, it would be given a name. He wondered what name Laila and Anjaan would decide upon. And then he smiled to himself thinking how silly he was to forget that the name could be decided only after the child was born, regardless of whether it was a girl or a boy. But his joy was swelling with each approaching day. He would ask Laila's aunts over for the aqiqah meal. He would ask Laila to send word to Fatima and Tahira too. By then the monsoons would be over, so there would be sunshine upon the yard in front of the shop for the family to sit, celebrate, and name the newborn child. But now the monsoons were drenching everything. The ground was filled with slush and the rains pelted incessantly. Even the narrow passage, between Ijaaz Miya's part of the house and that of Anjaan's, was muddy and slippery despite the bamboo awning joining the two. Roaring winds that lashed from the south swept rainwater through the open sides into the passage. It was during one such monsoon evening, when Laila was into the seventh month with child, that she heard her abba cough. She had grown heavy now for which sometimes her back ached. It took a great deal of effort for her to get up immediately and walk quickly to reach her abba. Now as she heard him cough, she rose slowly to go near him and check on him. She panicked, because the cough sounded more like a strangulated grunt, which forced out through a severely congested chest. She knew it had to be the damp, moisture laden air from the river that sat heavy on her abba's weakening lungs. Laila got up and walked over to his side of the house to warm him some water to drink. But before she reached her abba, she slipped and fell headlong on the slush in the passage, with the whole of her front down, her stomach hitting the ground the hardest. She shrieked in piercing pain and when Anjaan hurried to her and carried her to the cot, she left a thick trail of blood that merged with the ruddy burnt red of the monsoon slush.

Laila lost her child. A week after Laila's fall, Anjaan walked back the lamb that Ijaaz Miya had bought, to the Sutarkandi bazaar, and sold it off.

It would only be after many more years that Ijaaz Miya would once again go to the Sutarkandi bazar to buy a lamb for Laila and Anjaan Hazratkandi's child's aqiqah.

9
The Year Eighteen Ninety-Seven

The monsoon that Laila was with child again, Anjaan erected walls like those of the shop along the sides of the passage that joined his room to Ijaaz Miya's house. So that winds from the seas or the river at the back of the house would no longer chase rainwater into the passage and make it slippery. These days Anjaan helped with the cooking too, for he hoped everything to go well this time with the birth of the child. Ijaaz Miya too did not buy the lamb ahead of time, lest the river spirits once again cast an evil eye out of jealousy on Laila's yet unborn baby, like they did the last time. He would have six full days to buy one, he thought, after the child was safely delivered. This time round, Ijaaz Miya asked his sister, Laila's aunt, to come and stay with them since Laila had stepped into the ninth month of her pregnancy, to assist in the delivery. Whenever that might happen. Any day soon.

And so, on a bright sunny afternoon a couple of weeks later, a rustle of activities began in Anjaan Hazratkandi's room. Laila's aunt called for Anjaan from the shop while Ijaaz Miya sat on his morha and scraped out a thin long string of bamboo, not too thick but strong enough to make a neat, smooth cut through the tender umbilical cord. Ijaaz Miya scraped through the outer layers of the piece of bamboo to reach the clean, virgin part from the core. It was from here that he scraped out the bamboo string. He had seen the village midwife do it that way when Laila was born. As he sat scraping, he prayed. Silently, fervently. When the bamboo scraping was done, he walked upto the passage and standing midway between Anjaan's room and his side of the house, he called for his sister. She came out, took the scraping and hurried back in. Ijaaz Miya wanted to ask her if everything would be alright this time, but his sister didn't give the opportunity. And he was left pacing up and down the short length of the passage, his heart beating faster and faster, his chest feeling more congested with every step he took. Earlier, Laila's aunt asked Anjaan to call Mehroon bibi, who stayed just across the road, past the betelnut plantation. Mehroon bibi was almost as old as Laila's aunt and it helped to have more women in the house at such a time, Laila's aunt had said, women who knew the fine art of handling the birthing of a child. Mehroon bibi was one such woman. When Anjaan went to tell her and ask her to help, she immediately set out with him. But before he went, he had already started the fire and set the pot on it. So now between the two elderly women, there was much hushed activity. While Mehroon bibi stayed with Laila, her aunt rushed around the two rooms of the house, going into the kitchen to bring in the hot water, collecting washed, old dupattas, towels and throwing about random instructions and advice at Ijaaz Miya and Anjaan, instructions that failed to receive either understanding or compliance. When Laila's aunt brought the water into Anjaan's room, Ijaaz Miya was still there in the passage, but now he had stopped pacing up and down.

'Go sit and rest,' Laila's aunt called over her shoulder, 'I'll let you know.' And she disappeared into the room. But Ijaaz Miya remained standing there. He was scared even to cough, thinking it might come in the way of the delivery. And yet, he couldn't get himself to go back to his room either. And then, suddenly, all noise coming from the room ceased. There was absolute silence. The women stopped coming in and out of the room. The door to Laila's room was shut tight from inside. It was an eternity that Ijaaz Miya and Anjaan stood there at the passage, silently, scared even to breathe as they stared at the shut door. Anjaan fought hard to keep away visions of Laila dripping with blood, screaming, and clutching her stomach after her fall years ago just where he was standing, leaving her womb wrung, his heart wrenched, and the earthen floor bloody. Standing now at that same place, he looked down. The ground was dry and clean. His gaze moved to the closed door. And at that very moment, the silence in the passage was broken by the shrill wail of a child just born.

And so, that late but sunny afternoon of the autumn of 1897, a son was born to Anjaan Hazratkandi and Laila Begum.

'Hear his wails, Anjaan! Hear his wails!' Ijaaz Miya said, wiping away tears of gratitude, 'those are signs of healthy lungs. Bismillahir Rahmanir Raheem!'

Anjaan came up to the old man, clasped his hands and took them to his forehead and sobbed. Out of joy. Early the next morning Ijaaz Miya rode his bicycle to the Sutarkandi bazar to buy a lamb for the child's aqiqah. He had already sent word to Laila's other aunts and uncles to come and join them on the seventh day for the aqiqah. He had sent word to Fatima and Tahira too. Anjaan felt happy for his son, for he would grow up with his own amma and abba. And a nana as well. Anjaan would give him all the love that he himself had felt deprived of. Yet, Anjaan wouldn't be able to give him a family name. This one question always held back his joys from becoming whole. For the baby would still be called just a Hazratkandi. That night, Laila asked Anjaan, 'So what do you wish to name your son?'

'I don't know, Lailajaan,' Anjaan had said, 'but I want him to live free like the clouds in the open, unshackled and unchained skies.'

'Like the clouds?' she asked, amused, suckling the child at her breast.

'Yes, like the clouds, like baadal!' Anjaan replied, his eyes suddenly lighting up, 'Yes, Lailajaan, like Baadal. Baadal!'

And so it was. On the day of aqiqah, the lamb was slaughtered for the afternoon meal. Laila's aunts stitched little dresses for the baby and brought these as gifts. Fatima and Tahira helped with the cooking. And amidst the celebration, Anjaan and Laila's son was named Baadal. Baadal Hazratkandi. With a baby in the house, the days seemed to move by faster than the winds from the sea in the south.

When Baadal was old enough to sit astride the bicycle, Anjaan fixed a small seat on the horizontal bar between his seat and the handles of the cycle for Baadal to sit on and go for rides with his father. Anjaan and Baadal went for long rides along the Dooni, through fields of paddy and across little patches of vegetables fenced off from the rest of the field to keep cattle away. Baadal shrieked with delight and clapped his soft little hands when flights of wild ducks took to their wings at the sight of approaching humans. Anjaan was reliving his own childhood along with his son. Sometimes they got off the cycle and walked along the sloping banks of the Dooni, patting very small calves but fearing to go too close to the big ones. Anjaan kept talking to Baadal as they rode and walked, telling him of the waters in the Dooni, the egrets in the sky, and about his own amma.

'Your amma loves you more than anyone else, Baadal, and that's why, never go away from her, never forsake her.' He felt Baadal's tiny fingers squeezing around his. And everytime he said this, Anjaan unknowingly fell silent for some time, remembering that he had been made to do just that, had been made to run away from and forsake the woman who loved him more than anyone else. He remembered the woman who he came to call amma. Anjaan would get lost in thoughts till Baadal tugged at his hand and egged him on with more questions. Neither Anjaan nor Baadal foresaw that the foot track they rode along, feeling the carefree breeze on their happy faces, would one day have barbed fencing all along it, cutting through the open fields to give a part each to two different countries.

When Baadal started walking, he scampered around the cans and tools in the shop, picking up things and tinkering with them.

'Ah ha! My little shehzada!' Ijaaz Miya exclaimed indulgently, 'he is showing interest in the repair work, Anjaan, he'll learn fast and well.' Anjaan smiled while the old man continued, 'I can see the shop will not just continue but it will grow. And someday maybe my Baadal will own a carriage of his own. Drawn by horses. Like those of the silk merchants!'

Anjaan hoped he would own an identity, a name.

Ijaaz Miya loved nothing more those days than to sit on the bench with a friend and watch Baadal toddle around the yard under the gulmohar tree. And the child loved to watch how the red flowers gently fell upon the ground from the branches above his little head. Sometimes on Fridays when the shop was kept closed so that Anjaan and Ijaaz Miya could go to attend jumuah at the mosque, Anjaan rode through the fields and along the Dooni all by himself while returning. Baadal would be home then, lying beside Laila. During those noons, the breeze that brushed Anjaan's face was a pensive and melancholic one. He remembered all the afternoons that he slept hungry on those banks waiting for the clothes he had washed to dry. He remembered abba's last days in bed. All this reminiscence made him long to see the place that was once home, the hearth that nurtured him and showered on him the love that still warmed his heart. So one afternoon he cycled towards that house where he once lived with amma and abba. When he came by the narrow foot track that led into the courtyard, he got off the cycle and even though he wished to, he couldn't walk into the yard. Because it was now thick with undergrowth, small thorny bushes, grass and weed. What he saw made his heart weigh down with sadness and he stood staring at the house for a while, as memories flooded him. Scoops of earth had been dug away from the earthen plinth, maybe to raise someone else's house. Whatever, it had left the base of his amma and abba's house wounded and bruised. And how symbolically too, he thought. It was a pathetic skeleton of what it used to be when he ran out of that door all those years ago. One half of the door hung only from the lower hinge, precariously leaning outward. It was open. The other half had fallen off. As the afternoon sun warmed into the hut through the broken door, he could see a rectangle of light inside, on the ant-trailed, scarred mud floor, surrounded by a darkness that came more from abandonment. And that solitary rectangle of light was the place where amma used to wait for him. Outside, the cow shed was gone. He lingered on for a while before walking back to his bicycle. Earlier, he had thoughts of bringing Baadal this way someday, to show him where he spent his childhood. But after that day's visit he decided not to. What would he tell Baadal? That it was home? For it wasn't. That the loving couple who raised him were his amma and abba? For they weren't. The way the little boy was so full of questions, he might ask, 'Why were you here in this house when you were small like me and in nanajaan's house now that you are big and tall?' Anjaan would have had no answer then. These were questions he could evade. For now. But some day, before he asked Anjaan why they were named just the same as their village, Anjaan would have to take him to the hillock at Malegarh. Anjaan would tell him about his other grandfather, lying in peace under the earth there. He waited for Baadal to grow older to take him to the Malegarh graveyard. Now however, it was time for Baadal to go for lessons from the Qoran at the mosque. Baadal went to the same mosque that Anjaan had gone for his. Over time, Anjaan made sure that he completed his lessons of the Qoran. At the same time, he also wanted Baadal to learn more than just to write his name, and in a language that everyone understood. So, he sent Baadal to the Hazratkandi Primary School as well.

'We sat under a tree, ammajaan, and a crow above repeated everything we were learning aloud,' he said on returning home that first day, excited and waiting to go back the next day.

'Oh?' Laila teased him, 'but why? Don't you have classrooms with walls and a roof?'

'Oh! We sure do, ammajaan, we do! But the master thought we would have fun outside,' he said.

'And did you?' she asked.

'But ofcourse, ammajaan!' he giggled and added, 'only, I was hoping the birds wouldn't drop poop on us.'

Baadal loved school from the very first day. Boys from his class fell over each other to sit next to him, for he had an amazing knack to get them to like him. The few teachers who together, among them, taught all the classes, too loved *the little boy with the village for his surname,* as they called him. When other little boys quarrelled and punched and wrestled one another into an entagle, it was Baadal whom the rest would seek to disengage them. When someone was slow to catch up, the master said, 'Hazratkandi! Explain the lesson to him after class!' And when the boys made teams for kabaddi, every team wanted Baadal with them. And so as the years rolled by, he did well in his exams too and moved on easily from one class to the next higher one.

Soon Baadal was old enough and he no longer sat on the small seat between his abba's seat and the handles of the bicycle. He instead sat astride the bicycle's carrier at the back of Anjaan's seat while his father pedalled. Baadal would sometimes hold on to the back of Anjaan's seat and at other times wrap his arms around his abba and rest a cheek on his father's back. Anjaan wondered how a son might feel to remain thus with his father, whether he heard the father's heart thump with joy right across the back, and whether he felt assured of an identity, because he had a father and knew who he was. By then he had also removed the small seat in front. Their walks and rides through the fields and along the Dooni continued.

'The Dooni has seen me cry and seen me scared, Baadal, it didn't just quench my parched throat but pacified the agony in my heart too. Its rippling waters sang lullabies for me, and its banks spread out her arms for me to lie down and sleep when I was kicked in the stomach and made to slave through the pain and hunger. My hands were red and sore from scrubbing and chopping wood, Baadal, so I dipped them in the waters of the Dooni and then too, they cooled and soothed the singe. But long before that, I played on those banks and splashed in those waters with joy too, I too walked here when I was a child like you.'

'You came with your abba?' he asked.

Anjaan fell silent. He couldn't fill the child with truth that wasn't.

Baadal waited for an answer till a flight of birds made him look up at the sky.

'Abba, look! White kites!' he shrieked with joy.

Anjaan laughed. 'Those are egrets, son.' And as if he was narrating a painful past, he found himself saying, 'When night descends upon the sky and makes it dark, it is then that, white egrets, hurrying home, make you yearn for your own home, but then the heart grows heavy with fear and longing when you know you haven't one. And the night stealthily comes snooping on you, chasing you, scaring you. The more you run away from it, the more it is all around you. It was in moments like those, Baadal, that I desperately ached to be in my amma's embrace.' Anjaan stopped. He didn't know what made him tell a small child all of this. But he did. Maybe he thought Badadal should know.

And then one day, Anjaan decided to take Baadal to Malegarh. Baadal happily jumped on to the carrier and having gripped the back of his abba's seat, stretched out his legs. He was always worried that his sandals might slip off his feet.

Anjaan and Baadal rode past the Hazratkandi bazar and past Baadal's primary school. Like Anjaan, Baadal too was tall for his age and his limbs were strong. People said he looked like Anjaan. Though Anjaan thought his eyes looked like Laila's. So Ijaaz Miya would settle the matter by saying, 'As of now, parts of Baadal definitely look like both his abba and his amma but once he grows to be of my age, all of him will look only like me.' And the old man would double with laughter. While Anjaan was quiet and reticent in his demeanour, Baadal talked incessantly and never hesitated to ask questions. Long ago, however, Anjaan had been just like that. Rafiq used to get tired of answering all of Anjaan's questions. But that was before Rafiq changed. When the very people he started to talk with, and held hands and walked with, wringed the life out of his childhood, Anjaan Hazratkandi couldn't remain happily inquisitive and talkative about every little thing that passed him by. And the questions that continued to come, had no answer. That day too, like every other day that he went to Malegarh, he would once more seek answers to the only questions left in his life. The bicycle went past a small group of fishermen by the river and people waiting to buy as soon they would raise the net from the waters, if any fish came up on it. Ahead of the fishermen, they passed through fields of sugarcane and vegetables, before they came to a cluster of small huts at a distance from the Sutarkandi road. A little distance from those huts, they took a right turn and lowered the cycle towards the fields. From there it was a bumpy ride along a narrow foot track. Anjaan got off the bicycle, but Baadal still sat astride the carrier and made his best efforts to keep his feet pointing skywards to hold his flip-flops securely between his big and second toes. Anjaan slowly pushed the bicycle forward. He walked carefully today for there was Baadal astride the carrier. Otherwise, even though the path was narrow, he knew it like the back of his hand and cycled without getting off, jumping and bouncing along with the cycle. When the hillock came into view, Baadal almost shouted, 'Whoa! Abba! I have never seen this big a mountain before! Have we not come this way earlier?' Anjaan shook his head and continued to push the cycle towards the foot of the hillock.

'This, Baadal,' he explained, 'is not a mountain. It is not even a hill. It is a hillock.'

'How so?' Baadal was confused. They were getting closer to the hillock.

'Because mountains and hills are way too high and they have many peaks and stretch for long distances, many many miles together,' Anjaan tried to explain.

They reached the foot of the hillock and Anjaan helped Baadal get off the carrier. He then leaned the bicycle against a tree and before Baadal could take a free run out into the serenity of the wilderness, Anjaan quickly held him by his hand. The boy laughed. And the two remained holding hands as they walked up the hillock to where the graves lay.

'I know, abba! This hillock here looks like the heaped-up rice when amma hides a boiled egg in it to surprise me,' he giggled and went on, 'I think, abba, like the rice looked raised because of the egg in it, there must be something in there too to make it rise this much.' Baadal looked up at Anjaan and asked, 'Do you think there is something in there, abba? Something buried inside to make it swell up?' Anjaan walked round to his usual spot by the edge of the mound and sat down on the grass. Seeing him, Baadal too sat down beside him.

'Not something, Baadal, someone,' Anjaan replied. 'Someone.'

'Oh, I see! Because he is dead?'

'Yes, because he is dead,' Anjaan paused, thought over and went on, 'but Baadal, he is dead not because he was sick or old and weak. He is dead because he was brave. And gallant. He was a hero, son!'

'But abba, just one dead person buried in there can't make the land rise so high. There must be more of them. Have you ever counted how many?'

'I haven't, Baadal, but people say there were others who counted the dead buried in there.'

'How many, abba?'

'Maybe somewhere between twenty-five and thirty,' Anjaan tried to recollect the number Manik Roy told him, long ago.

'What brave act did they do, abba?' Baadal asked again.

Even Anjaan did not know what brave act they had done, or what exactly had happened at the battle of Latu near Malegarh during that cold, December night in the year eighteen fifty-seven. Anjaan wondered how he could explain to a nine-year-old about India being under British domination. He remembered how he himself was confused when Rafiq told him about invisible chains that held Indians as slaves.

'You know about the British?' Anjaan asked Baadal, expecting him to shake his head. The overhead sun was casting grotesque, short limbed shadows of them both upon the grass.

'Oh them!' he answered immediately, raising his voice, 'they aren't from our land and yet pretend to be, and behave like our kings, eh, abba?'

Anjaan went speechless. He realized how easily and in simple terms Baadal explained the complicated issue of British rule in India. Then slowly, when his amazement turned into amusement, Anjaan patted Baadal on the head and asked, 'Yes, son, that's exactly how it is. So where did you learn this? At the mosque or in school?'

'At home,' Baadal replied.

'Oh?' Anjaan was once again amazed. 'From?' he asked.

'Nanajaan,' the boy replied, laughing.

Anjaan could only smile.

'So abba, what about the British? How are they related to the dead in there?' he asked, pointing to the centre of the hillock.

'Those men in there, buried under the soil, are Indians like you and me. They fought and resisted the English from bringing more of India under their control,' Anjaan hoped he made it as easy as Baadal's nana's explanation. 'These brave men lying there and their fellow sepoys did not succeed that night, but they did succeed in making people here in Sylhet and this side of the country aware that, all over India, our countrymen were fighting and resisting these make-believe kings.'

'Ya Allah!' was all Baadal said, but Anjaan saw how intently he listened to the whole narration.

'So, these men here died fighting the British?' he at last asked.

'Yes, they did,' Anjaan nodded.

'Then they truly are brave men, abba, aren't they?' Baadal once more looked up at Anjaan, his eyes filled with awe.

'They sure are,' Anjaan said, looking back into those eyes, 'and you know something else, Baadal?'

'What?' he asked, slowly leaning against Anjaan's side, still looking up at him. How Anjaan adored this look in Baadal, the way he turned sideways and looked up at him whenever he needed to ask something. It was with one of those looks that he had his head turned up at him now.

'One of them here is my abba,' Anjaan said slowly, 'like nanajaan is your amma's abba.'

Baadal remained quiet for a long while as he stared towards the centre of the hillock and then his gaze slowly went all over the place as if searching for his grandfather.

'Where, abba?' Baadal asked, still searching across the Malegarh Martyrs' hillock with his eyes, 'might we be sitting on him?' he asked and suddenly stood up.

'I don't know, Baadal, I wish I knew,' Anjaan replied.

Their shadows began to get elongated towards the east.

'How was he to look at?' Baadal asked. He found a new hero to place on the altar of his mind. It fascinated him to know that his abba's abba had died fighting the British. For that matter, he now began seeing even his abba as a greater idol than he had already regarded him to be, because he was the son of a braveheart.

'I never saw him, Baadal,' Anjaan replied. How he wished he had seen him. 'He died before I was born. So I don't know how he was to look at.'

Baadal stared into nothingness and said, 'He must have been really strong and big, abba, stronger than you maybe, to be able to carry a rifle and shoot at the British. He must have ridden horses too! Wow!' Baadal paused and then asked, 'What was his name, abba?'

'Aryaan,' Anjaan replied, holding his breath out of fear at what was coming up next.

'Aryaan Hazratkandi?' Baadal asked.

This was where Anjaan found himself without an answer. Once again. Over and over again.

'it's a pity he died without my seeing him, abba,' Baadal rued.

'It's a pity, son, he died without even my being able to see him,' Anjaan replied.

Their ride back home was a quiet one through the dusk of an India yet undivided, yet unliberated.

10
The Year Nineteen Fourteen

Baadal Hazratkandi began to spend more time at the shop with his father while his grandfather began to spend more time inside the house. More carts and carriages started to arrive at Ijaaz Miya's repair shop, so Anjaan and Baadal both began working side by side. Baadal was quick at learning the trade, and because he knew how to engage people with good conversation, even if Ijaaz Miya hardly sat on the bench these days, a few of his friends continued to drop by, to sit and talk with the young, intelligent Baadal who knew how to gather news and to discriminately discuss and speak about them according to the listener's interests, likes and dislikes. Jalaluddin, the maulvi from the neighbouring village of Katigorah, was one among them. Earlier, when Baadal was small and used to be away at school, Jalaluddin often dropped by to fill air into his cycle tyres. If Ijaaz Miya happened to be around then, he would sit and talk for a while. But if Ijaaz Miya wasn't around and only Anjaan was at the shop, Jalaluddin yet made efforts to chat up with Anjaan. But Anjaan was a man of few words and Jalaluddin soon tired of the nods and shakes of his head and his smiles. It was however different with Baadal. Despite the difference in age, Jalaluddin loved talking to him. Most people did, Baadal had it in him. Often in the evenings, after they closed shop and after Laila made them salted black tea, Baadal would go and sit beside his grandfather. During those moments, Ijaaz Miya loved to hear from Baadal what happened through the day at his repair shop, who dropped by, and what conversations were picked up. It would be dark inside his room while outside, out under the gulmohar tree, the last of the sun's rays still lingered on for a while, pouring a mild touch of orange on the yard and on the small blades of grass around it. It was during those last moments of the day that Anjaan loved to sit on the bench and think, where he might find an answer to his questions. Or who might have them. Back in the house, Baadal sat with his nana till it was time for the evening prayers. He had long moved out of Anjaan's side of the house and started sleeping in the same room with his grandfather.

'Nanajaan,' he asked one day, 'have you ever been to the martyrs' hillock at Malegarh?'

'I've passed that way many times, yes, but haven't really walked up to the hillock,' his nana replied, propped up against the headrest of the bed with a pillow at his back. Laila brought in his salted black tea with some jaggery. Even if he didn't go to the shop anymore, it was by habit that Laila brought him his tea just before the muezzin's call for the evening prayer. It was also by habit that Ijaaz Miya looked forward to it. 'But your abba goes there often,' he said.

'Yes, I know that. Because these days, nanajaan, if the work isn't too much or isn't too complicated, the kind that abba felt I could manage by myself, I see him putting a trowel into the basket of his cycle and riding away. When I asked him once, he said he was going to visit his father's resting place.'

Anjaan had indeed started going to the graveyard more often. When he pulled out the weeds and grass-thorns from one grave, he wondered whether it was that or another one where his father lay. So, he went on to tend the one next to it. When he was done doing that he would again wonder if it was truly there that his father rested. Sometimes, when despair and loneliness overpowered him, he buried his face in his palms and sitting there among the dead, wept like a child. He wept like the times he had wept on the sloping banks of the Dooni. The solace that he once found on those slopes, he now found among these graves.

Anjaan began to look forward to Fridays, for it was then that from jumuah at the mosque, he took the afternoon for himself. On days when Ijaaz Miya accompanied them, while returning, it was Baadal who took nanajaan home. Earlier, Anjaan used to love going for a ride by the Dooni. But these days he spent the time tending to the graves at Malegarh. Many an afternoon he even went off to sleep on the grass there, while keeping off stray dogs, cows, and goats from dirtying the place. During autumn, tiny yellowing flowers and withered brown leaves from the large bokul tree in the adjacent land kept falling on the hillock all day and all night. If there was a breeze, along with the fragrance of the small white bokul flowers, even the leaves were carried as far as the graves and deposited there. So, some while back, Anjaan had brought a broom too from home, tying it across the carrier where Baadal used to sit as a little boy. And with that, Anjaan started to sweep the graveyard and rake in the fallen leaves. When done, he would push the broom inside the thickets over the edge of the hillock, so that no one could find it to take it away. As it was, no one liked to loiter around the dead. But that was during the autumn months. The summer months required weeding. As the seasons changed and time passed by, Anjaan did whatever the seasons called for, to keep the graves spruced up. Because somewhere there lay his father. That was the reason why he took a trowel in his bicycle basket.

One Friday afternoon, he saw that the graves were still clean and since there had been no rain the whole week, there was little unwanted growth. So there wasn't much to be done that day. So Anjaan instead rode to the Latu bazar to meet Subhroto Pal. Anjaan had known him since the time he started purchasing cycle bells and seats for Ijaaz Miya's shop. Entering the Latu bazar he got off the cycle and slowly started walking, pushing his cycle along. He loved to see the wares on display and to hear people haggling over bargains. It amused him to see little children throwing tantrums over toys and candies. The bazar, he thought, was so different from the graveyard. Here, want existed all around him, along with noise, chaos, people, jalebis, and sweetened semolina. While at Malegarh, there was absolute non-existence of want. It was so still and quiet that even his own breath felt like noise. And yet, it was to ask about that stillness and quiet that Anjaan had come to the noise of Latu bazar, to ask the living about the dead. He stopped in front of Subhroto Pal's shop. It was a low roofed room with a wide front, and Subhroto Pal sat on a high wooden chair behind a cupboard made of old Burmese teak, his ample belly blocking the drawers of the cupboard.

'Come! Come! Anjaan moshai!' he greeted cheerfully as Anjaan walked into the shop leaving his bicycle outside. Anjaan couldn't help smiling. He was the only one who addressed Anjaan as moshai. Anjaan happily allowed himself the privilege of this old man's endearment.

'Come pull yourself a stool,' he told Anjaan, without moving from his chair.

Anjaan pulled a stool from among a couple of them kept against the wall and sat down.

'Business must be good, eh moshai? For only last month you took some supplies,' he asked, 'good! When you do well, we do well!'

'Well, Subhroto kaka, actually,' Anjaan paused and then said slowly, 'I've come for something else.'

'Tell me, tell me,' Subhroto Pal encouraged Anjaan to talk.

'About the mutiny. At Latu...'

Even before Anjaan could finish asking, Subhroto Pal started to answer, 'Ah that,' he interrupted, running a hand over his bald pate as if wiping away the dust that had settled over the years upon his memory. Subhroto Pal always loved to talk about that December night way back in 1857.

'Were you around there that night, Kaka?' Might you be knowing who the sepoys were?' Anjaan asked.

'I remember that night as being exceptionally cold, Anjaan moshai, and I was a small boy those days. This place here sold only pots and pans way back then, not bicycle and carriage accessories. Those I added later so that the business could grow and improve. And by Jove! Hasn't it! Don't you think it has, Anjaan moshai?'

Anjaan nodded.

'You see, every one of my folks tells me that I have exceptional farsight!' and he exhaled a spurt of proud laughter.

Anjaan didn't have any need to know all that and yet, breaking the flow of his narration might make Subhroto Pal leave out significant details, that might otherwise be of help to Anjaan. So, he let him talk on and build up his mood.

'So, well, back that night, baba closed shop soon after sundown and I remember I got into bed early, right after supper and immediately fell asleep. Like, you know how cozy it feels to get tucked inside the warmth of a quilt on a chilly winter night,' he laughed and his belly shook. Anjaan nodded again.

'And then suddenly I woke up! To the sound of gunshots! It was frightening, Anjaan moshai, how they pierced through the silence and the fog!'

Anjaan listened without interrupting.

'More gunshots rang through the night. They jolted us awake and we sat up and huddled in bed, scared to go out and see. It was only two days later that baba brought news of the battle.'

'What news exactly did your baba bring?' Anjaan asked.

'That they were from Bradshaw ka Paltan.'

'Oh?'

'But the well informed knew it as the 34 BNI, Anjaan moshai, and my baba, because he knew important people in the paltan,' he looked out of the shop with a slight raise of his head and back again at Anjaan, with an air of importance, 'further said that it was the 34th Regiment Bengal Native Infantry. Bradshaw ka Paltan was what the sepoys and, you know,' he wrinkled his nose, 'the ordinary people called it.'

'I see! So what else did your baba know about Bradshaw ka Paltan,' Anjaan dared not bring himself to stand in rank with Subhroto Pal's superior knowledge, he let himself remain with ordinary people, 'and the battle at Latu, kaka?'

'They had revolted against the English,' Subhroto Pal regaled, 'by breaking out of prison and releasing other Indian prisoners too. Then they sat about ransacking and looting the armoury and also the treasury, maybe looking for stuff they could use for similar battle elsewhere and then they sat the barracks on fire.' Subhroto Pal then got up to light a few sticks of incense. He moved them in circles in front of an idol of Lakshmi that sat behind a tiny pot of water wrapped in a red cloth, in a small wooden altar perched on the wall. All along, he kept chanting a hymn under his breath. Then he stuck the sticks in a small holder in front of the idol and came back to sit and continue his story. He loved to repeat this story to good listeners like Anjaan Hazratkandi.

'So where was I?' he asked, settling on the chair.

'You were at the barracks. They had set them on fire,' Anjaan helped.

'Ah, yes! yes! So, the barracks, yes. After setting the barracks on fire, the sepoys were on their way to Manipur but on the way, they made the mistake of stopping by at Karimpur. Now look, moshai, there is something called destiny. Had they not stopped, they might have gone on to bigger revolts, more famous ones.....'

'...and most importantly,' Anjaan found himself chipping in without realizing, '...they would've lived. Atleast till...'

'Yes, yes,' Subhroto Pal interrupted, not really hearing what Anjaan said, 'destiny had it planned this way, you see Anjaan moshai, you can't undo what is planned for you. Now where was I?'

'Karimpur,' Anjaan helped once more.

'Yes, Karimpur. That's in Shahbazpur, on the border of the police station at Latu. So, when the commander of the 11th Sylhet Light Infantry, one Major Byng, heh, what a name,' and he guffawed before carrying on, 'came to know of the Indian sepoys halting at Shahbazpur, he marched towards them with around a hundred and sixty soldiers, so baba said, and confronted them.'

A grinning, scrawny youth, probably a worker of the shop, wiggled in with two small steel glasses of tea and put these on the cupboard in front of Subhroto Pal with nothing short of a jig. Subhroto Pal pushed one of these towards Anjaan and resumed. 'So, the two armies faced one another at Latu and that's where our brave men died. Twenty-six of them,' Subhroto Pal added.

'Did your baba bring news of who those twenty-six were, kaka? Their names?' Anjaan was hoping against hope that Subhroto Pal would say yes.

Instead, he said, 'That, Anjaan moshai, would be for the army's records.' Subhroto Pal felt himself superior to Anjaan, telling him so many things that he didn't know.

'Would you be knowing, kaka, where to find such records? Or whom to ask about such records? Or names?'

'Baba might have known.' Subhroto Pal was almost apologetic that he couldn't help Anjaan on this.

Yet, that day was the first time that Anjaan heard of the battle of Latu this elaborately. The wiggling youth reappeared and swept away the glasses like a kingfisher would a fish from the waters. Anjaan couldn't hold back his smile.

'The dead were then taken to be buried at Malegarh,' Subhroto Pal added, ignoring the boy.

Darkness had descended when Anjaan reached home. Baadal was lighting the lantern in Ijaaz Miya's room. His heavy cough pervaded through the house. So those days whenever hakim Sirajullah came that way, he brought with him small bottles of some paste and some little, round, pea sized pellets for Ijaaz Miya.

'Rub this paste on his chest,' he told Baadal, 'and if it dries up in the bottle, add some warm water before rubbing it in.' The paste smelt like it had mint leaves in it. 'And from these,' he said handing the pellets wrapped in a leaf, 'give one every morning and one each night.' Having instructed Baadal, Sirajullah would sit for a while and update Ijaaz Miya on news and gossip from all around. He went only after Laila gave him her special salted black tea, not strong, not weak, just right.

By then, monsoon thunders began to roll through the Hazratkandi skies. That night too sinister rainclouds were gathering to burst. Strong winds shrieked past their hut and threatened to take away with them their thatched roof. Strange, eerie noises rose above the waters in the river at the back and all of a sudden, Laila remembered her amma. 'Don't feel scared, Laila, my child, don't cry,' her amma used to say, 'it is only the fish jumping in glee, trying to catch the lightning. That's what the noises are.' She believed it then, she tried to believe it now too, but couldn't. And each time they drummed with flashes of lightening that cracked up the clouds, Laila trembled with fright and snuggled into Anjaan's bosom. He held her close, but his thoughts were far. He was yet to come close, unlike Laila on his bosom, to the answers he was seeking. As he lay awake holding Laila with his arms tightly around her, his mind raced to Malegarh at the speed of the same lightening that tore through the night skies of Hazratkandi. He lay thinking whether he should go and meet a few old men in the villages around the Malegarh hillock. Maybe they stood around and watched the sepoys of the battle of Latu being brought there to the hillock and while they were being lowered into the earth, maybe they heard names being read from their uniforms and had written them somewhere. Anywhere. Or maybe they just remembered the names they might have heard. If the rains stopped, he thought of going to Malegarh the very next day. To see if he could talk to people around the villages there.

The rains did stop in the morning and the skies were cloudless. There was no trace of the previous night's storm in the skies. But on the ground, the slush, mud, wet grass, and smell of rain-soaked earth evaporating from the paddy fields, all told tales of the storm of the night before. Anjaan thought of the narrow foot track off the Sutarkandi road, leading to the hillock. That track might have turned into a stream of slush, he thought, he wouldn't be able to go that day. He would make it next Friday after jumuah. So, he stayed back home.

In the evening as Baadal sat with Ijaaz Miya and rubbed on his chest the green paste that hakim Sirajullah brought, another thunderous noise rolled through the skies. It felt like the gunshots of an entire war came raging into their small hut.

'What thunder!' Ijaaz Miya exclaimed, 'it sounds like nothing I've heard in the more than eighty monsoons I have lived through.' He paused and listened. When he heard nothing, he asked Baadal, 'Son, is there no rain with that thunder?'

'That wasn't thunder, nanajaan,' Baadal said, pulling Ijaaz Miya's vest down over his chest and wiping his hands, 'that was an aircraft. A military aircraft. The world is at war.'

The world war that began in the west and came hurtling towards Sylhet was the only thing that men at the shop discussed those days. Whenever an aircraft roared through the skies, mothers pulled little children playing in the yards outside and hurried them under beds. A few adventurous little boys, however, hid from their mothers behind trees and watched the aircraft if they darted past the sky during the day, leaving a trail of thick cloud behind them. They would keep watching till that cloud melted from the sides and mingled with the air above Hazratkandi. How heroically those boys were then hailed by their friends! What amazing stories about the war and the aircraft they stirred up to tell them! But that was the little children's imaginative side of the war. In reality, too, the war had indeed spread its tentacles all over India and across both East Bengal and West Bengal, having reached Hazratkandi and Ijaaz Miya's shop too. In the latter, though, the war arrived not in ships and aircrafts but in heated debates and hushed opinions.

'But we here in India are being struck with a double-edged sword,' Sirajullah had said one afternoon, 'we're being hit both by the war in the west and our own struggle for freedom from the British. Am I not saying it right?'

Narayan Chandra Dey, who was listening intently all through, vigourously nodded his head.

Because with the world war raging, changes crept into the ruling systems among the zamindars and the nawabs in the provinces of Bengal. Their resources and power were lessened and seized, and some zamindars were even stripped of their titles alongwith their land. The resulting effects touched the lives of everyone who were one way or the other dependent on the nawabs, the silk merchants, the zamindars and their zamindari. So, when it came to Anjaan and his little family, the war touched them too, for there were now fewer carriages and carts coming from the homes of the zamindars and merchants to Ijaaz Miya's repair shop. Baadal still opened shop every morning, though work was considerably reduced. And people kept coming by to just sit and talk. The shop became a meeting point for people from quite a few villages across. Sometimes if Anjaan wasn't around and Baadal had work to attend to, people still came and sat under the gulmohar tree and talked among themselves. There was much to discuss and exchange those days. The war had thrown up new gossip and stories, some true, but most imaginary.

Lying down on his bed and listening to Baadal, Ijaaz Miya asked, his eyes slowly narrowing with sleep, 'Are we fighting the British?'

'No, nanajaan, we Indians are fighting the Germans, for the British. Every country in the world is taking sides.'

'But did we really have to fight side by side with the British?' Ijaaz Miya almost wheezed out the words.

'We had no choice, nanajaan. Outside India, whatever our people do, they do as representatives of our rulers.'

'Rehem, Allah! Rehem! I would've been at peace had I not lived to hear of this at my age, Baadal, what has the world come to!'

'The world has come to war, nanajaan, it is being talked about as the world war.'

Even as Baadal spoke, Ijaaz Miya dozed off. The massage always had a soothing, lulling effect on him. 'He looks so peaceful in his sleep,' Baadal thought. The green balm gradually eased his breathing and Baadal noticed that the wheezing became less and less audible. Baadal lowered his gaze to his nanajaan's stomach. It heaved and fell in a soft, gentle, and uniform rhythm. Baadal reduced the flame of the lantern but did not put it out. Leaving his grandfather asleep, he tiptoed out of the room. Ijaaz Miya slept through the night, never to wake up. When he was taken for his burial, he went on a bier held by Anjaan, Baadal, Narayan Chandra Dey and Rabishankar Guha, each shouldering a corner of the bier. Friends, both Hindus and Moslems, walked behind them, inconsolable at the passing away of an era.

While World War 1 raged through the nations, Ijaaz Miya lay in all the peace he had ever wished for.

11
The Year Nineteen Sixteen

It was summer once again in Hazratkandi. Anjaan would give anything to be on the bench under the gulmohar during the afternoons. The breeze during those afternoon hours comforted Anjaan's soul like nothing else did, when the boughs above him showered little specks of leaves with every whiff of breeze. The periwinkles along the corner of the shop's bamboo shutters were blooming brilliantly now, a happy mix of pinks and whites nudging through their lusciously deep green leaves. The gulmohar, much older than Anjaan, sieved into the yard just the right amount of sunlight. Not too harsh as to singe the skin and not totally cut off as to make the yard damp with monsoon moss. It was this very thing about the aged gulmohar that Anjaan loved the most. He didn't realize since when exactly he began to look up at the tree for company and solace. Mute and deaf, but it was always there, witnessing every joy, ordeal, and grief in Anjaan's almost sixty years of life. While Baadal worked in the shop, Anjaan stood in the yard in front, and watched Baadal. He was no longer a little boy. How time sailed by! It was just then that Kanu Saha walked in. It was a considerable walking distance from the village of Bouderbeel upto Hazratkandi, but the fifty something, sprightly Kanu Saha would cover it with the energy of a teenager. He taught at the Bouderbeel Buniyadi Vidyalay and sometimes played football with the school's boys too. That wasn't amazing though. What was amazing was that his dhoti never betrayed him during the football matches, during the most daring and limb flaying of the kicks, much to the disappointment of the boys who otherwise adored and respected master Kanu Saha. It was his umbrella that kept bringing him to Ijaaz Miya's shop. Even Anjaan was happily exasperated from mending it and had often suggested he bought a new one. But each time he said so, Kanu Saha would embark on a tale as a reason why he loathed doing away with that treasured umbrella.

'You see, bhaijaan, what the gulmohar is to you, my umbrella is to me!' he would say, beckoning Anjaan to come and sit on the bench for some gossip. Rain or sun, he always carried it with him wherever he went. 'There is something about an old umbrella which has been through life with you. You can't just discard it like scales scraped off a good hilsa, can you, Miya?' he would say, justifying his loyalty to the haggard umbrella. He loathed being called a miser. Even that day he arrived at the shop with the hooked wooden handle of his umbrella tucked into the neck of his kurta at the back.

'Anjaan miya! It's been long since I saw you out here. I met your boy during the last few times I visited. Knows a lot, your boy Baadal. Sure does!' He walked up to the bench and sat down. It made Anjaan feel proud to hear someone speak thus of Baadal. True, Baadal had indeed picked up work and picked up fast too. He was shouldering responsibilities at home as well on his strong, confident and youthful shoulders. Baadal bowed his head from inside the shop, as an acknowledgement of the praise, while still bent over his work. He was hammering into the wheel of a carriage.

'So have you heard, Anjaan miya?' Kanu Saha broached.

'Heard what, Kanu babu?' Anjaan came forward and sat on the bench.

'I was saying, Bengal is sending its youth to the war.' This he said with an air of immense knowledge.

'It is?' Anjaan said.

And while their conversation was beginning to build up, maulvi Jalaluddin too arrived from the village of Katigorah.

'Salaam Waleiqum!' he greeted cheerfully.

'Namaskar! Namaskar, Jalaluddin bhai! Come join us,' Kanu Saha greeted, sliding aside, and making space for Jalaluddin on the bench, 'we were just talking about the recruitments to the Bengali Double Company.' What they weren't talking of, because probably they didn't know till then, was that the Bengali Double Company would later be referred as the 49th Bengali Regiment.

'Ah yes, I've heard of it too,' Jalaluddin nodded, 'Mannan was telling me the other day about this recruitment. Don't know how true, but I've heard that sons and brothers of zamindars and nawabs who have been educated overseas and have now returned home are going to recruit themselves into the Company to fight the Germans.'

Rousing interest in the conversation brought Baadal out of the shop when he was done fixing the carriage wheel.

'Yes, I too got to hear of it,' he added, 'they are recruiting this year, from the thirtieth of August, so I've heard.'

'Anjaan, do you remember Mannan? The lively boy from Dhuliapore?' Kanu Saha asked.

'The one who drives a horse carriage?' Anjaan asked, 'if it is him, he came here a number of times, hasn't he, Baadal?' Baadal nodded. 'That same Mannan?'

'That same Mannan, yes, him,' Kanu Saha said, 'he was saying many young boys from neighbouring villages are thinking of joining the Double Company. He was telling me about boys from Hazratkandi and Bouderbeel too.'

'Mannan was here a week ago,' Baadal said, 'to ask if an extra seat could be fixed in his carriage. It seems some of our young boys have asked him to drive them to Dhaka.'

'I see, for that pre-recruitment awareness camp?' Jalaluddin asked. News of the recruitment had travelled fast around Sylhet, and all round East Bengal, trickling in to even small villages like Hazratkandi, Bouderbeel and the neighbouring Bhoumikpara.

'I guess so,' Baadal replied.

These days, people flocked around Mannan because he always gathered the latest news of the war from people who rode home in his carriage after having landed at the Dhaka sea port from Calcutta and other places.

'Must be,' Kanu Saha added, 'I heard that Subedar Purshottam Bandopadhyay, a representative of the Indian Army, will be visiting Dhaka sometime in the later weeks of June to meet prospective recruitees and get a fair idea and estimation of the capacity of the recruitees. Mannan will take the few of our boys who are going to Dhaka from Hazratkandi and nearby.'

'Will the boys be recruited in Dhaka?' Anjaan got curious.

'As far as I know,' Baadal said thoughtfully, 'the recruitment will take place in Calcutta. At fort Williams Cantonment.'

'You have a smart boy, Anjaan,' Jalaluddin said. He was impressed at the knowledge Baadal had, how he talked to people and made them comfortable and how well he looked after Ijaaz Miya's repair shop. Jalaluddin was one of those who had seen the growth of the repair shop and had also seen Baadal's contribution to it.

'Well, Kanu, when did you say the Subedar, the representative, is coming to Dhaka?' Anjaan asked, to be sure.

'Some time in the later part of June, so I heard. But,' Kanu Saha added as an afterthought, 'if boys going from here are hiring Mannan, then it is Mannan who will know exactly when the boys will leave from here and when they are expected back. So he would know when the Subedar will be at Dhaka.'

The men then went on to talk about the war in the west and India's own struggle for liberation. They sometimes even talked of organizing their own protest march against the British, but their march remained within that yard under the gulmohar and never really happened. They missed Ijaaz Miya in afternoons like these. As the day slowly began to wane, the men too got up one by one and began to leave. Kanu Saha picked up his much-patched, much-stitched and much-mended umbrella, and once more tucked it into the neck of his kurta, drawing much banter from the rest of the men. As the two men walked to the road, Anjaan noticed how Jalaluddin looked at Baadal as he left, with admiration in his eyes.

Anjaan and Laila had meanwhile moved into Ijaaz Miya's part of the house, and they now slept in the room where Ijaaz Miya used to. Baadal had shifted to where Anjaan used to stay. This shift was not merely a change of rooms, but it signified a sort of unspoken hierarchy in the family. The curtain that Laila had made from a dupatta many years ago, had long been torn and been removed. There was now a different curtain, of bright yellow cotton with small blue daisies all over. Baadal didn't have anything much to say, he never thought anything much of these things. Though Laila did ask him if he would like anything else on the window.

'If you are happy with it, ammajaan, I am happy with it,' was what he said. And so the curtain came to be. And the cot too, after long years, came to have just one pillow on it.

Anjaan woke up earlier than usual one morning. He went out to the yard under the gulmohar without disturbing Laila. In her sleep, she looked as pretty as she was on the day of their nikaah. Though it was summer, it was the time when early mornings were still cool in Hazratkandi. Anjaan thought of the recruitment that Kanu Saha and Jalaluddin were talking of. He thought of Subedar Purshottam Bandopadhyay.

'They said he was a representative of the Indian Army and would come to Dhaka with matters relating to pre-recruitment,' Anjaan thought to himself, 'in which case, he might have access to records of recruited sepoys, or at least sepoys stationed at Bengal, because he was being sent to the Bengal Province.' He walked up to the bench and sat down. Somewhere far, a cuckoo called, though it was well past spring. He smiled inwardly, 'Sometimes things happen belatedly, hope remains,' he thought. He wondered if the Subedar might know of the list of names of the sepoys of the 34 BNI, of the year 1857. If only he could ask Subedar Purshottam Bandopadhyay. Morning slipped into afternoon, but this thought lingered in Anjaan's mind. Laila noticed how absent minded he seemed. He worked around the shop, had his meals, and sat for namaz as he always did. Yet, he wasn't himself.

'Something seems to be bothering you,' Laila asked during supper. She hadn't yet eaten. She had served meal for Anjaan and Baadal and while they ate sitting on bamboo mats on the earthen floor of the kitchen, she sat fanning them with a hand fan, made out of the broad, dried leaf of a palmyra palm. The palmyra khajoor, as Ijaaz Miya used to call it. After a moment's silence, Anjaan replied, 'I was thinking, maybe, I should go to Dhaka.'

'But what for?' Laila asked. Even in the dim light of the kerosene lantern, through the rhythmic play of light and shadow caused by the fan in her hand as it moved to and fro between her face and the lantern, Anjaan saw the anxiety in her beautiful face. A few thin lines stretched out from the corners of her eyes and when he observed well, he saw a fine, almost negligible line running from her nose to the corners of her mouth.

'To meet Subedar Purshottam Bandopadhyay of the Indian Army,' he said, taking his eyes back to his plate.

Baadal immediately understood. But Laila didn't. It had to be explained. So Baadal took it upon himself to make his amma understand. When Anjaan had finished eating and gone outside to wash his hands, Baadal told his amma, 'Abba hopes to find out if Subedar Purshottam Bandopadhyay may have any information about the sepoys who died at the battle of Latu. Ammajaan, if he wishes to go, don't stop him.'

'Oh!' was all Laila said. She thought for a while and then asked, 'But how will he travel to Dhaka? It is far.'

'There are boys going from neighbouring villages, Ammajaan, and Liaqat kaka's son Liazul is going from our village. Abba probably hopes to go with them,' Baadal told her.

When Anjaan returned to the kitchen Laila asked him, 'How will you go?'

'Mannan is taking some boys in his carriage. I'll talk to him,' Anjaan replied.

'Won't that take days?' Laila asked, as she removed Anjaan's and Baadal's plates and brought down a fresh one from the meatsafe to serve herself now. Anjaan dragged his mat against the wall and sat down again, leaning on the wall, waiting as Laila ate.

'Yes, but there are musafirkhanas in some villages along the way,' Anjaan told her, 'Mannan usually takes his passengers to rest in a few that he knows when he ferries people for long distances.'

Though Baadal had finished eating, he hadn't yet got up. He too sat down and listened to the conversation, putting in his consent sometimes or a suggestion. Both Laila and Anjaan looked up to his decisions.

'Baadal,' Anjaan said after thinking for a while, 'will Mannan come by this way in a day or two? To the shop?'

'I don't know, abba, but I can send word to him through Hargovind. He stays very close to Mannan's village and often drops by our shop when he comes towards Latu bazar.'

'Do that then, son.'

The night outside was still and clammy. The air was calm, but a cloudy sky made the air suffocatingly dense. It was restless in an unseen manner. Just like Anjaan and his thoughts were at that moment.

In the days before going to Dhaka, Anjaan continued to visit Malegarh and one afternoon he rode past the hillock towards the village nearby. Most people in that village and even in those around the graveyard, knew him as Hazratkandi kaka from Hazratkandi village, who kept coming to tend to the dead. That day Anjaan went up to meet Nitairanjan Dey. He was old now, Anjaan guessed he would be around seventy. Or more. Certainly not less. Anjaan had occasionally bumped into him from the time he started visiting the graves. Both Anjaan and Nitairanjan Dey were younger those days and had more zest in their steps. Nitairanjan would sometimes be taking the cows to or from the fields and at other times, he would be returning from the bazar at Latu. Sometimes they smiled and nodded at each other but passed by without speaking. But after all these years, that day it would be different. Anjaan's steps were much slower, and his beard had long greyed. He could no longer see as far ahead as he could in those earlier days when he used to just smile at Nitairanjan as they passed, without actually talking. But that day he was going to talk to Nitairanjan. He had a few important things to ask him. Important for him, maybe not for Nitairanjan Dey. So he walked up to Nitairanjan Dey's house farther north of the Malegarh hillock, pushing his cycle alongside.

'Nitai babu, are you home?' Anjaan called out standing in the yard outside his house.

It took a while for Nitairanjan Dey to come out. 'Anjaan miya! Namaskar! What brings you this way today? Come, come!' he said, pulling a vest over his head and down his gaunt belly as he stepped down from the narrow verandah out into the small yard.

'I had been meaning to drop by often, but somehow found myself lingering over there,' Anjaan said gesturing towards the graves. He paused, took a step closer and said, 'I had been wondering for some time now, Nitai babu, if you were around when the martyrs were being brought over there,' Anjaan once again pointed towards the hillock, 'and buried.'

'I was, Anjaan miya, but my maa held me back inside the house,' Nitairanjan Dey said, staring hard towards the hillock as if that would make him see through foggy memories. 'A few people from our village watched the ongoings that time, but from afar. Because I was small, my maa was scared to let me go out and stand with them and watch.'

'Who were they? Who watched the ongoings?' Anjaan asked, hoping to meet atleast one or two of them.

'There was Gauricharan but the old man is no more,' Nitairanjan Dey replied after some thought. He then remained quiet for a long while, trying hard to remember the names of those who watched what happened at the graveyard that day and later told them stories of the battle and the burial. Meanwhile, Nitairanjan Dey's daughter-in-law brought out betelnut and offered that to Anjaan. Anjaan took one and picked a betelnut leaf as well. He then broke off its short stem, dipped it in the lime that came in a small earthen saucer next to the betelnut and smeared it on the leaf. By the time he rolled the nut into the leaf and shoved it into his mouth, Nitairanjan Dey remembered the name.

'Bholanath is there, just two houses away,' he declared with great triumph at his capacity to recollect.

'Can you and I go meet him now?' Anjaan asked.

Nitairanjan Dey nodded. 'Yes, yes, I can take you now, come.' He walked up to the verandah to put on his slippers and stepped out to lead the way.

As the two walked up to Bholanath Sarkar's house, Nitairanjan Dey let Anjaan know that Bholanath had become senile.

'Nevertheless, even when the old forget a part of their lives, Anjaan Miya, they do remember and retain in their memory another part. He may yet remember the part you wish to hear him talk about,' Nitairanjan Dey offered hope. Anjaan could sense the pity he felt for old Bholanath Sarkar.

Sadly, though, it was the part that Anjaan wished to hear him talk about that had slipped out of Bholanath Sarkar's memory. And so that visit too turned out to be like one of those many past efforts, futile and disheartening. Anjaan once more rode his bicycle back home with the same questions, unanswered, sitting heavy on his chest.

In the days that followed, Anjaan and Laila both prepared for Anjaan's journey to Dhaka. Laila put in a couple of clean kurtas, two lungis and a white, crocheted taqiyah on a clean, floral printed sheet. She folded a prayer mat and put it with the clothes. Then she rolled these things together with the sheet and tied up the bundle with a length of rope made of coir. She had a way of doing such things very meticulously. Now as she tied the bundle, she left two loops on top of the bundle in such a way that Anjaan may put his fingers through them and use them as handles to carry the bundle.

On the day Anjaan began his journey to Dhaka, Mannan arrived very early at the shop to pick him. It was still dark, the last few moments of the night still hovered above Hazratkandi. Liazul too had arrived there, to board the carriage together with Anjaan. The two sat on the bench with Anjaan's bundle lying next to them as they waited for Mannan and his carriage. Baadal kept walking up to the road to see if it appeared in the distance. Laila was in the yard too. This was the first time after they got married that Anjaan was travelling so far, and without her. Soon they heard the clip-clop of horses' hooves along the road approaching through the fading darkness of a retreating night. Anjaan picked up his bundle and got up from the bench. He looked at Laila. Her eyes were moist. She wasn't even sure if the Subedar would allow Anjaan anywhere near him, leave alone hear him or talk to him. But she never once spoke of her fears, not to Baadal, and certainly not to Anjaan. When Mannan reached the shop, he pulled the reins and the horses came to a halt. 'But I have to go,' he whispered close to her ear. Then he said aloud, 'Baadal, take care of your amma.' He climbed into the back of the carriage and Baadal helped him with the bundle. Liazul climbed in after Anjaan.

'We shall pick the other four on our way, Baadal bhai, don't worry, Anjaan kaka is safe with me!' he assured Baadal and Laila.

Baadal waved back as the carriage drove away.

Laila waited and watched till both the carriage and the sound of horses' hooves merged into the soft pale glow of a new dawn in the horizon.

Mannan knew the road to Dhaka well. He knew the road to most places around Sylhet and East Bengal. For he had been carrying people in his carriage for many years now. He knew the musafirkhanas and the dharamshalas on the way too. It was also in these rest houses and dharamshalas that he picked up information and news from other travellers about other places. In some stretches along the way, the ride felt jerky. Anjaan's old, unaccustomed bones cut into his sagging muscles. It hurt. Sometimes the horses shook their heads so vigorously that Mannan had to tug at the reins to calm them. They travelled through the changing colours of the day, through early dawn to a sunny morning and then to afternoon, just as the sun did above them in the sky. When they passed other carriages on the way, Mannan always made a courtesy wave or a call to the other driver.

'You know why I do that?' he asked turning his head a little sideways, so he could see the people at the back but addressing no one in particular.

'Why do you do that, Mannan?' Anjaan asked.

'It's an unsaid understanding among us carriage drivers, kaka, it is to ensure that everything on the way is alright. Because I am headed towards what he has already come past. Had there been anything untoward, he would have told me. And I would have told him if there was anything out of normal along the way that I just passed through.'

'Ah! That's really smart,' quipped Parimal Guha.

Mannan laughed, 'And then ofcourse, I also keep asking my passengers things like these and keep talking to them so that they don't fall asleep.' He laughed again, 'And you know why?'

'Why?' Haidar Siddiqui asked, amused.

'Because when my passengers fall asleep and snore, I too start feeling drowsy and am tempted to stop for a short nap. But don't worry, I'm wide awake this moment,' he said, as he urged his horses on. 'Ghraah! Ghraah!'

Around mid-day, Mannan pulled up his carriage at the dharamshala in Beerganj for a meal. The place had a separate meal section for the three other travellers, Manobendro Bhowmik, Dibyendu Sarkar and Parimal Guha, while Haider Siddiqui, Liazul and Anjaan walked towards the halaal meal section. So whenever Mannan had a motley group of passengers like he had that day, he preferred this place for a stop over. He released the horses from the carriage and took them to the horses' shed. Anjaan noticed that Mannan paid something to the boy in the shed, to feed and water them.

Soon, he too joined Liazul, Anjaan and Haider's section for his meal. When they resumed journey after a good lunch, the heads of some of the passengers started bobbing with sleep. But Anjaan was wide awake. Mannan sensed that.

'Now is the time when herds of cattle will walk back home, Anjaan kaka. If they're with a cowherd, well and good. If they aren't, Allah rehem! I need to keep looking out to see that my horses don't run into the cows.' They moved along large stretches of backwaters now, where villagers had left their jute plants to soak. When these plants rot, they would twist ropes out of them. Or pull out the fibre to make yarns with which they would make sacks.

'And so where exactly do we go to in Dhaka?' Mannan asked, to nobody in particular. Manobendro Bhowmik woke up with a start. 'Yes, Mannan?' he said, wiping away drool from the corner of his mouth.

'I was asking,' Mannan repeated, 'where exactly do we go to in Dhaka?'

'To the New Army Transit Camp,' Parimal Guha informed, 'though I don't know where exactly that is. We'll have to ask around once we reach Dhaka.'

'Trust this Mannan here! I know the place. It came up only after the war in the west broke out.' Anjaan felt grateful to be with Mannan. Towards dusk they arrived at Mirzapur and Mannan drove the carriage to a comfortable and homely musafirkhana.

'I know the person who runs this rest house.

Good man,' Mannan said, 'will take good care of us all including my horses. But if we leave this rest house and go farther now, it'll be past midnight till we arrive at the next. So, kaka, let's halt here for the night.'

'We are at your mercy, Mannan,' Anjaan smiled through his exhaustion. They resumed journey early next morning, stopping once again like the previous day, at a dharamshala, for their midday meal. From there, it would take them only about another hour or so to Dhaka.

When they reached Dhaka and the New Army Transit Camp, they were directed to a long open hall and asked to write their names on a register and wait. Anjaan's spirit sank. He would have to ask one of the boys to write his name for him. 'You will be called,' they were told by a sentry, 'and if you want water, there are pitchers at the back of the hall,' he pointed to the right, 'and if anyone wishes to relieve himself, go behind that coconut-frond barrier,' he pointed to the left. 'Ah yes, also, did you write your names correctly? Your names will be called out later and you all will be given a meal of rice, dal and curry. So I hope you have written your names properly. Otherwise some other will receive your meal and eat it.' Young men with newly married brides at home and younger boys, with just their first burst of beard and puberty voice, nodded and sat in groups, discussing the war and their dreams of going to it.

The sentry then came close to Anjaan and looked at him. Anjaan's head of grey hair and his almost white beard caught his attention. The past two days' journey had left deeper furrows between his many wrinkles, adding greater years to his age.

'You! Over there!' The young sentry beckoned Anjaan towards him. 'How are you here?' he asked.

Anjaan took hesitant steps towards him and pleaded, 'If I may please be allowed to meet Subedar babu, I just had a couple of things to ask. I will not bother him, nor will I take long.' He stopped and took a deep breath. The sentry looked at him well, walking all around him once and then again eyed him from the taqiyah on his head to the dusty sandals of black rubber on his feet, with great caution and suspicion at the same time.

'That cap on your head,' he said, pointing at the taqiyah, 'remove and show it to me.'

Anjaan obliged. He had no choice. The sentry stood on the toes of his thick black boots and ran a hand through Anjaan's hair.

'Nothing there?'

Anjaan stared at the sentry, shook his head, and then lowered his eyes.

'You sure aren't hiding any weapon underneath that long kurta, are you?'

'Khuda gawah! Why would I, huzur!'

'Raise your arms,' he said, beginning to frisk Anjaan.

The sentry moved his hands down Anjaan's back and sides, then bringing them down the legs and between them.

'No homemade grenades squeezed in there?'

Anjaan felt like he had been stripped and molested. Had the sentry known that a soldier's blood ran in the old man's veins too, would he then dole out the same treatment? Anjaan wondered.

'Who are the other young men with you?'

Anjaan turned to look at Haider, Parimal and the rest of them waiting to be called in.

'Boys from villages near mine. They have come for the pre recruitment mela.'

'They're not sending you as a bait?'

'Huzur, what do they have to catch, that they use me as bait?' he coyly asked, putting the taqiyah back on his head and dusting off with his hands the defilement from his kurta.

'You know this is a high security campus. You do?'

Anjaan nodded slowly. He was already left much exhausted from the travel and now having to face this questioning further weakened his knees and his morale.

'Alright, I shall ask to let you in. I'm not sure though, if you will be allowed. And if allowed, and if you show up any tricks, you're dead meat. You can't get away from the army, remember that!'

Anjaan nodded, remembering a similar warning from his childhood, many years ago, on a dark night when he arrived at the 9 Periphery Supply Camp. A strange kind of fear engulfed him and he suddenly wished he hadn't come.

'I am honest in my submission, huzur, I have no tricks, none at all. Only a couple of things to ask, please kindly seek permission for me from the subedar to let me in, huzur, please!' Anjaan felt humiliated and hurt, but at the same time he knew that the sentry was only doing his duty.

'And what are these *couple of things*?' the sentry asked.

Anjaan faltered in his speech. He hadn't come all the way from Hazratkandi to talk of the only purpose of his existence to a sentry. His identity was sacrosanct to him, if not to anyone else. He hesitated to speak of those couple of things to the sentry.

'Oh, alright! Alright! Let me go in and talk to the subedar. And what shall I put your name as?'

'Anjaan.'

'Anjaan what?'

At almost sixty years of age, Anjaan was now well used to be asked this.

'Anjaan Hazratkandi,' he replied without waiting.

But before the sentry went in to talk to the subedar, he put another on guard at the hall. Then he was gone for a long time. Anjaan began to wonder if his entire travel had been a waste. All of a sudden, the thought that he might be arrested and held back under suspicion flashed through his mind and he was gripped with terror. He wanted to run away before the sentry reappeared, but at the same time, he realized that his cramped, fatigued legs wouldn't carry him even till the boundary gates of the transit camp. He sat down, not knowing what he had landed himself into. He longed desperately for Ijaaz Miya's bench under the gulmohar. As the moments went by, he even began to think that the sentry might have forgotten about him and his request, so insignificant he was in the whole situation, with all the important people in that place. But soon the sentry emerged. He waved at Anjaan from a row of individual blocks of makeshift houses at a distance, within the campus. When Anjaan walked towards him, the sentry led him into the house, one that looked busier and more important than the rest. When Anjaan walked into the room, Subedar Purshottam Bandopadhyay was looking at a large map rolled out on an equally large table in one corner of the scantily furnished room. He was looking at the Bengal Province and the locations of the various camps, regiments, supply depots and periphery supply centres in Sylhet, East Bengal. Along with that, he was familiarising himself with this part of Bengal. He was wearing a pair of khaki trousers and a full sleeved, brass buttoned, blue shirt with many an ornamented badge pinned to the flap of his breast pocket. That uniform, the row of houses, the sentries everywhere, the rigidity of the entire army campus and the ambience as a whole took him for a fleeting moment to that first night when he had entered the 9 Periphery Supply Camp. He felt that same fear and that same ache haunting him all over again.

'Well, I am told you are Anjaan Hazratkandi,' the Subedar looked up from the map and spoke, though still standing by the table. 'But how is it that your last name is Hazratkandi? Isn't that a village towards... hmm...' he looked down at the map again, searching for Hazratkandi. 'Ah here it is. Hazratkandi,' he said, tapping with a map pointer at the small dot marked Hazratkandi on his large map, 'that's close to the Malegarh Martyrs' graveyard.' He now looked up once more at Anjaan Hazratkandi. 'But why are you here? We are not exactly looking for men of your elderliness, Hazratkandi.'

'Mwaafi, huzur,' Anjaan replied with all humility, 'it is that graveyard that you mentioned just now, which brings me here.' And Anjaan narrated to the Subedar what he came searching for. He had to be brief, for he wouldn't be allowed the whole morning. At the same time, nervousness kept the right words from coming to his mind and then on, to his lips. It helped, however, that the Subedar had a sound knowledge of the battle of Latu.

'Even if huzur may not have the names right here and now, Allah rahem, I shall remain indebted if huzur may generously look up or speak around, after going back to Calcutta from here, or mercifully puts me in connection with someone who may have them, the names.' Saying that, Anjaan stopped. He was once more in the grip of terrible anxiety, wondering how the Subedar would react to his strange plea.

But the Subedar had heard out Anjaan's story with patience. He felt pity for the old man. He had earlier, during post-battle rehabilitations, seen the plight of refugees, orphans and the displaced on many occasions. And yet, Anjaan Hazratkandi's tale seemed to be different from all other tales he had known.

'I don't have a list of the Latu martyrs' names right now, Hazratkandi, but I can definitely ask.' He could see that as Anjaan spoke, he frequently swallowed saliva to wet a throat that was parched out of fright and apprehension. So he offered Anjaan a glass of water.

'Go now, Hazratkandi, but before you do,' he walked up to his desk, picked a pen and a copy like the ones Baadal used to take to school, and gave these to Anjaan, 'write your address here.'

'Mwaafi, huzur, I cannot write beyond my own name in Arabic,' Anjaan said, lowering his eyes. A fresh wave of shame rose from the feet where his gaze rested and drowned his self respect, whatever little of it was left with him anyway.

Subedar Purshottam Bandopadhyay, on the other hand, felt another twinge of sympathy for the man standing with hands folded and palms together in front of him, a man maybe older than his own father.

'Oh! No problem, you tell me, I'll write,' he offered.

And so as Anjaan Hazratkandi spoke, Subedar Purshottam Bandopadhyay noted.

Anjaan Hazratkandi
Village: Hazratkandi, Sylhet Province, East Bengal, India.

Below that, within brackets, he wrote *Ijaaz Miya's cycle shop by an old Gulmohar tree, with a wooden bench under it.* For that was what Anjaan mentioned, when the Subedar asked him for any prominent landmark.

Anjaan then bowed and took his palm to his forehead the same way he did many years ago when he walked out of Superintendent Edward Fidley's office on the last day at the Central Supply Depot.

'I shall do my best, Hazratkandi,' Subedar Purshottam Bandopadhyay said as Anjaan left the room. And in his heart, he meant it.

Anjaan waited around with Mannan while Parimal Guha, Dibyendu Sarkar, Manobendro Bhowmik, Haider Siddiqui and Liazul, all of them were taken in one by one, to be with several others gathered at the open hall for the initial and informal interactions and information. They would be briefed about what was expected of them and what they could expect. It was afternoon when they were done. Immediately after, the men were asked to sit in rows on the floor of the waiting hall. Two sepoys walked in carrying between them a large saucepan, while a third trotted behind, ladling out scoops of rice from it onto the leaf plates laid in front of those sitting. Two more sepoys came in, this time carrying a saucepan of dal. They sat the saucepan on the floor after every few plates and with a bowl, dropped out a scoop onto the rice from a height that caused a great part of the dal to splash out of the plate. The next sepoy followed with a bucket of a curry of mixed vegetables. This he served with care and sympathy. Anjaan sat down to eat but a strange, aching disquiet began to pound at his heart and travel down to churn his stomach. His hunger disappeared. He wrapped his meal in the leaf plate it was served on, got up and walked away towards a mongrel that had sauntered into the camp at the smell of food. He fed his share to the dog. 'I'm sure you too don't have a name,' he told the dog under his breath, 'but you know you belong around here.' The dog looked up once at Anjaan and he whispered to it, 'It's okay, eat, you deserve it more than me. I could neither write my name nor am capable of serving in the war. You atleast bark, and raise alarm. Go on, eat.'

Mannan suggested they start the return journey immediately. Because it was well past noon, night would fall when they would still be a long distance away from Mirzapur, where they halted the previous night.

'There is a musafirkhana at Devitola too,' Mannan said. 'They don't take in people late at night but the old lady who looks after it is a relative of mine. We will have to help her out though, in preparing the food.' There weren't too many options to disagree to the offer. And so Mannan and his passengers spent the night at Devitola. Despite the physical and emotional fatigue that bore down on him, Anjaan could not sleep.

In the entire return journey of two days and one night, the young men were enthusiastic and talked of the ongoing war and their own anticipations of serving the army in it. Anjaan was the only one who sat quiet, his thoughts running amok from the 9 Periphery Supply Camp to the Central Supply Depot at Narikuli and to the New Army Transit Camp at Dhaka. But eventually, they always seemed to reach and settle at Malegarh.

Setting out early from Devitola, Mannan drove his carriage even though a light drizzle dampened the horses' coat.

'Should we have waited?' Parimal Guha asked.

'My horses!' Mannan exclaimed, 'lovingly slapping one of them on its back, 'are weatherproof, Parimal bhai! Never let me down, come hail or cyclone. Unfortunately, it doesn't snow here in Sylhet.'

'Had it snowed?' Manobendro Bhowmik asked, picking up the fun.

'Had it snowed, bhai, they would have pulled you even through that! Hah! Bravo! Carry on, boys! Go on!' he said once more slapping the horse.

Soon they left the drizzle behind and came upon a small township. The summer sun was pushing through the clouds.

'Wow, look! That's a palatial bungalow!' Haider Siddiqui said, craning his head out of the carriage to look at a large mansion behind equally large, ornate gates on the right of the road. Bright red terracotta tiles lined its many domed roofs. But the sheer magnificence of the mansion stood out like a sore thumb among the rest of the small, low cottages that made up the town.

'Oh, that!' Mannan said, taking a quick look at the place and turning his gaze back to the road, 'that is Jaffar Alam's house. He is a merchant, trades in silk and jute yarn. Filthy rich.'

'Yeah, can see that,' Liazul remarked. 'You know him?'

'Everyone around here does,' Mannan replied. 'Gave more gifts to the Nawab here than the taxes he ought to have. This got their taxes heavily discounted. But now, I hear the British have stopped giving the Nawab the right to collect taxes. That has brought an end to Jaffar Alam's tax evasions and with the war in the west at its peak, trade too is in an all time low, so I hear. His lavishness has come down.'

'Most traders and merchants are in a similar plight,' Liazul added.

'So, there we are,' Dibyendu Sarkar reflected, 'rich or poor, illiterate or educated, we all have been touched by the war and the freedom struggle. Haven't we, Anjaan kaka?'

Anjaan was shaken out of his own thoughts. 'Yes, yes. We have,' he replied hastily, to mask the gloom that shrouded his heart. No one probably understood that better than him. He was both poor and illiterate. The double-edged sword, like Sirajullah said, had struck him once more.

'By the way, is it just my stomach that's rumbling with hunger, eh?' Manobendro Bhowmik asked turning his head to look at all his co-passengers, 'Mannan, feed us, boy, stop your horses at some decent place.'

The sun was now directly overhead, and the sky was without a clump of cloud. Sweat trickled down Mannan's hairline at the back of his neck but that in no way could exhaust his spirit.

'Meal time! Of course I have it in mind,' he laughed, 'just ahead. A little distance now, bhai, sing a lullaby to quieten your stomach. For just another half of an hour. And we'll be looking at steaming rice and fish curry. Trust me.'

The steaming rice and fish curry at the Tetultol dharamshala was indeed a treat. The horses too were well fed and rested. Mannan treated himself to some dried betelnut as well. He plonked one big piece into his mouth and put a few more into the pocket of his kurta.

'That should keep my mouth busy,' he said, 'otherwise I'm prone to two vices.' He paused for reaction. The rest were slowly climbing back onto the carriage

'And what are they?' Parimal Guha laughed as he asked.

'One, is to doze off,' he paused again, waiting for more reaction, as he reined in the horses and got ready to mount.

'And two?' Liazul asked.

'Jabbering so much as to bore you all to sleep. Which again would infect me.' And he roared with laughter. At least his laughter did infect all of them now and they laughed heartily as the horses resumed their journey. All of them, except Anjaan. He only smiled because, otherwise, it would look impolite.

And amidst chatter, discussions and a few inescapable nods of dozing heads, the carriage moved on, just as the sun too sailed past small tufts of clouds towards the western sky. Mannan took the horses past fields and backwaters, and villages where little children created a happy cacophony climbing mango trees, to pick the last ones for the day.

The setting sun warmed their backs as they approached Hazratkandi. But before reaching his village, they had to stop several times on the way to drop off the rest of the passengers. When Anjaan was left alone at the back of the carriage and the familiar sights of Hazratkandi somewhat soothed his frayed being, his thoughts began to return home. To Laila. To Baadal. To the shop. The war had taken its toll on it. Even if Baadal and Anjaan worked hard to bring back its recent good times, they would not be able to do so without customers. And these days customers were few and far between.

It was dark when Anjaan reached home. Baadal hurried out on hearing the horses' hooves and Mannan's voice calling out to him. Quietly, he helped his abba down the cart and carried his bundle in. Laila was waiting at the doorway.

'Could you meet the Subedar?', Laila asked with her eyes. She did not say a word though.

Anjaan's thoughts went back to the New Army Transit Camp at Dhaka. To Subedar Purshottam Bandopadhyay's office.

'He said he would do his best,' was all Anjaan could tell her then.

Later in the night, lying in bed next to her, he told her everything, he emptied out all that he held in his defeated soul. The way he felt his insides bursting with shame, heaped as they were one atop the other, when he had to tell the Subedar why he was a Hazratkandi like the village on his map, and that he couldn't write beyond his name, that too only in Arabic. He hid his face in Laila's bosom and said through a muffled voice, 'The sentry felt me all over with his hands, thinking I might be carrying some weapon underneath my kurta.' He reached out for her hand, clasped it and said, 'he made me remove my taqiyah to check under it.' And finally, he took a deep breath and said haltingly, 'he felt between my legs, searching for firearms.' In the dark, Laila bit her lips till they bled, to hold her cries. She wouldn't cry, not now. She was Anjaan's strength. 'But he was just doing his duty. These are times of the war, aren't they?' Anjaan said between his chokes, though he said it to console himself, if not Laila.

Even in the dark, inside the mosquito net that hung over the bed like an upturned box, Laila saw that he was sobbing, releasing the lid over the pain that he was carrying in his chest through the journey back from Dhaka.

'It'll be alright,' Laila comforted him, putting an arm around him. 'The Subedar has kept your address and said he will do his best. So I'm sure he will. I believe he will.'

When Laila kissed him to sleep, Anjaan got the salty taste of blood from her lips on his tongue. That taste veered his mind to their first night after the nikaah.

Laila's belief made Anjaan wait the rest of his life for news from Subedar Purshottam Bandopadhyay.

12
The Year Nineteen Thirty-Two

When the world war came to an end in 1918, a slow but steady flow of customers once again started to trickle into Ijaaz Miya's shop. On some days just one or two and on other days, none. But gradually, things began to look up. Friends, however, continued to come as they always did for the usual exchange of news and gossip. They talked of the war and they built their own war stories around a piece of blue, flat iron that Dilhajur found in his paddy fields. They talked in whispers of how hundreds of people were shot at on orders of a British within a closed area, and how many more jumped into an abandoned well to escape the bullets, at the Jallianwala Bagh far away in Punjab on the day of Baisakhi.

'Qazi was saying, it was some Brigadier General, by the name of Reginald Dyer,' said Narayan Chandra Dey.

'You never know, it may happen to us here in Sylhet too,' lamented hakim Sirajullah. 'Maybe not firing within an enclosed park, but some other form of massacre. Any form, you see, you don't know to what extremes people can go, to establish their might.'

Anjaan nodded. A trail of all the viciousness inflicted upon him flashed through his memory. 'Yes,' he agreed, 'they can do anything to establish their might. You've said it right, hakim.'

They would talk about the zamindars in Sylhet, about who among them were favoured by the British and were granted the princely titles of Maharaja and Raja, only because these zamindars lent their support to them. They also discussed those zamindars whose titles were made to fall in rank because they did not side with the British. They talked of how steady, long-term changes were creeping into Bengal's social and political structure. But outwardly and immediately, the numbness of the world war was beginning to fade, and things were slowly beginning to crawl towards normalcy, though the war definitely left its scar. Work at the shop was picking up once more and Baadal took care of almost all of it. He had his father's long and strong limbs, and his mother's eyes, while Anjaan attributed his easy way of conversation to Ijaaz Miya. Anjaan felt confident leaving him in the shop to take care of work as well as customers. He, on the other hand, began to spend more time around the villages at Malegarh and at the martyrs' hillock. Once he spent a whole afternoon scraping soil from the edges of the graves and heaping it on top of them, to make each of them stand out as prominent and individual graves. He then gently smoothed out the loose soil with his bare hands, as if he was caressing someone who was sleeping.

Back at the shop, Mannan dropped by to replace a broken screw and stitch a part of the torn awning of his carriage. So, while Baadal mended his carriage, Mannan sat down on the bench on the edge nearest to Baadal, and began to update Baadal about happenings from all over. He just had to be incited.

'So what's new, Mannan?' Baadal called out from inside the shop.

'Nothing much, Baadal bhai,' he paused and then suddenly remembered, 'Oh yes, this thing they're mentioning as the Khilafat movement.'

'And how did you get wind of that?' Baadal asked, still bent over his work. It would take a while to stitch up the carriage's torn awning.

'The other day I had to drive Rasool master to the post office at Mohiniganj,' Mannan was saying, when Anjaan walked into the yard. He had taken a brief afternoon siesta and now came out to see Baadal at work.

'Salaam waleiqum, Anjaan kaka!' Mannan greeted.

'Waleiqum assalam, Mannan my boy!' Anjaan smiled, 'so travelling anywhere far?' he asked, motioning at the awning being mended.

'Not far, not as of now, Anjaan kaka,' he replied, 'that tear in the roof happened when a stone apple dropped on it some days back while I was travelling towards Bouderbeel, passing under a large stone apple tree by the wayside.'

'Allah rehem, it fell when it did, Mannan, it let your head pass by!' Anjaan said.

'True! Kaka, true! Never thought of that.' Mannan ran a hand over his head, as if to assure himself that his head was there and in one piece. 'With the monsoons approaching, I won't get passengers with a torn roof on my carriage. So here I am, at Baadal bhai's mercy,' he laughed.

It reminded Anjaan, even Laila was asking if they could get a change of thatch before the monsoons. Over many a monsoon storm, the thatch had become sparse in places. Moreover, the smell of mildew and fungus from the thatch percolated into the rooms below, driving Laila into tearful sneezing fits. There have been times when insects dropped from the rotting thatch onto the cot. Nothing petrified Laila more. So, she was asking about changing the thatch. Anjaan and Baadal were hoping instead to replace the thatch not with new thatch but with corrugated iron sheets. They would be able to afford it now, if only customers kept growing at the same pace as they were at the moment. Had the world war not sent their business spiralling down, the new corrugated iron sheets would have been up long back.

'So, Baadal bhai, what was I saying?' Mannan tried to reconnect.

'You were saying about taking Rasool master to the post office,' Baadal helped.

'Ah, yes! At the post office, yes. Your memory is sharp, Baadal bhai! So yes, as I waited outside the post office at Mohiniganj for Rasool master, I came to know that the post office had the electric telegraph system.'

'But hadn't that been in operation since the war started?' Baadal asked.

'It had,' Mannan smiled sheepishly, 'but Baadal bhai, I came to know of it only the other day!'

That made Baadal laugh too. He was putting in the last few stitches on the canvas of the awning.

'When I asked Rasool master about it on our way back, he said that it was installed to stay updated on war status and situation reports. And also to stay connected with the Madras and Bengal Presidencies.' Mannan looked towards the awning.

'Just a few more stitches there, Mannan. You'll be done in another fifteen minutes,' Baadal said.

'No hurry! No hurry! Baadal bhai,' Mannan said, vigorously shaking his head, 'unless ofcourse you're fed up of seeing and hearing me,' and he laughed heartily. Mannan's cheer spilled out into the yard, making even Anjaan break into laughter. 'Also, Baadal bhai,' he resumed, 'chatting this way doesn't give me the guilt of procrastination or gossip, because at the same time I'm getting my repairs done too!'

Even Baadal enjoyed Mannan's company. This boy was a genuine source of information and news.

Anjaan walked up to the bench and sat next to Mannan. 'So how do they operate this electric telegraph system, Mannan? They send a question and then receive an answer directly?' he asked, interest building around the telegraph system for certain obvious reasons. Baadal noticed which way his father's queries were heading.

'Well, I'm not really sure, Anjaan kaka, but I guess they type out a message which goes through the air as some kind of code, then reaches the post office which you have indicated as its destination, where it is decoded into a language we can read. Then the postman takes it to be delivered at the address given on it.'

The interest Anjaan found in all of that had an underlying reason. He thought hard about the possibilities of this thing called the telegraph bringing him some clue towards his search. So the day after, he walked down to the post office at Mohiniganj. He had two things in mind as he walked. He would send a message to Subedar Purshottam Bandopadhyay and also, ask the people at the post office if they could connect him to anyone outside Hazratkandi, outside Sylhet and Dhaka, who might have some whereabouts of the names of the sepoys of the 34th Regiment Bengal Native Infantry during the battle of Latu. It wasn't the whole list that mattered to him. He searched for just one name on the list. But to look up that one name, he would need to ask for the whole list.

'You will need money to pay for the messages,' Laila reminded, as she saw him off under the gulmohar tree. She knew he wasn't in the habit of carrying money unless he planned to drop by at the bazar. And that day, he had only the post office in mind. 'Here, take some,' she said, drawing the free end of her saree's pallu to the front over her shoulder and opening a knot in one corner. There were a few coins knotted in the folds there, enough for small payments at the post office.

Mohiniganj was far but not as much that Anjaan couldn't walk till there. He was used to walking great distances. In fact, these days he preferred to walk because pedalling left him out of breath and when he got off the cycle, his legs felt limp. When he arrived at the post office, he saw people standing in queues, in front of a row of tiny windows cut into grills, in a small hall. These windows opened into small cubicles with wooden walls, inside which sat the employees of the post office. Anjaan didn't know where to start or what to start with. He felt lost. Usually, it was Baadal who went there for any kind of work, for he could read. He could write as well, in a language that everyone in Sylhet understood. But Anjaan couldn't. The people, the noise, the queues, the signs and boards, everything inside the post office made him feel as if his spine was collapsing into a freezing pool. Other people who walked in after him looked at the white letters on the red boards fixed over each window, read them, and took their place in the queues according to their requirement. A surge of anguish once again rose from his reeling stomach and hit his heart. He didn't know how to read those letters. And while he waited and looked around for someone whom he could ask, the queues got longer. Neither was there anyone he knew. The people who sat behind the grilled windows, just wide enough to push hands, paper, and money in and out, seemed too busy and too important to entertain the illiterate Anjaan.

'Er...bhaijaan, excuse me please,' Anjaan hesitantly asked a middle-aged man who had just entered the hall and who, Anjaan thought, wouldn't mind helping him. The man turned and looked at Anjaan.

'Can you please help me?' Anjaan asked.

'Well, how?'

'Can you please tell me in which queue I need to stand for the telegraph?' Anjaan asked, shame and humiliation making him feel hot beneath his taqiyah.

'You mean, the telegram?' the man asked.

'Oh yes, that, I guess so, yes.' Anjaan replied. Now he was a little embarrassed too.

The man read through the boards and pointed towards the corner window. Anjaan was grateful for that was the window with the least number of people standing in front of it. By the time he turned and smiled at the man to express his gratitude, the man had already moved on. Anjaan walked over to the window and took his place in the queue. When his turn arrived, the man sitting inside the cubicle asked without looking up, 'Whom to?'

'Subedar Purshottam Bandopadhyay,' Anjaan replied.

'Address?' the man asked.

'Hazratkandi, Sylhet,' Anjaan replied.

Now the man looked up.

'The Subedar stays at Hazratkandi?' he asked, bringing his eyebrows close to each other.

'No, huzur, I do,' Anjaan replied.

'And why may I need your address!' The man said nonchalantly, letting his eyebrows immediately dart away from each other. 'Tell me the Subedar's.'

'Oh! Mwaafi, huzur, the Subedar's, yes,' Anjaan said apologetically, 'the Subedar's. It is 49th Bengali Regiment, Calcutta.'

This time the man stopped writing and looked at Anjaan for a while.

'Huzur?' Anjaan meant to ask if there was anything else he wanted to know about Subedar Purshottam Bandopadhyay.

'Look, miya,' the man bawled, 'the 49th Bengali Regiment had long been disbanded. Maybe around two years or so ago. When was it, Satish?' he asked his colleague sitting at the window next to him.

'August thirtieth,' Satish looked up a chart and replied, '1920.'

'Yeah, it was then,' the man behind the telegram window confirmed, looking back at Anjaan.

The surge of anguish that rose from his stomach and hit his heart a while ago dropped with a resounding thud back into his gut. It was a thud that kept hammering at his insides for long, till they rose and reached between his ears to create a dulling throb in his head. Another thin ray of hope was slipping away from his reach. He slowly stepped out of the queue, making way for those after him. There were just two of them. Anjaan waited for them to finish. As he waited, he watched people filling forms and sending money. That probably was what Baadal said was money order, Anjaan thought. Then he slowly approached the man behind the telegram window once more.

'What now?' the man asked, slightly gentler. It might have been out of pity, or it might have been for the fact that he would now be able to take a break with no more people in the queue of his window.

'Huzur,' Anjaan began slowly, 'I was told you can send direct messages to people in Calcutta.'

'Most places, yes,' he said, leaning back on his chair, 'but it has to be via telegram.'

'Can you please send a message for me to anyone in Calcutta? Or in Madras? To someone who might have a list of the sepoys of the 34th Regiment Bengal Native Infantry during 1857? During the battle of Latu?' Anjaan said all of it in one breath. He was scared that if he paused in between, nervousness might hold him back from remembering all that he needed to tell. Or the man's sympathetic mood might come to an end. He felt relieved when he had finished saying all that he had to.

'Once more like the last time, we will need an address,' the man behind the window replied, leaning forward and bringing his elbows to rest on his desk, 'Do you have any?'

Anjaan shook his head. 'Huzur, but could you maybe send to anyone whom you might be knowing? At Calcutta? At the post office there? Or maybe to someone at the army office there? Any office?'

Exasperation was once again beginning to show on the man's face. His eyebrows were closing in. 'What message do you exactly wish to send? Whom do you wish to send it to?' he asked.

'I do not wish to send any message, huzur, nor do I wish to send it to anyone in particular.'

The man flayed his arms and clicked his tongue.

'I wished only to get some information,' Anjaan said, the feeble confidence that he was attempting to garner slowly slithered down his spine. 'And it is for that same information that I wished to send word to Subedar Purshottam Bandopadhyay.'

'With such vagueness, no, miya, it just can't be possible,' the man said, once again leaning back on the chair. He and Anjaan kept looking at each other for a while.

Anjaan Hazratkandi's heart sank and the corners of his mouth drooped. A man came up behind him and stood at the queue. 'Now give way please, miya, don't hold the line,' the man behind the window said with a wave of his hand. Anjaan moved aside and looked around. With slow steps and still looking around, as if he was searching for something, something that he didn't know if he would ever find, he came out of the post office and sat on the steps for a while. He had been standing for long inside the hall in queues and now his knees were aching. And his shins were pulling. The thought of walking the distance back home further drained his energy. It wasn't, however, the falling energy in his legs that fatigued him. It was the falling hope in his heart.

* * *

Some months later, Anjaan reached home from the graveyard at Malegarh, to see maulvi Jalaluddin, from Katigorah, waiting to meet him under the gulmohar. He had brought a nikaah proposal, of his daughter Firdaus Begum, for Baadal.

'I would be only too happy, Jalaluddin,' Anjaan had said then, 'but I cannot commit without asking Baadal and Laila. Let's see what Baadal says.'

Jalaluddin nodded, running one hand through his beard,' I understand, Anjaan, I shall wait.'

Though Anjaan almost knew what Baadal would say when asked about Jalaluddin's daughter Firdaus

Begum. He would say, 'If you and abba are alright with it, ammajaan, I am alright with it.'

And that was exactly how Baadal consented to the proposal.

Baadal, though, wanted some time. He planned to pull down all the thatch and put up a new roof of corrugated iron sheets, for both the shop and their dwelling house. Only after all that was done would he be ready to bring in his bride. Meanwhile, Anjaan and Laila set about making preparations for the nikaah. Anjaan accompanied Laila to the Sutarkandi bazar to buy clothes and jewellery for the bride.

'During our nikaah when I came to buy a saree for you, Lailajaan,' Anjaan remembered fondly, 'I was at a loss. I didn't know how to pick one. Even when I had picked one, I wasn't sure if you'd like it. I was scared you'd mock my choice.' The wrinkles and the grey hair nonetheless, Anjaan felt his blood rushing to his face at the confession. He could hear Laila giggle through her hijab.

'I wanted to buy you a pair of sandals too, but I didn't know what size would fit you.'

'You did? Then maybe you can buy me a pair today? Now?' she smiled.

So, it was a saree, bangles, earrings and a jhumar tikka for the bride and a pair of sandals for Laila that they had purchased. Anjaan then looked this way and that, as if trying to find something

'You're looking for anything?' Laila asked, 'is there anything left to buy?'

'Yes,' he nodded, awkwardly smiling like a child who had come to the bazar with his mother and not like an aged man with his wife.

'What is it?' Laila asked.

'Roasted grams!'

By the time the new roof was up, relatives and friends had been invited for the wedding. People passing that way had to shield their eyes those days from the blinding sunlight that reflected upon the new roof of Ijaaz Miya's shop and Anjaan Hazratkandi's house. Though Ijaaz Miya was no more, the shop continued to be called as Ijaaz Miya's and Anjaan wanted it to remain so. With its new sheet iron roof, freshly mud-plastered walls, and pruned periwinkles by the bamboo door of the shop, the house was now all set to receive its bride.

It was in Mannan's carriage that Baadal set out to maulvi Jalaluddin's house in Katigorah, to wed his fourth daughter, Firdaus Begum. It would also be in this carriage that he would bring her to his own home. The embroidery around the neck of the bright blue sherwani he wore emphasized his strong, square shoulders. Anjaan stole a sideglance at his son. He was indeed a fetching youth, he thought. He gently laid a hand on Baadal's. It felt strong and taut under his own coarse and shrivelling one. Maybe, Anjaan thought, he did not feel as much about being without an identity as he himself did. For he had a home to return to, and people to love and be loved. No one had repeatedly and forcefully told him that he belonged nowhere, that he had no roots, and that the village of Hazratkandi wasn't to be called his home. His soul probably did not bleed with stab after stab of being asked a name and of fending for himself. Anjaan raised his gaze to his head. He was wearing a taqiyah with a thin, light blue lace around the edge, to match the blue of the sherwani. He looked special indeed, like a groom ought to. Or maybe, Anjaan wondered as he brought his own hand away, Baadal did, after all, feel the agonies of being called by the name of a village they didn't know they belonged to or not. If he did, he disguised it well.

'Baadal bhai!' Mannan called cheerfully while they were on their way, 'today at least I am not going to charge you for this ride. This is my wedding gift to you!' And he let the whip set the horses moving. 'Go, go, boys! Nothing more important and no greater responsibility ever had been entrusted upon us three. Go boys! To Baadal bhai's bride's house! Go! Go! Go! Bhabhijaan must not be kept waiting!' He chuckled, 'Go Boys!' His zesty words made even Baadal's pulse beat faster. Mannan had a habit of talking to his horses. For him, they were more of brothers than horses. That day he was not in his usual yellowing white pajama and kurta that smelt of horse. He was dressed in a new, shining green kurta with a set of chained buttons down the opening on the chest. Baadal's friends, uncles and cousins followed the carriage, most on foot, some riding bicycles. They played drums and sang songs as they walked and danced along the way. Jalaluddin's house was one of the first houses upon entering Katigorah, from Hazratkandi. That day it was decorated with strings of festoons made of coloured paper, hung along the foot track leading from the road to their yard. The moment Baadal stepped into the yard, women suddenly emerged from all corners like bubbles on the surface of boiling water. Baadal heard giggles and whispers emitting from within the veils, and a few ran back in, to tell Firdous how her groom looked, and what he was wearing. Those who went with the groom were made to sit in the yard on cane mats spread out on the ground. Baadal could sense the excitement in the household. Little girls dressed in bright, colourful salwar kameez ran around the yard, their kohl lined eyes yet to go behind the hijab. While they sat, the aroma of halwa and gosht wafted from somewhere at the back of the house. And when Baadal pronounced 'Qabool! Qabool! Qabool!' giving his consent to the nikaah, to wed Firdaus Begum, he did so with his abba beside him. Anjaan felt both happy and sad. Happy, because his son did not have to think who would be by him as he got married. Sad, because the nikaah would bring on a grandchild, if Allah willed, and from the moment of its birth, that child would be another Hazratkandi without an identity. Guilt tugged at his dead conscience like ants did a dead grasshopper. For he could have put an end to the misery of living a nameless life for his descendents, had he not sat for nikaah with Laila. But passions of youth and yearnings of a lovelorn life blinded foresight, at a time when he could have stopped the Hazratkandi lineage. When he had longed for company himself, it was only fair that Baadal too be given the choice. And now that Baadal was getting married to Firdaus, Anjaan's hopeless heart wished for a grandchild. He knew it all and yet he didn't seem to understand any of it.

Later that day, Laila, her aunts, Mehroon bibi and a whole lot of womenfolk and children waited under the gulmohar to receive Baadal and his bride. When she arrived, they walked with her into the lone room at the end of the passage. Little children ran around her, and older women gave each other random bits of first night advice, intending the new bride to hear them. They giggled among themselves and pushed and nudged one another as they laughed, sharing wedding anecdotes from their own lives. Firdaus took small steps, so it took her a long while to walk that short distance from the yard in front of the shop to Baadal's room, allowing the little procession all the time they needed to make merry and even sing a few songs. As Laila held Firdaus's hand and led her into the room, she remembered the day she stepped in there as Anjaan's bride. How time flew! The cot in the room was no more the one Anjaan bought. It was a new one, a bigger one. Once more there were two pillows on the cot and the curtain this time was a blue one with white egrets on it. Laila had hung a mirror too, on the bamboo wall beside the cot, next to the window. It had a wooden frame around it. This was to be Firdaus and Baadal Hazratkandi's new home.

From early the next day, people started coming over to see Baadal's bride. For this wedding, there were more people than there were during Anjaan and Laila's. Fatima and Tahira came with their children, children-in-law, and grandchildren too. Laila cooked for her son's nikaah what her mother was no more there to cook during her wedding, a curry of shutki. She had cleaned and sun-dried the fish at home herself and cooked it the way she saw her ammajaan do it. Anjaan had walked to the Sutarkandi bazar a week ahead of the nikaah. There, he looked through a number of lambs before picking a plump one, and brought it home for the feast. He could well afford it now. Laila's aunts were old, but they were very much there, lending full gaiety to the wedding. They could no longer cook vermicelli with jaggery and dates but they ate to their full from the one that Liazul cooked. He had brought with him two others from Rashipur to cook for the wedding. And this time, it was Anjaan who spread upon Ijaaz Miya's bench a new sheet with bright yellow sunflowers on it. That day it was Baadal who sat there, like Anjaan did so many years ago. Firdaus, like Laila, sat in an inner room, surrounded by young girls and womenfolk. When Anjaan stood and watched the newly-wed couple from a distance, he thought he saw Ijaaz Miya too, sitting next to them. He seemed to be smiling at Anjaan.

Anjaan missed him like perhaps he would his own father.

Laila made it easy for Firdaus to settle down in her new home, in her new family. Just as Baadal was fast and good at learning things from Anjaan, so was Firdaus, at learning from Laila. The first thing Laila taught her was to brew salted black tea, just right. Not strong, not weak. After many years, since her amma left her, Laila once more found a confidante at home in Firdaus.

When four summers had gone by and Laila still hadn't called in Mehroon bibi for Firdaus, people around Hazratkandi and Katigorah began to whisper and gossip once more about the ill omen that the bastard had brought upon Ijaaz Miya and his family.

'Mind, Firdaus,' she was told by a friend at the market once, 'you will find yourself sharing your man and his cot with another woman, if you can't beget a child, a son rather, soon enough.'

A visibly unnerved Firdaus asked Laila the next day, as the two were washing by the river, 'Might I be barren, ammajaan?'

'And who mouthed such impudent filth?' Laila shot back, thrashing the clothes harder on the tree trunk that had lodged itself in the riverbank for many years now. Laila too got to hear such comments, though they were made behind her back. Some even thought that, in these many summers, a child might as well have been conceived, which never survived. As indeed it had happened years ago in that same house. Laila's first. But Laila had faith in her God and in her love for the girl who came to be by her Baadal.

'Have patience, child,' said Laila, as she removed her blouse and draped her cotton saree over her breasts, stepping into the water now to bathe herself, 'without fail you will beget my Baadal a son. It just might be in their veins to impregnate late.'

Firdaus covered her mouth with a palm and giggled. She too stepped into the river, saree and all.

'If it is a girl, ammajaan, I want her to have dimples like you,' she said, splashing water over her bare arms.

'And if it is a boy?'

'I want him to tend to the graves.'

True to Laila's words, a few years from that day, Firdaus was with child. As she grew heavier, squatting in front of the fire in the kitchen and cooking would make her feet swell. So, Laila took it upon herself to do the cooking. But Firdaus would still hover near her, running small errands and keeping her mother-in-law company, chatting constantly.

'Baadal often tells me about the graves, ammajaan.'

'That is the purpose of their existence.'

'He feels sad for abbajaan. Very sad. But he doesn't want anyone to see it.'

Laila sprinkled some salt into the curry.

'Yes ammajaan, he had asked his old school teachers too if they knew anything about the martyrs in those graves.' She paused and said, 'I asked my abba too, because there are so many people who keep coming to meet him, just in case anyone among them might know anything.'

Laila looked up at Firdaus. Her heart went out for the young woman, carrying her progeny in her womb.

'But no one seems to know more than what Baadal already knows,' she said, looking out of the window towards the river.

'Do you regret, Firdaus, that you are about to mother another nameless, identityless Hazratkandi?'

'All names began somewhere, with one man, ammajaan, and then the name came down through generations to become a family name. So has ours begun with abbajaan and you. Through generations, we too will grow to be a family name. Isn't it something to be proud of, rather? To begin a lineage?' Laila had never thought of it this way. Firdaus sat down near Laila and slowly leaned her head on Laila's back. The appetising aroma of a simple curry of bottle gourd filled the kitchen.

Sometimes when Firdaus's feet got too swollen, Laila would take them one at a time on her lap and gently massage them. During those moments, she told Firdaus stories from their childhood, about the pains Anjaan suffered and about the mark on his left forearm.

'Even Baadal didn't know about this, ammajaan?'

'No. He hasn't asked, we didn't mention. It would hurt him more.'

Soon Laila sent word to Mehroon bibi to remain prepared for she would be needed any day soon. And when the time came, Anjaan once more went across the road through the betelnut plantation to fetch Mehroon bibi. It was a winter afternoon and the sun warmed Anjaan's face. He suddenly realized that he was enjoying that warmth. He wondered whether he too had arrived at that age at which Ijaaz Miya used to enjoy nothing more than sitting out in the sun and warming his creaking bones and aching muscles. Maybe when grandfather-hood came upon him, he would be able to indulge in such leisure. But for now, he quickened his steps. Laila had asked Anjaan to get her a packet of razor blades a few days earlier. Now, as Anjaan set out to fetch Mehroon bibi, she dipped one of those into boiling water, keeping it ready to cut the umbilical cord. Baadal stood in the passage like his nana had done a long time ago. Only, he wasn't pacing along it. He was waiting, just in case his amma needed help outside the room. Anjaan arrived soon after, and Mehroon bibi went straightaway into Firdaus's room. It was only a while that she was gone, but those few moments sent unbearable anxiety through the men waiting outside.

Laila's face soon appeared through the door, holding it only half open, and she announced excitedly, 'A son, Baadal! A son! Firdaus's doing well!' Then she looked at Anjaan and said, 'See? Didn't I tell you? That she'll beget my Baadal a son?' and she hurried back into the room, tears of joy glistening in her eyes.

And so it was that a son was born to Firdaus and Baadal Hazratkandi in the winter of the year 1932. Baadal would love him to be like the wide-open skies, always free. And yet, at the time his son was born, even the skies were about to be divided and partitioned with unseen lines and boundaries. But, right now, when Anjaan looked up at the sky to offer his gratitude, the sky was still one. Undivided. Free, wide, and unbroken. He would like his grandchild to be like that sky. Like that Asman.

And so, on the day of the aqiqah, a lamb was slaughtered for the feast and Firdaus and Baadal's son was named Asman. Asman Hazratkandi. The third in the lineage of the Hazratkandis. When Laila brought the child and placed it in Anjaan's lap for the first time on the day of the aqiqah, Anjaan wept. 'Rahem, Allah! Rahem, Asman!' he said to himself, and let the tears trickle down.

Those were tears both of joy and of regret – for he sought the forgiveness of the innocent child looking up at him, as if to ask his grandfather, 'Who am I?'

13
The Year Nineteen Forty-Three

*A*njaan Hazratkandi looked forward to the times when Laila spread a mat out in the sun and had by her a large aluminium tub of warm water. She also had by her a small bowl of mustard oil heated with a few pods of garlic and a sprinkle of fenugreek seeds in it. She set the oil aside till just the right amount of warmth was left in it. Then she sat on the mat, spread out her legs in front of her and asked Firdaus to put baby Asman on her knees. She then undressed the child and dipping her fingers into the warm oil and with gentle strokes, massaged the baby and stretched its limbs. And the child looked up at the sky lying on her knees, fascinated by the birds that flew across it. He blinked and gurgled, kicked his feet against Laila's stomach and put his tiny fist into his mouth, sucking on it. As Laila massaged the baby, she incessantly kept talking to it. 'This,' she said, stretching the legs, 'will make your limbs strong. And this,' she said, rubbing the oil in circular motions on his chest, 'will keep the heart healthy and clear when the moist wind from the sea in the south and the river blows into it.' Anjaan sat beside Laila and the child, never taking his eyes off him even for a fleeting moment.

'He's looking at the sky, Lailajaan,' Anjaan would say, 'do you think he hears you?'

'Ofcourse he does,' Laila would reply, 'he gurgles in response, can't you see?' She would then look at the baby and say, 'That the sky holds you enthralled, Asman, is because you are its namesake. Grow up to be ceaseless like it, embracing both birds of free flight and clouds of cyclone. Be like that sky, my Asman!' Anjaan hoped with all his heart that Asman became all that Laila wished him to be. For deep within him, he knew it would be all the more painful, when he would grow up to realize that no people and no place embraced him.

After the massage Laila put the child in the tub of warm water and gave him a bath. When the bathing was done, she quickly wrapped him in a soft towel and hurried inside the house. 'The winter winds like to catch a clean, fresh, baby,' she would say over her shoulders to Anjaan. These few moments of the morning made Anjaan's day.

As the child grew, Firdaus was fraught with sleepless nights. For she could not suckle the child to its full and hunger made the baby wail unsettlingly into the cold stillness of the night. Her nipples became sore and red, she herself remained drained and wasted. It was then that bracing the cold and the mist, Laila would go out at dawn looking for stems of the taro by the fallow land, all along the river, and farther. This she cooked with lavish measures of black pepper, dropping in a few small dried fish, if there were any in the house.

'Eat, Firdaus,' she offered the hot curry with steaming rice, 'the taro will fill in the milk and the pepper will heal the womb. Eat, child,' she would say, while she tried to calm the baby.

When Asman was old enough to go out with his grandfather, Anjaan picked the choicest seat from among the small ones meant for children in their shop and fixed it on the horizontal bar between his own seat and the handles of the cycle. Like he did many years ago for Baadal to sit on. Anjaan then took Asman riding through the fields and along the Dooni, past the mosque and around the Hazratkandi Primary School where Baadal used to go.

'You too must come here, Asman, and learn to read and write more than just your name!' Anjaan told the child.

'Now, dadajaan?' the child asked.

'Not now, but when you are old enough,' Anjaan said.

'How old is old enough?' he asked.

Anjaan laughed heartily. 'Maybe five years? Maybe six?'

It didn't matter to Asman, though, how old he had to grow to be old enough. Because for now, he felt safe and assured sitting astride his dadajaan's cycle with the warmth of his grandfather's bosom on his back and the support of his aged arms by his sides. Anjaan, however, realized he could no longer pedal as fast as he could during the times when he used to ride with Baadal. Sometimes he got off the bicycle and pushed it alongside. Even then Asman felt the breeze blow across the fields and caress his face, making his eyes squint. And because Anjaan could no longer take Asman riding as much as he took Baadal, he brought an old car tyre from Subhroto Pal's shop at Latu bazar and hung it on a long thick coir rope from one of the sturdy lower branches of the gulmohar. Laila folded an old saree and placed it as a cushion on the tyre. While Baadal worked at the shop, Anjaan sat little Asman on the saree cushion in the tyre's groove and pushed the tyre ever so gently to make it swing. How Asman loved those moments! When the tyre swung high, he bent his head backwards and looked up at the sky, ecstatic and radiant with the blood rushing to his joyful little face.

'Wheee! Look, dadajaan, look!' he squealed with delight, 'look at the sky! It doesn't end! It's wide and free and spilling all around me! Look!'

'Yes, Asman, isn't it really!' Anjaan laughed, giving the tyre another little push, 'your dadijaan wants you to be like it.' The child laughed in glee, his hair coming over his face as the tyre came low and went high again.

Asman soon started going to the mosque with his abbajaan and dadajaan for jumuah. He also began his Qoran lessons there just the way his abba, and before him, his dada had done. Then, the year Asman turned five, Baadal took him along so he could be enrolled at the Hazratkandi Primary School. The school registration recorded his details as,

Name: Asman Hazratkandi
Age: Five years.
Village: Hazratkandi, Sylhet Province, East Bengal
India.
Year: 1937

Asman loved going to school and made many new friends. He could now climb onto the tyre-swing all by himself. Sometimes he would also scamper about the shop. He was growing tall too, tall for his age, like his abba and his dada. While swinging on the tyre one day, he asked his dadajaan, who was sitting on the bench watching him, 'My friend Imdad has many cousins, dadajaan, and all their names have Siddiqui after them.' He went on swinging but seemed to be trying to recollect something.

'That's their surname,' Anjaan replied.

'And Jagdish Basak was saying,' Asman said, at last remembering, 'that they have almost an entire village of uncles, cousins, and relatives, all Basaks. They were asking me about my cousins, dadajaan,' he remained quiet for sometime before saying, 'do I not have any cousins? Cousins who have Hazratkandi for a surname?'

Baadal looked up from his work towards Asman. 'Now run along inside and ask amma to make tea for us all. Ask her to give you some extra jaggery. Go run along now.' Baadal hoped to divert the child and spare his grandfather the anguish. Asman jumped off the tyre, ran in and did what he was asked to. But he quickly came back, and this time sat on the bench next to his dadajaan. Then he looked at his grandfather, turning his head sideways and tilting it up just a little, exactly the way Baadal used to when he needed to ask something important.

'Dadajaan,' he said, tapping Anjaan on the arm, 'when Qarim master was telling us today about zamindars and their zamindari, Sudipto Kar said his great grand uncle was a zamindar. They used to live in a large house in Matiapool. He has other uncles too, staying all over. Two of them are in Calcutta. Where are our ancestors, dadajaan?'

Anjaan realized that the time had come for him to tell Asman about his great grandfather. To tell him, that his grandfather was braver than all the zamindars, and his name was more revered than all other ancestors. But then Asman would ask what his great grandfather's name was. And Anjaan would have nothing to tell him. So as the child talked, Anjaan sat quietly and listened to him.

'But Asman,' Baadal spoke from the shop, 'your dadajaan, you, me, your dadijaan, your ammajaan, aren't we all so many Hazratkandis?' he tried to sound cheerful.

'Oh, abbajaan!' Asman said, slapping his forehead with his palm, 'but these are the only Hazratkandis there are. That too, all in just one house. We have no other Hazratkandi anywhere else, like my other friends have their relatives with the same name all over. They go to visit them too, and their aunts and uncles also come to stay with them, along with the cousins. Why don't we go visiting?' He thought for a while and said, 'and Sudipto, like Jagdish, doesn't go to the mosque. They go somewhere else they call Durgabari. Sometimes they come with a smearing of some red powder on their foreheads.'

Firdaus brought out the tea and Asman hopped off the bench for his share of the jaggery. Sipping his tea, Anjaan said, 'Asman, child, one of these days I shall take you to meet my father.'

'Aha! He's here?' Asman asked, his eyes lighting up with the late afternoon sun glinting in them.

'He's no more, Asman, he died a brave death.'

'Oh!' was all the child said, and fell silent.

When Asman passed the last exam in the primary school, he started going to the Hazratkandi High School, just a few steps away from his earlier school. He was now old enough to sit astride the bicycle's carrier, so his dadajaan once again removed the small seat in front. However, it was mostly with his father that he rode thus. Because his grandfather could no longer pedal across the fields and along the Dooni with the same ease that he used to a few years earlier. Nor did he have a firm grip on the handles. His hands shook and his fingers felt limp. But Anjaan and Asman still went out together. Only, instead of cycling, they walked. It was during those walks that Asman heard stories from his dadajaan about the 9 Periphery Supply Camp and of Balraj Sandhu, Sujit, Mahib and Dinbandhu. It was also then that Anjaan told Asman about Superintendent Edward Fidley and Manik Roy of the Central Supply Depot at Narikuli. Earlier when Anjaan used to bring a young Baadal for rides along the Dooni, they used to sit on its sloping banks because little Baadal wanted to pat the calves and count the cows. But now as he brought his grandson for walks, they sat on the banks because Anjaan got exhausted. His breath became short and rapid. So, while they sat, Anjaan told Asman of the battle of Latu.

'Ramnath master once mentioned, dadajaan, this battle of Latu,' Asman said, 'he told us what had happened.'

'Did he also tell you who the brave sepoys were, who fought the British led by Major Byng?' Anjaan asked.

Asman shook his head. He picked up a pebble and flung it into the waters of the Dooni, making the pebble leap like a frog in the waters. It made Anjaan smile. A vision of himself doing that so many years ago flashed through his memory. That made him feel confident that he wasn't getting senile like Bholanath Sarkar in the village of Malegarh. And he had to have full control of his mind, because he had answers to look for.

'No, dadajaan, Ramnath Master didn't tell us who the sepoys were.'

'That's because Ramnath does not know, Asman, that your great grandfather, my father, was one of them.'

Asman jumped up with excitement. 'He was, dadajaan? He fought the British?' Then he abruptly sat in front of Anjaan and punching his right fist into his left palm, said, 'Now this I am going to tell Jagdish, Sudipto and Imdad. They are going to swoon when they get to know that I belong to the Hazratkandi lineage, of the Hazratkandi who had fought and resisted the British at the battle of Latu. Bang! Bang! Bang!' Asman said animatedly, shooting an imaginary rifle into the air. 'What was his name, dadajaan?'

'Aryaan.'

'Yes! I am going to tell everyone in school about sepoy Aryaan Hazratkandi!' he said, elated on finding out what he just did.

'No, Asman, you don't,' his grandfather said.

'But why?' Asman asked, surprised.

'Because Aryaan wasn't a Hazratkandi. I don't know what he was, I don't know what his family name was, or where he belonged to. Or if his name was even Aryaan. For that matter, Asman, I don't know where I belong to. Do you not see, our name is the same as that of our village?' The boy calmed down, sat beside his grandfather, and nodded.

'Why, dadajaan?'

'Just because I was born here and that was all I had for a name,' Anjaan replied. Sooner or later, Asman had to know. And strangely, Anjaan felt a wave of relief settle on him after it was said and done with.

Asman looked into his dadajaan's eyes. They were clouded. Just like his identity. He couldn't make out if those eyes were clouded because of the eighty years of life they had seen, or because of the cloud that hung over his identity. Even through his own tender years, he sensed the suffering in his dadajaan's heart.

'I have been searching for that name, Asman, my child, I have gone to Dhaka too, looking for people who I thought would be able to tell me something about that soldier, that martyr, so that I may know something about me. And about you and about your abba.'

'Doesn't anyone know?' Asman asked.

'Someone somewhere surely does, but I have not yet been destined to come across that person. I'm still searching, Asman. I'm still looking for answers to so many questions about my being, your being, our being. Being a Hazratkandi.' He paused and took a deep breath. It seemed like a resigned sigh to Asman. 'If I die without finding my answers, the Hazratkandis will forever remain without an identity,' his dadajaan said, staring away into the far horizon across the fields.

Asman slowly leaned against his grandfather and let his head rest on his arm.

'Dadajaan, if that happens, I'll continue the search for you.'

Anjaan smiled and let his own head lean towards Asman's. He gently slid his arm away from under Asman's head and wrapped it around his grandson. Both Anjaan and Asman sat holding on to each other quietly for a long while on the banks of the Dooni, listening to the ripple of the waters and the flapping of wings in it as wild ducks frolicked, splashing water towards them too. A trickle of tears ran down Anjaan's clouded eyes and disappeared into his white beard. While his eyes were only clouded, his soul was a frenzied, gyrating tornado.

'So shall we go to visit the Malegarh hillock soon, dadajaan?' Asman asked.

Anjaan nodded. 'But for now, let's go home.'

Asman helped his dadajaan get up and held him by the arm as they walked back home along the Dooni. Even in that small, eleven-year-old hand, Anjaan found so much strength and confidence. While his own were trembling. He looked down at his grandchild. When he was his age, he had already been forced to be on his own.

Anjaan and Asman were yet to visit Malegarh when famine struck all of Sylhet and the whole of East Bengal in the year 1943. It was one of the most dismal and calamitous famines that Anjaan had lived through. Cattle and humans alike were dying every day while disease and illness brought by starvation and malnutrition spread like the rise of the sea waters during high tide. Rats, snakes and foxes, anything that escaped death, were hunted down by the famished people and eaten rapaciously, before someone else snatched it away from them. Thieves were always on the prowl, thieves not of silver and money but of grain and livestock. And when the wind blew in from the river in the back of their house, it brought with it the foul smell of rotting corpse. When people walked in the dark, they stumbled upon skeletons covered only partly with maggot-infested, decayed flesh. Most times these were of cattle, but sometimes these were of human too. Once when Asman saw large birds hovering in the skies towards the north, he had said, 'Dadajaan! Look! They are almost like airplanes!'

The boy was thrilled but was scared too. He ran behind his dadajaan, still looking up at the sky.

'Those are vultures, Asman,' his grandfather said, looking up. How sinister they could make even a brilliantly azure sky appear! 'There must be corpse somewhere below there.'

'How do you know, dadajaan?'

'Because vultures feed on the dead.'

'Dead cattle?'

'In these times, who knows, Asman, it might be dead cattle or dead humans.'

In the early days of the famine, there were fewer people coming to Ijaaz Miya's shop but, as the famine got worse, they completely stopped. They had neither urgency nor resources to repair mundane things like bicycles and carriages when their stomachs were gnawing at their insides and people were killing eighbours even for a fistful of grain. Many even gave away their umbrellas and cycles in exchange of whatever food they could get hold of. Laila fell ill during the time of that devastating famine, but hakim Sirajullah could no longer make his herbal pellets and pastes and bring them over to Laila. He was himself ill and dying. Firdaus dug out whatever arum and tapioca there was in the fields behind their house by the river and boiled these in small quantities to make a meal. The luxury of jaggery and black salted tea had long been forsaken.

Each morning Firdaus took the trowel and wandered off along the river at the back of the house in search of edible roots and arum. The soles of her feet had begun to crack and chafe, and her nails had started to grow dark and brittle. The skin around her fingertips began to harden. When she tried to peel them off with her teeth, they bled. One morning as she was digging out some tapioca by the river, she saw another woman, haggard and hungry, clawing among the weeds and growths for scrap to eat. When she saw Firdaus and the few tapioca near her, the woman suddenly darted forward, picked up the tapioca and fled.

'You swine! You thief!' Firdaus shouted and cried as she gave chase.

The woman turned to look once and continued to run, laughing hysterically. 'Give those back, you bitch, those are mine! For my abbajan! And my ammajaan!' Tears rolled down Firdaus's face while her own stomach wobbled with the water with which she filled it, to quieten the pangs of hunger. Her heart raced. And for that one fleeting moment, hunger and rage called the devil into her mind. She picked up such speed as is fuelled only by desperation and ran across the scraggly field and hurled the trowel at the woman who was by now slowing down. Firdaus's hijab fell from her head, but she could not be bothered to stop and pick it. Her ammajaan and abbajaan meant more to her than her hijaab. She trampled over it as she ran.

The trowel found its mark. It hit the woman on the head, and she screamed and fell to the ground. But as quickly, she got up and staggered away, leaving the tapioca scattered on the ground. Now it was Firdaus who laughed hysterically. That's what the famine and hunger did to people.

She hurried to the spot, picked up the trowel and the tapioca and walked back home with steps that were unsteady from weakness, hunger and the running, not bothering to wash off the woman's blood on the edges of the trowel. For she had first to hide the tapioca for her ammajaan and her abbajaan.

In the afternoon, she boiled a little of whatever rice there was in the house for Laila to keep her going. They could afford only one paltry meal now. When Laila came to know of it, she stopped eating, saying she had cramps in the stomach if she ate and that she had no appetite. Instead, she made Firdaus keep the rice for Asman. For two nights she feigned nausea to make Firdaus give the rice to Asman. On the third night, while she lay in bed, Anjaan cajoled her into taking a small morsel out of his hand. She swallowed it with great pain but immediately threw up all of it. Anjaan thought she needed water. When he put a little into her mouth, it trickled out of the corner of her lips. She had thrown up her last breath with that last morsel of food, though her eyes remained staring at Anjaan. Laila did not survive the famine. With people dying and ill in every household, there was no one who could come to make a bier and carry her on it for her cremation. So Firdaus pulled out the bamboo mat from under the mattress of Laila's bed and spread an old saree on it. Firdaus's heart broke to send Laila away thus. She cried disconsolately. Laila had been more than her own mother and all those moments the two shared by the river, by the fallow field, while drying fish, over chores in the kitchen, and while raising Asman, all those moments whirled through her mind now, making her head feel dizzy. It was Laila who made her see why Baadal and Asman must continue to search for their identity. Firdaus had said she would do her bit. That time had come. And now to send this very woman off like a bundle of rags lacerated Firdaus's soul. Anjaan and Baadal then gently placed Laila on the mat, rolled it up and tied it around with thick ropes of coir. And Laila left the only home she knew, the home that was both her father's and her husband's, bundled like the garments she rolled up for Anjaan to carry to Dhaka. And yet, all of them together could not tie her up as finely as she did Anjaan's bundle. Asman carried a hoe while Anjaan and Baadal bore her during that last journey, not too far from home. They carried her to the fallow land at the back of their house, close to where Firdaus had dug for arum roots and tapioca a few days ago. Baadal dug the ground with the hoe and all three of them gently lowered Laila into it and covered her with soil. First in fistfuls with their bare hands, then on with the hoe. Anjaan did not cry, not then.

'La ilahaillallah Muhammadur Rasulullah,' was all that he said softly under his breath. His Lailajaan was gone. The famine had dried out even his tears.

But later, alone at night in his bed, he sobbed himself to sleep late towards the wee hours of the next day. His last link to a past he had treasured had fallen.

14
The Year Nineteen Forty-Seven

It took Sylhet a couple of years to come out of the grip of that calamitous famine of 1943. And it took a few years more for Ijaaz Miya's shop to recover from the slump. While Sylhet and Ijaaz Miya's shop were limping back to normalcy, the English were slowly starting to pull away from their camps and bases in India. India had resisted the British, fought for freedom, and won it. Parts of the country rejoiced while parts of it were left torn and asunder, its people displaced. Once again, Anjaan didn't know where he belonged. Among those who rejoiced at being liberated from the British or among those who were left displaced and torn, in spirit and nation. For along with freedom of India came the partition of Bengal. East Bengal was made to become a part of the newly formed nation of Pakistan. Anjaan's small village of Hazratkandi remained where it was, by the Dooni, and yet, it remained no more in India. With partition, the village of Hazratkandi was made part of Pakistan. It came to be known as East Pakistan.

Anjaan couldn't sleep during much of that sultry night. He stretched out his hand, but the bed was empty beside him. Laila was long gone. He tossed over and thought how similar his existence was both in his new nation of Pakistan and in Ijaaz Miya's house, which he now called home. Both were borrowed dwellings, both separated by land corridors that weren't part of the main abode. At home, there was the passage between where he now stayed and where he first came to stay, at the lone room behind the shop. And in his new nation of Pakistan, there was this entire stretch of India in between East Pakistan, where he lived, and West Pakistan. He sat up in bed thinking, what if Subedar Purshottam Bandopadhyay sent him any news. His address had changed. From India to East Pakistan. Though he remained right there at his two landmarks of the gulmohar tree and Ijaaz Miya's cycle shop. Even if any news came, he feared the post man might send it back to that part of Bengal which was still India. If that happened, answers to his many questions would once again be lost.

He didn't realize how long he sat in bed, awake and thinking, his thoughts moving across nations and people while he himself sat alone and belonging nowhere yet again, in the darkness of a borrowed room of a doled-out home. He heard birds chirping outside and a rooster crow somewhere far. Day must have dawned, he thought. The same birds, the same dawn, in the same village of Hazratkandi under the same skies, the same soil, between the same latitudes and longitudes. And yet, all of these didn't belong to India any longer. Just because someone somewhere decreed that Hazratkandi be shoved into Pakistan. Strange, he thought, that whims of a few had been generally accepted, while the land over which so much hue and cry was raised, so much blood and tears were shed, and from which so many had been uprooted, that very land never budged a hair's breadth. Anjaan felt drained and worn out, he didn't want to come out of bed. He heard the rumble of army trucks outside. Those days whenever he sat under the gulmohar tree on the bench, he saw them pass by in twos and threes. Never alone. Sometimes there were jeeps too in the convoy. They darted through the bazars of Latu, Hazratkandi and Sutarkandi. The English armies were leaving. Every time those convoys drove past, they left a cloud of dust behind them. Some of the dust would come to settle on the bench. There always seemed to be dust left in Anjaan's life, dust raised never by himself. Then he suddenly remembered that he promised Asman to take him to the Malegarh Martyrs' graveyard. He'd rather do it while he still had strength left in his legs, he thought. He forced himself out of bed.

The ride to Malegarh seemed so different that day. Whoever they met on the way was either talking of independence or of the partition that was a fallout of the independence. Anjaan nodded to passersby he knew but didn't stop to join them in their discussion. What seemed to matter most was that his father lay in Malegarh in India, and he was now in Pakistan. Asman sat astride the carrier and Anjaan rode the cycle but every now and then they stopped by the wayside. Sometimes Anjaan sat on the grass and at other times he just stopped and waited a while to get his breath back. There were stretches of the road when Asman pushed the cycle alongside and his dadajaan just walked beside him. His steps were getting slower.

'You know dadajaan,' Asman said, 'remember I told you about my friend Sudipto Kar?'

'Well, yes, but what of him?' Anjaan asked.

'They are leaving Hazratkandi. He won't come to our school from next year,' Asman said looking straight ahead into the road. He was feeling sad.

'And where will they go to?' Anjaan asked.

'You remember, dadajaan, I told you they had relatives all over and he had uncles in Calcutta too?'

Anjaan nodded.

'They have an uncle in that Bengal which is still with India. They will go away and stay with his family. I'll miss him a lot.'

'But why are they going away?' Anjaan asked.

'I don't know. But it seems Sudipto heard his father say that because they belonged to a faith different from most in Pakistan, they may not be allowed to live in peace in the freedom that has just come,' Asman replied. Heavy words for a boy of his age, Anjaan thought. But then times were such that, at schools, mosques, temples, and bazars, those were the only things that were being talked about. So young and old, such words were on anybody's lips.

'But who are *they*?' his dadajaan asked.

'Those like us who go to mosques.' Asman paused. 'Moslems.'

They were almost reaching Sutarkandi. Far off from the road they could see the cluster of huts. Usually when Anjaan passed those huts around that time of the morning, he saw much activity around the place. There were people in the fields, there were children walking to school and sometimes there would be women folk washing by the stream and cattle grazing too. That day, however, it all seemed very silent, like the entire village had gone into hiding. Nothing seemed to move around the huts except the cattle. Even those were fewer than before. Maybe, Anjaan thought, the villagers there too had moved away like Sudipto Kar's family. A little distance after passing by the Sutarkandi bazar Anjaan noticed a makeshift check gate. It consisted of nothing more than a couple of canvas tents erected on the side of the road. In one there was a collapsible sheet iron table with a few long registers on it, like the ones on Edward Fidley's table at the Central Supply Depot at Narikuli. A few sentries sat around the table while a couple of them stood outside by the road, stopping passersby, and making brief enquiries.

The second tent, a slightly larger one, probably housed the sentries, for Anjaan saw cots and utensils in there. He had never seen these tents at that place, not before independence, not when the whole place was just one nation. India. When they neared the tents, the sentries stopped them.

'Where to, kaka?' one of them asked.

'To Malegarh. Why do you ask? I have been going there for so many decades that I lost count. I was never stopped here, never asked a thing,' Anjaan replied.

'Those times were different, and the nations were one, kaka, you were then riding within the same nation. But now you are crossing over to India from Pakistan. You will have to write your name and address there,' he said, pointing to the register inside the tent. Anjaan's fingers began to tremble even more, his feet felt cold.

'And will I have to do this everytime I come to Malegarh?' he asked, slightly intimidated.

'Yes, from now on,' the sentry replied. He wanted to say that he was only doing his duty. But he didn't say anything. Anjaan Hazratkandi didn't know that India would establish the Indo-East Pakistan border outpost at Sutarkandi only from March of 1948. He didn't need to know. Where he was stopped that day was an interim arrangement to keep a record of the people crossing over and returning. What lay heavy on his old, weakening heart was that independence took him a nation away from his father's grave and from his search. It felt strange.

'Come in this way, fill the register,' the sentry motioned.

Leaving the bicycle just outside the tent, Anjaan and Asman walked towards the table. The sentry sitting there opened the register and handed Anjaan a pen. 'Write your name and address here. As for the time of your crossing over to India, we'll do that.' The pen was too thin for Anjaan's fingers to get a grip on it. Even if they could, he wouldn't be able to write. Asman looked at his dadajaan's eyes. They always remained somewhat foggy now-a-days. He put out his own hand and held his grandfather's, as if to assure him.

'Can I write on his behalf?' Asman asked the sentry.

'What is he to you?' the sentry replied.

'He is my dadajaan. My grandfather,' Asman said, looking at his dadajaan.

The sentry agreed. 'Well then, you may write.' Then he paused and said, 'Then write your own name and address instead and, below that, add that you are accompanied by your grandfather.' The sentry who was sitting now pushed the register towards Asman and he filled it in. Anjaan watched as Asman wrote neatly in Bengali

Name: Asman Hazratkandi
Age: Fifteen years.
Village: Hazratkandi, Sylhet, East Bengal,
Pakistan
Year: 1947

Seeing Asman write thus made Anjaan feel proud.

The sentry looked at the name and said, 'Hazratkandi. Hmm. A mistake there? With your name and the name of your village? They're the same.'

'No mistake,' Anjaan replied, looking straight into the sentry's eyes, hoping to discourage him from asking any further on this. The sentry shifted his gaze to Asman and said, 'When you return, you will have to sign here once more.' Asman nodded.

When they were done, Anjaan motioned him to sit astride the carrier and they rode away. From there it was a slow ride, and a quiet one.

'You never had to do this earlier, dadajaan?' Asman asked.

Anjaan didn't say anything but from behind, Asman saw that he shook his head. When they turned and came upon the narrow foot track, both got off the cycle and while Anjaan pushed the cycle, Asman walked behind it. On reaching the foot of the hillock, as always, Anjaan let the cycle lean against a tree and the two walked up the Malegarh martyrs' graveyard.

'Isn't it quiet up here, dadajaan!' Asman exclaimed. Anjaan remembered how he had asked the same thing to Balraj Sandhu the first time when he had gone to Malegarh with him and Sujit.

'It is, because the dead don't make any noise,' Balraj had said to him that day. He said the same to his grandson now.

'Those are really well kept for graves on a lonely, far-off hillock,' Asman remarked, looking around him.

'Aren't they! That's what I do every time I come up here, child, I tend to those graves so that my father may feel loved and cared for, and may feel he belongs, in case this is foreign land for him,' Anjaan replied.

'And how do you know which grave is your father's?' Asman asked.

'I don't know, Asman, that's why I spruce up all of them.'

Asman went around the graves, sitting next to each one for a while to look at it well enough, trying to see if he could find any clue that nature or fate might throw up at him. The grass felt smooth when he ran a hand over them.

'You must have tended to them for many years now, dadajaan.'

'I did. Otherwise, you would not have been able to come here and walk around.' Anjaan pointed towards the thickets and said, 'I used to have a broom of fine, thin bamboo sticks over there, child, go and see.'

Asman walked up to where his grandfather pointed and brought out the broom and the trowel. He tried to rake in the stray brown leaves around his feet as he checked out the broom.

'The first ones I brought here got worn out and the trowel got rusted and broke. These are later ones.'

'You miss him, dadajaan? Your abba?' Asman asked.

'I never met him, to miss him.' He paused before saying, 'He probably didn't even know about my existence. When the beginning of your life is such, Asman, and when the rest of your life is lived by the name of a village you don't know is yours and yet go on living in it like a refugee because you don't know where else to go and because you are held here for you want to find out where you actually belong and who in reality you are, then it's a wretched life indeed, Asman, it's a wretched life. Existence, yes, but a failed and lost one. A life that no man would want to live. And yet, I am living it. You know, child, each day that passes without any answer or clue, sees a little bit of me dying. I'm dying each day and yet living this life, Asman, I am. Because I have a search to finish.'

Asman came closer and sat next to his dadajaan. His dadajaan seemed to be looking at something beyond the horizon, searching for something. 'My own lifetime is over and wasted, it is for you and your abba that I need to carry on my search for our name. Keep in mind, Asman, the name Hazratkandi has been thrown at us out of disgust. When I was asked my name for the first time outside Hazratkandi, I had said *Anjaan*. I was asked for a surname. I didn't have one. So, I said, *Anjaan, of Hazratkandi*. And I was labelled a Hazratkandi. Hazratkandi isn't our family name. We have no name, no identity. But what kills me with remorse, Asman, child, is that I have passed these on to you. This existence without identity.' The old man's clouded eyes began to well up. The cloud in them was raining. Asman's heart went out for his dadajaan. 'It wasn't my fault, Asman, that I didn't know and still don't know who I am. Or where I belong. But yes, it is my fault that...' now he started to shake with sobs, '... that Baadal and you are living lives like me.'

Asman shifted closer to his dadajaan and put his arms around him.

'I tried my best, Asman, I did. But with my limitations, I am yet to find my answers. And I am still searching.'

Asman quietly promised himself once more to carry on his dadajaan's search. 'Dadajaan,' he said softly, 'if destiny has it then someday, something or someone will surely come up, which will unearth all that you are searching for.'

His grandfather looked resigned. 'I'm not even looking for much, Asman, I'm just searching for a name and a grave. Of which I know only one part. If only that is the real part.'

They both sat quietly for a long while, watching the occasional brown leaf from the bokul tree fall on the ground and listening to the stray crow fly over the graves.

'We have become free from British rule, yes, but it is freedom of a different kind that I am desperately still searching for, Asman, it is the freedom from existence without identity.' India and Pakistan had been liberated, but not Anjaan. He was still shackled to namelessness.

'Shall we go home now, dadajaan?' Asman asked gently, 'amma will be worried.' He stood up and held out a hand for Anjaan to hold and get up. Still holding on to the hand, Anjaan walked around the graves, bending to brush aside, with his free hand, dried twigs and fruit seeds dropped by birds on some graves. He showed Asman which graves had ants nesting in them, and which ones had roots of banyan.

'Don't let the banyan roots dig deep, Asman,' he said, 'or else they will strangulate the one sleeping inside.' He knew every grave like it were his child, Asman thought. Or his father.

'And during the last couple of summers,' Anjaan said pointing towards the bokul tree, 'a pair of emerald doves has been building their nest there. Don't disturb them if they come again next summer. Let there be new life and birth even among the dead, Asman, they bring me hope.'

As they began to walk down the hillock, Anjaan turned back once more to look at the graves.

'I wish I knew which one,' he said, before walking down to his cycle.

On their ride back home, they had to stop at the Indo-East Pakistan Interim Check Gate at Sutarkandi. This time there were a couple of other people too, signing before them. They had come to villages across Sutarkandi to visit relatives and were now returning.

Asman wrote his name and the sentry put in the time of their return and let them go. This was the beginning of many more times that Asman would write his name there. It would soon become the Sutarkandi Indo-East Pakistan Border Outpost.

On the way, Anjaan asked, 'What were the names the men before us wrote?'

Asman tried to recollect and said, 'One was Mafijul Alam Haque and the other, mm, well, some Bhowmik.'

Anjaan closed his eyes and ran a palm across them. Asman knew what thoughts might have passed through his mind.

Asman would pass across the Sutarkandi border many more times. Because this visit to Malegarh was the first of many for him. It was also the last of many for Anjaan Hazratkandi.

15
The Year Nineteen Fifty

Anjaan Hazratkandi's limbs began to tremble more and more with each passing year, and he soon took to bed. He became more reticent too. During those times, Asman went to Malegarh with his abba and every time he went there, he came back home and sat by his dadajaan to tell him what he and his abba did at the Malegarh graveyard that day. How they raked in the dried leaves of the bokul tree and burned them in a pile, pulled out the grass thorns, and cleaned some graves of goat droppings. Anjaan listened intently, never interrupting. His friends still dropped by at the shop to sit and share stories from all over, but they were fewer now. Kanu Saha and his family had moved away to West Bengal. Hakim Sirajullah was no more, he didn't live to see the British retreat. Had he been there, he might have had some pastes and pills for Anjaan's wasting limbs. Mannan and Liazul kept coming, and since they were closer to Baadal in age, they would sit for hours and talk of all that was happening around them. Anjaan, however, no more seemed to be willing to know or hear of anything other than that which concerned the graves at Malegarh.

That summer, Firdaus saw saplings of the gulmohar sprouting on the ground underneath it, near the bench. The bench itself had, meanwhile, undergone one more replacement of legs. And yet, its age showed on the seats where the colour of old wood had faded from much sitting and turned into that of rice husk. As the bench faded, the gulmohar's trunk grew in girth. Firdaus let its saplings grow a little more before she gently dug them out one morning with clumps of soil still holding on to the roots to help them grow in a new place in new soil. She gave three of these to Asman to take to the graveyard and plant them there.

'When you plant them, Asman,' she told him, 'see that you place them in such a way that when the trees grow big and their branches spread out and start to flower, they spread out equally over all the graves there. So that when the flowers drop, they drop not just on a few graves but on all of them. See to it,' she said again. Baadal put the saplings in the basket in front of his cycle and with Asman astride the carrier, they rode to the graveyard. Asman noticed how quickly they arrived at the Indo-East Pakistan Border Outpost at Sutarkandi. Because his abba could pedal so much faster than his dadajaan. At the outpost, the sentries began to recognize Asman, but he still had to fill the register and write his name. Only, on days when he went with his father, he had to write *accompanied by father* and then add Baadal's name and age. The sentry would then motion with his hand for them to go ahead. The makeshift tents of the outpost were gone. In their place, there was a house of brick and mortar with a roof of corrugated iron sheet. Even through this concrete structure, Asman felt its makeshift character. Had his dadajaan seen it, he would have found it somewhat similar to the temporary house that was Subedar Purshottam Bandopadhyay's office at the New Army Transit Camp at Dhaka. But Anjaan Hazratkandi could no longer visit the graves at Malegarh. Nor could he visit any place else. When Baadal and Asman came upon the turn at the narrow track off the Sutarkandi road, both got off the cycle and started walking, Asman keeping pace behind his abba and the cycle.

'Abbajaan, have you wondered how the graveyard remains so oblivious and at peace even now while all over Bengal there is so much unrest?' Asman asked, 'Why is it so, abbajaan, that the lightness that freedom was supposed to bring hasn't yet come?'

'For the rest of Bengal, it may be because some among us are no longer feeling secure here. Between us and them, a wedge has been planted.'

'Them?' Asman asked.

'Like you yourself once said, Asman, *them*, who go to temples. Hindus.'

'Oh, I see, abbajaan.'

'For us, it is because the freedom that your dadajaan, you and I are looking for hasn't yet come, Asman. But those lying here know who they are, they know where they came from. They didn't use as their surnames the names of the villages where they lived. Hence, they are at peace.'

At the foot of the hillock, Baadal left the cycle leaning against the same tree where Anjaan used to, carefully picked the saplings from the basket, and walked up the hillock. Asman went a few paces ahead, heading towards the thickets where his adajaan kept the trowel. He pulled it out and walked back towards the graves.

'Ammajaan asked us to see that all the graves get equal shade and flowers once the trees grow big and branch out and start to flower. She asked us to pick the places that way to plant the saplings,' Asman told his father. Baadal smiled. Firdaus never came there but in her own way she showed she cared. Baadal and Asman picked three spots around the graveyard, dug them out neatly and put the clumps of soil holding the saplings gently into them, one sapling in each. They then heaped the soil that had been dug out back at the base of the plants. Standing up and shaking the loose soil off his hands, Asman said, 'But abbajaan, if we leave the saplings like this, cows and goats will chew them up.' So that day after returning home, Baadal cut up equal lengths of bamboo sticks, long enough to reach higher than the top of the saplings. While he prepared them, Asman went and sat near his dadajaan and told him about the saplings they had planted. Anjaan smiled feebly.

'And tomorrow, dadajaan,' Asman told him about their plans, 'we will take sticks to put around the saplings and will wind coir ropes around them to make small fences so that cows and goats cannot get at the saplings.'

Anjaan slowly turned his head towards Asman and said, 'On days when there is no rain, you will have to water them, Asman, you will have to carry a bucket from home.'

They did as Anjaan said. When the monsoons passed by and autumn came, whenever Baadal or Asman went to the graveyard, they carried a bucket hanging from the handle of the cycle. They then fetched water from the pond by the fields where the cows grazed, across the narrow foot track, and watered the saplings. Sometimes Baadal gathered dried cowdung from the fields and heaped them at the base of the saplings. All three of them survived and were growing healthy too. Baadal would also pull out the undergrowths around them so that weeds did not suck away the nourishment from the dung. And when he raked in the dried leaves and burned them, he let the ash cool for a day before sprinkling them on the newly sprouted, tender leaves of the gulmohar saplings so that insects may not feed on them. Over time, the plants reached upto Asman's chest and their roots went deep enough not to require any more watering with the bucket. But out of habit, Baadal continued to tend to them and to the graves. On evenings when Asman got late in the shop, Anjaan would ask for him. Those few moments with Asman when he got to hear of the graves was what he looked forward to all day long, lying in bed. One evening just before the onset of winter, when dawns and dusks were turning chill, but the day was still warm, Anjaan asked Asman, 'Has any letter or telegram arrived for me, son? I'm worried because lying here on the same bed on the same land, I now am in Pakistan, but the letter will have India on its address. I'm anxious.' He took a deep breath as if even those few words sapped out all the energy from his frail being. 'Or might it have gone back, undelivered, because the address was not found?' The old man sighed deep and heavy.

'Who would it be from, dadajaan?' Asman asked, lightly pulling each of his fingers in turn.

'Subedar Purshottam Bandopadhyay,' he replied. He kept his eyes shut. Asman remained quiet. 'You know, Asman,' he carried on, still keeping his eyes shut, 'When I entered his room that day, the Subedar's room, he looked at the map he was reading and asked me if the Hazratkandi in my name was the same as the village on it.' Asman gently squeezed the fingers to let him feel assured, to tell him, never mind even if he did.

'But that too would be alright, Asman, had I known that I belonged to it. I don't know where I came from, I don't know my lineage, if there is one at all. That one name in the grave took away everything with it. Everything of me has been buried in there, child, my being itself is buried there. It is the search for that being which kept beckoning me there, to the graves. So, when I tended to the graves, I felt like I was tending to my own pains.'

These words were to haunt Asman till his last.

'I will look out for the letter, dadajaan, I will,' Asman promised. A tear trickled down from his grandfather's closed eyes. 'Do you want me to go and enquire at the post office, dadajaan?' Asman asked. Anjaan opened his eyes, blinked and nodded, 'Please do, if you can.'

The next morning and once every week then on, it became a routine for Asman to cycle down to the Hazratkandi post office and ask if there was any letter or post card or anything that may bear news for Anjaan Hazratkandi from Subedar Purshottam Bandopadhyay. And he despised himself for having to tell his dadajaan on returning home that there was no news, not yet. And each time on hearing that, Anjaan would turn his head away from Asman, towards the wall. Anjaan often heard him sob at that moment.

Meanwhile, winter had fully arrived in Hazratkandi. The sun was warm on the bench in the yard under the gulmohar, but Anjaan couldn't go and sit there anymore to let his limbs soak in the sun.

They wouldn't carry him anymore to the bench from his bed. These days Firdaus heated mustard oil with garlic and gave it to Asman to rub into his dadajaan's soles and palms to keep them warm. Just the way Laila used to, to massage Asman when he was an infant. That evening too as Asman massaged the oil into his soles, he kept talking to his dadajaan as he always did. 'Next spring when the rains start, dadajaan,' he said, 'and when a whole lot of periwinkles burst through the ground underneath the few bushes we have by the corner of the shop's door, abbajaan and I will pick them and take them to the graveyard. We will plant them there, in a fine spot.'

'Yes, that would be really nice.' Anjaan said, trying to search his grandson's face with his near-dead eyes.

Asman pushed the bowl of oil forward and moved towards his grandfather's hands.

'Here, dadajaan, give me your hand,' he said, reaching out for the shrivelled hand with his own, while Anjaan dragged his hand as much as he could towards Asman's. As Asman massaged, his grandfather asked, 'Have you been going to the post office?'

'Yes, I have, dadajaan.'

Anjaan might have forgotten that just a few days back Asman returned from the post office and told him that there was no news yet. Or it might be that, for him time seemed to have stretched so much that even a day felt like a week and so in just about two days he was again asking about news from the post office.

Asman didn't have the heart to tell him that there was no news. Anjaan didn't ask either. He just said, 'If ever there is any news, Asman, even if it arrives after I am no more...'

'But why speak thus, dadajaan?' Asman interrupted.

'Hush, my boy, listen now,' Anjaan stopped him. And Asman fell silent. He sat listening quietly, rubbing the oil into his dadajaan's fingers and pulling and stretching them. The fingers that held him and taught him to stand and walk. The fingers that gently pushed him on the tyre swing. The same fingers, but they had lost all strength and will now. Just like dadajaan himself.

'So, if news comes after I am gone, open up the letter and read it well. If it asks you to follow any lead, do so to your best. He is a kind man, the Subedar. Your dadijaan believed he would try to put me through some connection somewhere. She was rarely wrong.' He paused for a while before saying, 'She also knew how to keep hope alive in the most desolate of hearts.' He paused once more and took a few deep breaths. 'Asman,' he said, motioning under his head, 'here, look under the mattress.'

'What for, dadajaan?' Asman asked, reaching towards where Anjaan had showed.

Anjaan gave a feeble tug at his hand as a reply. Asman did as he was told. Under the mattress he felt something soft and woolly. He pulled at it. Anjaan shifted his head ever so lightly to make it easier for Asman to lift the mattress a little more. When he dug his hand further under the mattress, he thought the woolly thing felt like pompoms. They were! He pulled out the whole thing. It was a small, round cloth bag with draw strings, the pompoms attached to its ends.

'Keep that, child,' Anjaan said, 'I kept this all these years as a custodian for your dadijaaan. Since the day I gave this to her as a nikaah gift, it became hers. She never used anything from there though. Said I already gave her all that she ever needed and so she didn't have any need to use anything from this bag here. Keep it, Asman, use the coins in it if the need arises, in the search for our name. But please, child, never give up the search. Never!' Anjaan used every bit of strength left in him to give that one last heave to his head to bring it towards Asman. Asman quickly bent forward and held the head, bringing it to his bosom. The old man reached for Asman's shoulders with both his hands and managed to let them rest there. But in the effort, the bowl of oil got pushed to the edge of the bed and it dropped, spilling whatever oil was left in it on the earthen floor. 'The graves may yet tell you something, child, search for the name. Don't die nameless. Don't die unbelonged like me. Don't let the search remain unfinished! Don't! Don't!'

Close and tight as Asman held his dadajaan's head, he suddenly felt it slacken, and his hands dropped from Asman's shoulders. He was gone. Atleast, in death, Anjaan Hazratkandi was held lovingly in his grandson's bosom. Sound of the falling bowl had brought Baadal and Firdaus hurrying to the room, just after Anjaan had already breathed his last.

Baadal dug Anjaan's grave close to where Laila lay, around the patch of arum and tapioca. Mannan, Liazul and Asman carried Anjaan's bier along with Baadal and gently lowered him into the ground to be by his Lailajaan. There were no Hindu friends to say goodbye.

Anjaan, of Hazratkandi, left just as he arrived. Without a family name, without an indentity. But the search of the Hazratkandis continued.

16
The Year Nineteen Seventy-One

In the years that followed, Asman helped Baadal in the shop and cycled down to the Hazratkandi post office once every week to find out if there was any news for Anjaan Hazratkandi. These days he also began to look up the Bengali newspapers that were now being kept on racks along the wall inside the post office for people to browse through. He read through every headline to see if there might be any news regarding the Malegarh Martyrs' grave or the battle of Latu. Anything, that might give him a lead. Back at the shop, Mannan and Liazul often dropped by but to Baadal, the exchanges no more seemed to be as free as they used to be during the times of Ijaaz Miyaa and Anjaan. Some uneasiness loomed when Tapan Bhowmik or Jadav Saha joined in. The road to Malegarh too had changed since the British left. There were the same fields that Asman rode through with his dadajaan and his abbajaan when he was a child, and there was the same Dooni. Yet when some people passed through the villages, chatting would abruptly stop, laughter would hush, and all of these would resume in hushed tones only after the people passed by. Trust between temple-goers and mosque-goers left along with the British.

It was only at Malegarh, among the graves, that Asman got to be by himself, alone with his thoughts. The white and pink periwinkles he and Baadal planted that first monsoon after Anjaan passed away had rapidly grown and spread. Each spring then on, Asman picked a few and planted them around the graves. As they continued to grow and spread, he removed a few more and planted them along the foot track he used to take to reach the place where Anjaan used to sit. For long hours Asman sat where he used to with his dadajaan and during those pensive moments, everything that his dadajaan said, passed through his mind again and again. Asman was very young those days but he remembered his dadajaan filling with remorse for letting the misery of namelessness pass down to Baadal and him. Asman looked at the white periwinkles. They looked so pristine in the sunlight. The pinks looked seductive towards late afternoon. He remembered his dadajaan wondering often whether he even belonged to Hazratkandi. His dadajaan made it obvious, especially to Asman, that Hazratkandi was not where he ought to be. That sense of shame when people asked his name during his early years, that sense of abandonment that he felt when he was asked to stop calling the woman who raised him as amma and that sense of confusion whether he would grow a beard and read the namaz or get a shave and ring the bell at a temple, every one of those feelings left him living only for that one quest. His quest for identity. He never found it as long as he lived, but that the quest passed on to his son and grandson made him feel all the more wretched. During his dadajaan's last days when Asman used to sit with him during the evenings, he saw the ache, the remorse and despair, and the shame of an entire lifetime spilling out of those clouded eyes. And now all that agony weighed heavy on Asman's heart too. He began to feel the pain of his grandfather. Now as he sat among the graves, he wondered which could be his dadajaan's father's. If only he could find out. If only he could at least find out the name. But time wouldn't wait. And the seasons rolled by.

One day at the post office, newspapers from two days ago were yet to be removed from the rack and so Asman looked through them for the latest one. He browsed through the dates and pulled it out. It was still crisp and a faint smell of kerosene and machine oil from the printing machine lingered on the black letters of the paper. He looked for the date. *Thursday, March 25, 1971*. There was still no news and no article on the battle of Latu. The rest of the day was like any other, that uneventfully slipped into a silent night at Baadal and Firdaus's house. Asman stayed till late evening in the shop. During such evenings, sometimes he worked at repairs and at other times he sat tuning the small transistor radio that he picked up from Subhroto Pal's shop at Latu bazar. Subhroto Pal was no more though. His son Devabroto Pal ran the shop now. Rarely did Asman look for songs and plays through the channels in the radio. He mostly tuned in for news. Or discussions and commentaries relating to undivided Bengal during the times of India's earliest struggle for freedom around 1857. That evening however, he was doing neither. He just sat by himself trying to make sense of all the thoughts that passed through his mind. It was only when Firdaus called him for supper that he dragged the bamboo shutters of the shop together before chaining through them and locking them up. The next day was a Friday and Baadal would have to wake up early for the first namaz of the day before going for jumuah.

However, even before day broke on Friday morning, the muezzin's call was drowned by shrieks, wails and horrified, panic-stricken shouts of men, women, and children from the villages north of Hazratkandi. Gruesome calls of cattle being slaughtered collectively rang through the false dawn. Birds, terrified out of their nests, cried like the ominous banshee, to announce death. Cries of 'Allahu Akbar!' rant through the air and Asman was jolted out of his sleep. He sat up in bed and listened for a while. It took sometime for his eyes to get used to the darkness in the room. But when the screams went on and on, he got down from bed and ran out of the house. Stopping under the gulmohar, he saw that the northern sky above the villages of Bhowmikpara and Bouderbeel, and the Hindu villages of the Sahas, the Sarkars, Basaks and also the Kars, was turning grey and sooty instead of the soft orange of dawn. The horizon was fast getting shrouded with thick smoke bellowing from huts, haystacks and barns which had been torched and set ablaze. Acres and acres of cultivated fields were thrashed through with long swords and sticks. If plants could cry and bleed, the fields would have been soaked with their tears and reddened with their blood. Above Asman, the branches of the gulmohar cast an eerie silhouette against the black of the sky as approaching smoke played hide and seek among the branches. Cattle that escaped being slaughtered fled from their blazing sheds and ran amok among squealing people. Asman took a few steps towards the road to see better. But just then Firdaus and Baadal too came running out of the house and Firdaus pulled Asman back inside with her. She would not let him stand out on the road to watch a demonic day rise in the horizon. Baadal too hastened back into the house with them. Firdaus did not let Asman go back to his room to be all alone, the three instead remained together in Baadal and Firdaus's room. It was the same room where Laila used to sleep as a little girl with her mother. It had a window that opened towards the river at the back of the house. Now as Asman walked towards it to open and look out, Baadal pulled him back.

'Don't Asman, there might be a mob out there! Don't!'

In the wee hours of that Friday in March, all three of them stayed together, fearing even to talk loudly, waiting for whatever was happening to come to an end. They listened hard for any impending, alarming noise, whether stealthily approaching footsteps or a shouting mob in a killing spree. Asman wished for some noise behind their house. Any noise. Because the silence, enhanced by the sordid greying of the village outside in that neither hour between night and dawn, was driving him insane. It was more torturous not to hear anything, keeping the tension looming. They feared to speak but, in their hearts, each made their own assumptions, of a massacre. Of faith against faith. Of Moslems against Hindus.

There were fewer people at jumuah that Friday. It was only at the mosque that Asman came to know of the previous night's carnage.

'Three villages have been completely razed,' Mohsin Haque told the few that stayed on after jumuah. 'Not to talk of all the rest that have been left crippled. They'll not recover from this bloodbath, at least not for one whole generation.'

'But who were they? What was the motive?' Rahim asked.

'Our own people,' Mohsin replied, in what seemed like a whisper. 'It would be neither safe nor wise to talk of any motive standing here at the mosque now, when blood might yet be trickling out of dagger-wounds on the dead bodies that are still warm. We all have seen which people were targeted.'

Asman felt a shiver crawling up his bones.

'Whatever, it's no more going to be the same again between our two people here,' Mohsin continued, 'no more!'

Many had heard a buzz in the days before of such a fallout.

'It had to happen, it was waiting to happen.' Mohsin Haque said.

'But are you aware,' Qarim master announced, 'that we have seceded from Pakistan?'

'So where are we left now?' Rahim asked.

'We are a new nation.'

Asman remembered something that Sirajullah had said long ago when he was still a little boy. The comparison had amused him then, it made him think hard now. Sirajullah had said, 'Bamboo, once split, never becomes whole. With whatever or however you attempt to bind it.' Sirajullah's bamboo was the bond between the Hindus and the Moslems of Hazratkandi and its neighbouring villages.

The wedge had been struck. And struck deep.

'I was told they are still pulling out charred torsos and severed limbs from underneath burned corrugated iron sheets that had shrivelled like the skin of potatoes roasted in ember,' Liazul added. Baadal froze. He often used to walk through the fields across those villages with Mannan and Jadav Saha, till a few days back.

'Some tried to run away and hide in the fields among the tall sugarcane plants, but it seems they were chased like hare and dragged out and hacked till all the blood in them ran out into the soil in the fields,' Qarim said, looking over his shoulder, scared that there might be someone listening, someone who shouldn't hear. 'They tore down bells from the temples and defaced the idols inside. They flung chopped heads of cows into the temple ponds, laughing with sadistic pleasure.'

Asman was too shocked to even speak a single word all through this animated but whispered exchange. He had friends in those villages with whom he'd played football with a shaddock when they were in high school. He had visited many of those homes, many a time. He used to call those friends' mothers *kaki*. How they adored Asman and always spared some kheer from Durga Puja for him. Those same friends had sisters who prepared coconut laddus for Asman on the day of *Bhai Phota*. Asman's soul cringed as he now stood listening to horrendous tales of how their chastity was maligned the night before. Many of their fathers came to Ijaaz Miya's shop often, Asman remembered that very well. Sometimes to mend cycles and umbrellas but mostly to just sit and idle away time over a chat. Though for some time now, they had stopped coming. Standing in the mosque listening to their slaughter now, their faces swam through his mind as his pulse raced. Sinister smoke spilled over an otherwise beautiful March sun above the mosque at Hazratkandi, making fear grip the hearts of those standing under that sun.

'When people ran into the Kali temple on the banks of the big pond at Bouderbeel and hid in there, the killers bolted the door from outside and set the temple on fire,' Mohsin whispered.

Even in that horrified and numb state of mind, Baadal was faintly reminded of a discussion long ago, under the gulmohar, of the Jallianwalabagh massacre.

'Brothers,' Qazi said, 'stay on the alert, mind your movements and your acquaintances.' When Qazi said this, he particularly looked at Asman and Baadal. 'Such massacres often pave the way for retaliation. Sooner or later.'

Shaken to the core, Baadal and Asman returned home in silence. The roads were empty except for small clusters of people here and there flocking around mutilated bodies recovered from ditches and under bridges, from thickets and fields. Villages along the road to Sutarkandi too were drenched in blood, of both men and cattle. The soil of Hazratkandi had turned a ruddy maroon. For days after that, villagers saw corpses and carcasses floating down the Dooni, their stench reeking through the spring air. The cycle repair shop remained closed that day, like it had been since the time of Ijaaz Miya, because it was the day of jumuah. Had it been any other day, even then it would have been kept shut.

Later that evening when Firdaus sat by the earthen stove blowing into the fire and preparing the evening's meal, Baadal and Asman too sat in that small kitchen, on bamboo mats on the earthen floor, leaning against the bamboo wall. Baadal looked down at his feet, his stoic face veiling the fear that was threatening to erupt through his eyes any moment, at any sound coming through the night. He wondered if he should tell Firdaus about all that they heard at the mosque. He slowly raised his gaze to look at her and then at Asman. The dim flicker of light and shade from the kerosene lamp on their drawn faces accentuated the tension in them. All else outside was as silent as the dead could be. Even the cicadas were quiet that night. Firdaus and Baadal sat waiting for Asman to tune in to the radio for some news. When it started, Firdaus stopped blowing into the fire and sat still. All three of them listened intently. East Pakistan had seceded from that part of Pakistan, which was far away from the western side, with around a thousand miles of India in between them. It would now be a new nation. It would be known as Bangladesh. Baadal dropped his head into his hands. The fire Firdaus was lighting suddenly rose with life and in that burst of glow upon her face, Asman saw terror and apprehension writ large in her eyes. She pulled out a piece of firewood and set it aside, letting the fire ebb. The news went on, tough the transmission crackled with heavy disturbance. There was mention of *Operation Searchlight*, that it was a planned military operation targeted at those Bengalis who might have stood in the way to West Pakistan's independence. Asman and Baadal looked at each other. That was what had happened at the kali temple of Bouderbeel and at the village of Bhowmikpara, and at the villages of the Sahas, and Kars and at that of the Sarkars and the Basaks. Asman wondered how his friends could have ever been that hindrance to West Pakistan. There had been brutal killings at Dhaka too, the news said. Baadal asked Asman to switch off the radio when the news shifted to other happenings. Firdaus resumed her cooking without saying anything.

'Bengal will not be the same,' Baadal said shaking his head, still holding it in his hands.

It wouldn't.

'The village of Hazratkandi will be in the new nation of Bangladesh,' Asman said.

'So where would we be put now?' Firdaus asked, still confused.

'Bangladesh,' Baadal replied.

She quietly brought down two plates from the meat-safe standing on three legs and one brick against the corner and put them in front of Baadal and Asman and served them their supper. Not that anyone had any hunger or appetite. Just that, it was a habit and a ritual. While they ate, she gathered the used pots and pans and was about to take them out to clean them, but Baadal stopped her.

'Leave them here tonight, Firdaus,' he said, 'clean them tomorrow when day dawns. Don't go out in the dark.'

Fear and distrust had made their way into the hearts of two people who chatted and laughed under one tree sitting on the same bench. March was otherwise a beautiful time around these parts of Sylhet. As a child Asman remembered waiting eagerly to hear the first calls of the cuckoo. Soon after, the gulmohar would burst into flaming red flowers covering almost the whole of the canopy. But the spring of 1971 was so different from all those past springs. The cuckoo did call, but it was the piercing shriek of kites that filled the air, and vultures ruled the sky.

Asman continued to cycle down to the graves at Malegarh. Though his country changed, the sentries at the Sutarkandi border outpost remained the same because they were on the Indian side of the border. Only, it would soon start to be known as the Indo-Bangladesh border outpost, from Indo-East Pakistan border outpost. Every time Asman approached the outpost, he got off the cycle and walked towards the small room where the register lay on a table, to write down his name. But the sentries recognized him well by now and they would call out cheerfully, 'Asman Hazratkandi, isn't that you?'

'Yes, huzur,' Asman would reply.

'To Malegarh, eh?' the sentry would ask. To which Asman nodded.

'You carry on, Asman bhai, we shall put your name on the register ourselves. Returning by afternoon?' the sentry would ask.

'Yes, huzur, by afternoon,' Asman replied, 'maybe even earlier.'

And the sentry motioned with his hand for Asman to pass by.

That spring, during one of his trips, Mannan picked up a couple of yellow oleander saplings from underneath a bush that was filled with the yellow blooms. It fascinated him so much that he stopped his carriage to pick up a few saplings. But then, he didn't know what to do with them. So he left them with Firdaus. Firdaus planted one near the graves of Anjaan and Laila and the other right outside her kitchen door.

'When it grows and starts to flower, I'll keep watching the blooms,' she said with anticipation. But that was never to be. Spring soon made way for summer and the rains.

Soon the saccharum began to bloom and sway in rows by the receding waters of the Dooni. And they reminded Asman that autumn had arrived. They always heralded the festive spirit of Durga Puja in the villages north of Hazratkandi. But this year those villages were left deserted, pyres still burning in them. Then late one afternoon on the eve of that Durga Puja, when

Baadal was working at the shop, a few men walked in towards him. Baadal looked up. He recognized them, though they were not from Hazratkandi. They had come earlier for small repairs. A few more arrived immediately after.

'Uh, well? What's to be repaired?' Baadal asked, something tightening inside him.

The men didn't speak but closed in around him. Even before Baadal could stand up from where he was working and move away, they kicked their way through the tools and pliers on the shop's floor, caught hold of Baadal by the neck and shoved him out into the yard in front of the shop, under the gulmohar.

'Informer, were you?' one of them yelled at his face and spat on it.

Another pulled out a machete from his waistband over a dhoti as he shouted, 'Gossiping harmlessly with friends, eh? Good front you put up, miya, when all the while you let your shop be used to plan and root us out, you sly scoundrel!'

'Intelligent, huh! You instigate and get others to do the killings!'

'And yourself sit calmly tapping at those cycle wheels, huh?'

Baadal never knew what it felt like to be struck by lightning, but he thought it must have felt like what he felt at that moment. Never in their wildest nightmares did any of the Hazratkandis and Ijaaz Miya imagine that all those beautiful hours of sharing and chatting, the light teasing and laughter over little things of life, the exchange of news and lending support and shoulder during hours of grief and death with friends from the villages of the Basaks and the Haques, of Siddiqui and Saha would ever be interpreted this way. The men didn't give Baadal a chance to speak. And explain. A few of them held him back while the machete dug through his stomach and slit it sideways, ripping his insides apart. Baadal screamed but his energy was already draining. What he emitted was merely a hoarse, faint grunt, calling out to Firdaus and Asman. Which of course didn't at all carry to Malegarh, from where Asman was returning at that time. The machete then struck his head and when the men released him, Baadal instantly dropped to the ground. Firdaus came rushing out of the house hearing all the commotion. But Baadal did not get to see her. They had already killed him. When she saw the men and then saw Baadal lying under the gulmohar tree like a slaughtered lamb, she didn't know which way to go. She cried to come to Baadal and at the same time she knew she had to run back into the house if she was to escape the men's fury. And before she could decide, one of the men pounced on her, dragged her out under the tree by the hair and banged her head again and again against the hard trunk of the gulmohar, shouting each time, 'Tell us, you witch, where is that son of yours! Tell us!'

'He isn't home,' was all she managed to groan.

'Not home you say? Take that,' he said, banging her head again on the tree trunk. A few gulmohar flowers dropped on her as the lower branches shook. At last when she collapsed, they left her lying on the ground to die. Some of them went into the shop, ransacked it and stormed into the house looking for Asman. When they couldn't find him, they vent their wrath on the shop and set it on fire. And into that fire, they threw Ijaaz Miya's bench. The same bench, that stood as a silent witness through the chronicle of grief and longing, birth and death, hope and despair, and most of all, through the search for an identity, of the nameless Hazratkandis. Like an omen of the times to come, the bench was burnt to ashes. Old rubber tyres of bicycles kept in a corner burned and emitted thick, nauseating smoke as it spiralled menacingly towards the sky, just as the smoke above the villages of Bouderbeel and Bhoumikpara only a few months back. One of the men brought out Asman's transistor and hurled it at the thick trunk of the gulmohar. It broke and fell next to Baadal, with its insides scattered out on the ground just like Baadal's. It was only after a while that Asman arrived from Malegarh. The men had left by then. Dropping the cycle, he darted towards the gulmohar and heard his amma's feeble voice, gasping and grunting. People had already gathered and were trying desperately to douse the flames that were fast feeding on the dry, bamboo walls of the shop and threatening to spread towards the inner house.

Asman hurried towards Firdaus, sat down beside her and broke down seeing her bloodied head and face. Only her eyes were blinking. The rest was all a thick, pulped mess of gruesome red.

'Ammajaan!'

'Parimal Guha,' she said between gasps, 'Madhusudan Saha, Banikanto Roy....they chanted.... Jai Ma... Jai Devi Ma...' And Firdaus shut her eyes with the name of the goddess.

'La Illaha Ill Alla Muhammadur Rasulullah...,' Asman said under his breath, bringing her warm, bleeding head to his cold, shivering bosom. He sat holding her that way for a long time while people scurried about fetching water from the river across the fallow land behind their house and hurled buckets and buckets of it into the fire. Leaping tongues of flames had in the meantime licked up much of the lone room behind the shop, the room that used to be Anjaan's first place in that house. When Asman stood up, he did so not knowing who he was, a Hindu or a Moslem. He looked up at the darkening sky, not knowing where he belonged, to Bangladesh or to Pakistan. He was left all alone. The only thing he knew was that he would let no more Hazratkandis ever be.

Asman, of Hazratkandi, would be the last, he vowed.

17
The Year Two Thousand

It had taken everything of Asman to rebuild the shop, over decades. But how could he do that with his life now? The lone room, in which Anjaan had first come to stay, remained ravaged and full of debris. The rest of the house still bore tell-tale charred marks of that fateful night. Asman just let them be that way. He had lost the will to build the house over again. The shop he had to attend to, because he had to eat as long as he lived.

Two days after the fire, he walked into the remains of the shop. In places, the ash still felt warm, as he looked around for any tool or thimble that the fire left fit to be used again. Umbrella shafts lay twisted and bent as if they were as pliable as the hair in his amma's neat long braid. Nothing remained that he could find solace in. Not any tool, no spare rubber tyre or umbrella shaft but most achingly, not ammajaan. He would have to start all over again. He didn't know how he would do that.

Sitting among the graves at Malegarh a few days later, he had been contemplating the round cloth bag with the pompom drawstrings. Since his grandfather handed it to him, he had tucked it away in a tin trunk, stashed among old clothes that belonged to his dadajaan and abbajaan, and some school marksheets. Those were his own. He never looked inside the bag. He wondered how much money there might be in it. It was anyway only a small pouch. He looked at the graves around him. How oblivious they were to the turmoil in his heart. How unmindful they lay of the guilt that he held in his conscience about the thought of using the money in that pouch. For, hadn't his grandfather said, 'Keep it, Asman, use the coins in it if the need arises, in the search for our name.'? And here he was, thinking of using it to rebuild the shop. He felt a lump in his throat. He looked at the bokul tree. The dove-nest that his grandfather had showed him was not there any longer. But in grooves higher between the branches, there were many more nests. He wondered what catastrophe had broken the earlier one, but the doves had put life together again over the years. He would too.

Coming home that evening, he brought down his trunk from the bamboo rafters in his room, dusted it and opened the lid. It squeaked at the hinges. He dug among the things and pulled out the pouch. His heart beat faster as he pushed his fingers into the slit at the mouth and drew it apart.

'Forgive me, dadajaan, forgive me if you can!' he said to himself, his voice choking. The pouch weighed down with coins. *Annas*. He emptied them on his bed just as his dadajaan had done decades ago, on his bed in the dormitory at the Central Supply Depot at Narikuli. He too was then thinking of starting life anew. Just as Asman did now. He picked a few of the coins on his palm and brought his hand close to the kerosene lantern to take a good look. They had imprints of the Queen and King of England. Each of them. Putting them down, he picked a few more. They too were coins of the British era of the 1800s, and were obsolete in the Bangladesh of the year 2000. The guilt in his heart erupted and he sobbed aloud as he put the annas back into the pouch. There was no one else beside him to hear his sobs and come running to him, to hold his head and wipe his tears. No one, besides the darkness. He could cry as much as he wished. He pulled the drawstrings to close the pouch. The pouch and the coins had now become even more priceless to him. He put it back into the trunk among the clothes and marksheets and stowed the trunk away on the rafters once more. He slept very little all that night, thinking of ways to rebuild the shop.

Early next morning, he looked under the eves of the thatch roof outside the kitchen. Baadal used to keep the fishing net there, tucked between the bamboo post and the kitchen wall. It was still there but he had to shake off soot and cobweb as he brought it down. He didn't remember the last time when he or anyone else at home used it. He did remember, however, others from the village borrowing it on a few occasions. It had tears and holes in places, the net would require mending. So the next few days he devoted himself to the mending. And when it was ready to dive into the waters and catch fish, Asman took it first to the river behind their house. When he caught big fish, he took it right away to the market at Sutarkandi. But on days when he caught small fish, he spread them out on banana leaves to dry them under the sun on the fallow land by the river. Dried fish sold for more money. Sometimes he even folded the net, clamped it on the carrier of his bicycle and rode to the Dooni and even farther to the Sonai. He would sell fish, till he managed to put Ijaaz Miya's shop together once more. Though he never again placed another bench under the gulmohar tree.

But even as he fished, he often thought he felt his hands trembling, like he saw his dadajaan's. Sometimes his vision felt clouded too. Age was catching up. But more than that, a lack of will to live, coupled with loneliness, drove him faster to the trembling. Sometimes, he thought he found it difficult to breathe. He cycled down to the graves at Malegarh every day. And on days that he did not go there, he went to the Hazratkandi post office. Even the post office had changed since that first time he had gone there to ask if there was any letter for Anjaan Hazratkandi, from Subedar Purshottam Bandopadhyay. The old post office had been replaced by a new, bigger building. Outside, however, the couple of red letter-boxes still bore white stains of lime, like smudged fingerprints on some postal form, all over them. But inside the post office, there were a whole lot of new windows where he saw people depositing money for themselves. Like in a bank. But these were not his concern. His concern was a letter and that was yet to arrive.

Sometimes on Fridays after jumuah he rode along the Dooni across the fields like he did in his childhood with his father and grandfather. The fields were still there but no more as vast and open as they were those days. They were ripped apart by high, barbed fences monstrously running through them, throwing one part to Bangladesh and the other to India. Maulvi Jalaluddin's fields in Katigorah too were sliced through. Now when his grandsons came to work in the fields, they had to step into a foreign nation, into India, through large gates that were manned by armed sentries. Then before dusk, before the gates closed for the night, they returned to their homes back in their own country. The children of Firdaus's other cousins in Katigorah brought in their cows to graze in that part of their own field which lay in India across the international border through those large gates in the morning and took them back in the evening. At

Khaiboor's home, his dwelling house got left behind in India and the kitchen got shoved to Bangladesh. And his wife Amina bibi shuttled between the two nations from dawn to dusk, looking after the family. Sometimes Asman stopped by the Dooni and sat on its banks, looking up at the sky. Maybe, he thought, the air in those skies were divided too. Even at sixty-eight, he could still pedal upto Malegarh because the roads were now wide and smooth and coated with asphalt. Cars zoomed past him every now and then, but there was still enough space on the road for him to carry on pedalling. He didn't need to stop, get off, and lift his cycle to the far edge of the road to let them pass by, as he had to earlier. At the Sutarkandi Indo-Bangladesh Border Outpost, the sentries changed over time but each time a new batch arrived, they too came to know Asman Hazratkandi, and they too let him pass by with just a wave of their hand. Now there was also a very large and high, overhead green board spanning the entire width of the wide highway where the Sutarkandi border outpost was. Had Asman known how to read English, he would have read the words in white letters in one corner of the board as *Indo Bangladesh International Border Sutarkandi*. When he looked at it from below, it looked like a fence that separated the open sky of his childhood into the skies of Bangladesh and India. He cycled under that fence everyday to go to the graves at Malegarh. The roads on the Indian side were now dotted on either side with concrete structures that housed many a government office and hospital, for both men and cattle. The narrow foot track, off the Sutarkandi road, which had been an inseparable part of his life, and which led to the graves, was no longer narrow, though it was yet to be gravelled and coated with asphalt. Asman sometimes felt like a living record of all the changes that had come over the land through all these years. On his person too, his hair had grayed, and his skin seemed more than was needed to cover his shrinking body. The yellow oleanders that Firdaus had planted were abundant bushes now, and flowers from the one by the river always kept dropping on the graves of Anjaan and Laila. Baadal and Firdaus too lay close by and there were bright yellow oleanders on their graves as well. Every monsoon, new saplings sprang forth underneath the mother bush. That spring, Asman picked one sapling from there and planted it at the centre of the Malegarh graveyard. With the periwinkles at Malegarh too spreading every monsoon, Asman picked the excess, and lovingly replanted them around each grave. He continued to pull out the weeds and the grass thorns. He even traced and then made a neat path from the edge of the graveyard right upto the other side, to the spot where he used to sit with his dadajaan as a child. He lined this path too with periwinkles. The trunk of the bokul tree had by then acquired a much greater girth than him and dropped even more brown leaves. Asman had to rake in the leaves every day.

One afternoon when he was approaching the graveyard, he saw a couple of cars at the foot of the hillock, near the old tree where he always leaned his bicycle. There were a few men around the cars and some more up in the graveyard. When Asman hurried there, he saw that they had very long measuring tapes and were taking some measurements around the graves. Two of them were making some sketches on white paper and writing down things and making calculations on note pads. They carried calculators too. Asman walked up to one of them and asked, 'Huzur, why the measurements?'

'There'll be some construction here,' was all he said, with obvious importance, and went back to his work.

Asman lingered on. For the first time in all these years, he felt intruded upon. This was the only place where he found some comfort, this was the only place which he thought he could call his own, where he could be by himself. But now even that seemed to be slipping away from him. The men then talked among themselves and one of them beckoned Asman to come to them.

'We were told, someone has been tending to the graves. These flowers, that path, any idea who? Might you be knowing?' he asked Asman.

Asman lightly bowed his head. 'I know huzur, because it is I who has been tending to these graves.'

'Oh! Does anyone pay you for this upkeep?' The man asked.

The thought of payment in lieu of tending the graves had never occured to Asman. He shook his head.

'Then why do you do it?' the man asked, visibly surprised.

'My grandfather's father lies here.'

'In these graves?' the man asked.

Asman nodded.

'He's a martyr? Of the battle of Latu?' He asked, his surprise turning into reverence. Asman nodded once more. The man gently put a hand on Asman's shoulder and said, 'That surely is something to feel proud of! Did you know that now this place is going to be done up like a monumental park? Grave-slabs are being proposed for each grave, there will be a plaque dedicated to those brave soldiers and there will be a boundary wall too.'

Asman listened intently and in wonder. Suddenly he turned around and stared into the man's face with a flicker of renewed hope in his aged eyes, and asked, 'Mwaafi, huzur, but will you also inscribe names on the grave-slabs?'

Asman's movement was so abrupt that the man was taken aback. His head moved backwards, and his arm slid off Asman's shoulder. 'Well? Oh that! We don't know. That part will be taken up by others. Our job is to do the initial survey and start the construction.'

Asman looked around at all the pink and white periwinkles, at the gulmohars now grown into graceful and stately canopies and at the small yellow oleander sapling that had just steadied itself in its new soil. 'And these, huzur?' he asked, with a swing of his hand towards the flowers and the gulmohars.

'Let's see, we shall try to save the gulmohars, but these,' he said, pointing at the periwinkles, 'will have to go for now, I'm sorry. I won't be able to help it.'

Asman felt as if a boulder had been dropped on his chest from a great height. He waited for the men to leave. Then he sat for a long while at that same place where he used to since he was a child. He didn't know where to go from this point in his life. He closed his eyes out of fatigue, a fatigue of the mind. And then, behind those closed eyes, he saw the graveyard as it was when he first came there. That was the year his land got liberated from the British. Land, he reflected, without attaching a name to it. The name having changed over and over, he didn't know what name he could call it by. Those days, the graves were neat, but there were no flowers and no gulmohar. A car horn pierced his thoughts and broke his reverie. Fifty-three years had passed by within those few moments behind his shut eyes and now when he opened them, the graveyard was full of periwinkles and gulmohars, with one oleander waiting to bloom. He stood up and walked slowly towards the thickets where he kept the trowel. He brought it out and dug up as many periwinkles as would fit into his cycle's basket and carried them home with him. He would save them and let them grow there till the grave-slabs and the boundary wall were built. And when all the construction work would be completed, he would again bring them back to Malegarh and plant them around the graves. But it saddened him to think of the fate of the gulmohars.

Soon Asman started seeing trucks at the foot of the Martyrs' hillock at Malegarh, unloading bricks, heaps of sand and stones and sacks of cement. Another day, he saw iron bars being dragged up the path that he so lovingly traced from the base of the hillock to where the graveyard began to roll out. It felt like they dragged over his chest, leaving bruise marks he could see along the track on the ground and those that he couldn't, in his soul. It gave him a sense of defilement of the graveyard. But then he consoled himself by forcing to think that all of it was happening to beautify the place. Asman kept going there even though he could not tend to the graves as long as the construction was going on. He went and just sat there and sometimes walked among the workers. His heart broke to see the periwinkles trampled upon and pulled out without the least of remorse. Those that were waiting their turn to be pulled out were, meanwhile, coated with thick films of sand and cement dust. Asman could no longer make out which ones were pink and which ones were white. They all appeared the same dull grey. He looked for the oleander. He couldn't find it, not where he had planted it. When he looked around, he saw it lying broken and wilted a little distance away. Two of the gulmohars had been chopped down, their roots pulled out to make the ground even. Asman cried like a child into his pillow that night. They had even dug up all around the graveyard to erect the boundary wall. They were also laying concrete steps from where he used to leave his cycle upto the edge of the flat top of the graveyard. Asman noticed that they had laid these steps along the same path which he had traced and which he had then lined with flowers. As he sat and watched the monstrous iron cauldron of the cement mixer roaring and rotating as it mixed the mortar, and as the workers bend iron bars and laid the bricks in the graveyard which he thought belonged only to him and he to it, Asman wondered if Indians felt the same as he was feeling now, when the British first came and started usurping things into their hands. He could only sit and watch helplessly and let the graveyard be taken over. Guilt whipped his soul because he could no longer keep the place tranquil, that he could not do anything to stop the peace of the dead from being disturbed. At the far edge towards the other side of the graveyard, opposite the entrance, they put up a sombre plaque of black granite with white inscriptions on it. The bottom half of the inscription was in English, so Asman couldn't read that. The top part was in Bengali and this Asman could read. He read it many times over right from the day it was unveiled.

In the memory of those who sacrificed their lives
In the great mutiny of 1857,
for the freedom of the country

There were also blue boards near the entrance to the graveyard, narrating the story of the Battle of Latu. They made an arched gate too at the entrance. On that gate, there were some letters. In English.

'What do they say?' Asman had asked the superviser at the site one day.

'Malegarh War Memorial,' he read out.

Those were harrowing months for Asman. He was told that the graveyard was now a monument and would soon become an international heritage site. Asman didn't understand how that would make any difference to him or to those who drew him there. But the constructions in the graveyard went on all the same. He saw them through, in the hope of seeing the next lot of workers arrive to inscribe names on the grave-slabs. But nowhere, not on the blue boards, not on the black plaque, nor on the graves were there any mention of the names of the martyrs. And then finally one day, their work over and completed, the workers packed up all their machines and tools and left. The graves looked neat and fresh, but the smell of kerosene and new paint lingered among the dead. No longer was it the smell of leaves crushed under feet, dry barks of aged trees, small wild flowers, and the unmistakable smell of cows and goats that every whiff of breeze blowing into the graveyard carried with it.

Asman Hazratkandi began to tend to the graves all over again. He replanted the periwinkles and yellow oleander and planted a few gulmohars along the boundary wall, to make those lying in those graves feel belonged and at home, unlike him. Though construction work at the graveyard was now long over, his own search was far from it. And as the years passed by, he continued to visit Malegarh just as he still visited the post office at Hazratkandi once every week.

Then one cold December morning on his way to the graveyard as he approached the Sutarkandi Border Outpost, he noticed that there were many more sentries than there usually used to be. Asman saw new, unfamiliar faces among the sentries, side by side with the familiar ones. And unlike other days, that day he was stopped, and asked to write his name on the register, and sign it.

'But I have been allowed to pass by for so many years now, huzur, they all know me, they all know where I go to, and that I return by afternoon,' Asman said, a little curious, a little wary.

'Yes, we understand, but today is different,' a new unfamiliar sentry was trying to explain to Asman. Just then, another sentry who knew him, walked up. 'We know, Asman Hazratkandi, that you pose no threat,' he said. 'However, we are duty bound today. At the Malegarh graveyard, where you are headed, there will be a big gathering today, of very important persons from both the countries of India and Bangladesh. It is a high security day today.'

'But why?' Asman wanted to know further.

'Some anniversary is being observed at the graveyard today,' one of the sentries replied.

'It is the anniversary of the Battle of Latu,' another added.

Asman quietly walked up to the register. His weakening fingers found it difficult to hold the pen. He remembered his dadajaan during his first visit to the Malegarh graveyard and how he took the pen from the sentry to write on the register on behalf of his dadajaan because his fingers could not hold the pen. That was his dadajaan's last visit to the Malegarh graves and that recollection brought a strange sense of foreboding in him. Like some omen. His trembling fingers formed scrawny letters on the register, but he did manage to write. In Bengali.

Name: Asman Hazratkandi
Age: Eighty-five years
Village: Hazratkandi, Sylhet,
Bangladesh.
Year: 2017

He put the pen down slowly. The sentry picked it up and said, 'We shall put in the time.' He paused and asked, 'Returning around noon?'

Asman nodded. He once more read what he had written on the register. *Bangladesh.*

As he resumed cycling towards Malegarh, the thought that passed his mind was how just that one thing kept changing over the years. He remembered his abbajaan writing India as his country in the year 1937, when he was admitted to the Hazratkandi Primary School. He also remembered writing East Pakistan as his country in the year 1947, when he first came to Malegarh with his dadajaan. And today he had written Bangladesh. For a moment he thought his head reeled. But he pedalled on. He just had to be at the Malegarh graveyard that day. From afar, he saw that the hillock was swarming with people. There were a whole lot of policemen too. Villagers crowded along the roadside. The whole graveyard wore a festive look.

But when Asman neared the foot of the hillock, he was stopped.

'No, Asman, not today. Not now!'

18
The Year Twenty Seventeen
Indo-Bangladesh Border Outpost, Sutarkandi

As Asman lay fallen and unconscious by the wayside, the one hundred and sixtieth anniversary observations of the Battle of Latu at the grave of his great grandfather began and finished. He did not get to see the lighting of the ceremonial earthen lamps, nor did he get to hear what all the important people, the ministers, the officers, and the social activists said on the occasion. He did not get to hear the small children in their neat school uniform sing India's national anthem. When the VIPs left and Jaising Hmar's duty at the venue of the event was over, he climbed on to the back of the Border Security Force truck along with his troop to return to his post at the Sutarkandi border outpost. But even as he did so, he turned around again and again, his gaze searching the crowd of villagers still lingering by the road and walking up to the graveyard. He was searching for Asman. Of Hazratkandi.

Asman woke up to the sprinkling of water on his pale face. His white, crocheted taqiyah was lying next to him on the grass. Except for a few people, the roads were beginning to empty out. The VIP cars were all gone as was the van that came to telecast the event live from the Malegarh War Memorial. Asman wondered how he didn't hear even the siren wailing out from the escort and pilot vehicles accompanying those cars with their beacon lights. He looked around for Jaising Hmar, but he too was nowhere in sight. Nor was there any other policeman or security person. The people near him helped Asman to sit up. He didn't know them, though he heard someone among them telling the rest that he knew him as the person who kept coming to the graves and tended to them. Only after he sat up did he remember that he had been pushed and that he fell to the ground. Still sitting on the grass by the road, he looked towards the graves. There was no one there but for a few people who were winding up after the function and cleaning up the place. A few others were putting up candles along the steps leading to the graves and below the black granite plaque. They were also sticking candles all along the boundary wall and around each grave. They didn't yet light them though. They would do so only after dark. The cold December wind was starting to reach his old bones through his kurta. He looked towards the Sutarkandi high road. The ungravelled road leading to the high road ahead seemed very long that evening. Dusk was gathering around the horizon, and it would soon spill over. He turned his gaze back to the graves.

'Get up, Asman miya,' said the man who knew him, 'it'll get dark soon, and cold too.'

People helped him on his feet and picked his cycle. Asman's arms felt like they were being pulled down with great force towards the ground and they refused to obey him. Someone helped him lift them and placed them on the handles of his cycle. And Asman slowly walked away from the grave of his great grandfather. The road ahead was lonely and dismal, his mind was blank, and his heart ached with every breath he took. As he neared the Indo-Bangladesh International Border outpost at Sutarkandi, he saw the green fence cutting across the skies. The same skies, which he had known since they were one. The large white letters on the green fence seemed a blur as he came closer and closer under the fence. Dhaka, it was written on that fence, was two hundred and ninety kilometres from where Asman was, though Sylhet was only forty-five kilometres. Hazratkandi was much closer. On the wide central portion of the fence was written *WISH YOU A HAPPY JOURNEY. THANKS. ASSAM P.W. BLDG. & NH DEPT.* Asman never could read it, even during those times when his head was not bleary. But all the same, his journey home to Hazratkandi from Malegarh in India's Assam was never happy. Today when he came under the fence, he bent his head back and raised his eyes to look at it. He felt as if the fence was swirling. He felt as if it was falling on him. The skies of all the countries which had mocked him, pretending to make him feel that he belonged to them, seemed to go round and round, faster and faster, till they blended into one. By then, he had already dropped onto the asphalt road right under the green fence, under the border gateway between India and Bangladesh. The back of his head hit the road with the heavy sound of a boulder being dropped on the mud embankment of the Koshiara river, followed by a sharp splitting noise. His skull cracked and blood first began to trickle out from under the broken head and then flowed profusely, but Asman Hazratkandi felt no pain. With his face up and his eyes open, he saw his dadajaan smiling at him. He was showing Asman a beautiful flight of white egrets flying in the pattern of an airplane across the sky that was once again one and limitless. His open eyes were calm. His unbelonged soul flew out through those open eyes to catch up with his dadajaan and the egrets in their flight home.

A commotion stirred up at the otherwise quiet outpost. A car came to a screeching halt just next to Asman's body, but the sentry quickly motioned it to move on. They did not want an undue gathering at the border that day. For reasons of security for both India and Bangladesh. The sentries who had known Asman also knew that there would be no one coming to look for him. A few sentries gently carried his body away and prepared for a funeral while another picked his cycle and put it leaning against the outpost's outer wall. Others brought out buckets of water to wash away the blood from the road.

At Asman's burial late that evening, a lone soldier named Jaising Hmar, of the Border Security Force of India, lit a candle near their outpost at Sutarkandi, while hundreds of candles lit up the Martyrs' Memorial at the Malegarh hillock in memory of Asman's great grandfather.

If only he knew in which grave his great grandfather lay, if at all he was laid to rest there. If only Asman of Hazratkandi knew that martyr's name in full....

Epilogue

- **Debatable date of the occurrence of the battle of Latu:** Insufficient records regarding the date of the Malegarh Mutiny of 1857 have left the date debatable. While the official history of the Sylhet Light Infantry records the event as having taken place on Christmas Day, 1857, which would point at December 25, 1857, an old obituary of Major Byng records his date of death as December 18, 1857, at Latu, the site mentioned in the story.
- **Records of the rebelling 34th. Regiment Bengal Native Infantry (34 BNI)** and names of sepoys therein, were removed from the official records soon after the mutiny of Latu. That is regretful standard military practice since times immemorial. So what is available today is primarily the names of the British officers, though there are also the names of a few "faithful" Indian Subedars, etc.
- **Bradshaw Ka Paltan** was the way that the sepoys referred to the 34 BNI, according to the custom of

calling a regiment by the name of its founder. From the sepoys, the name spread among the locals too.
- **The Sylhet Light Infantry later became the 1st Battalion, 8th Gorkha Rifles** but, at the time of the battle of Latu of 1857, it had sepoys from Awadh, Bihar, and other hillmen, including Gorkhas.
- **Operation Searchlight** was a military operation undertaken by the Pakistan Army to demoralize and check the growing resistance of freedom-loving Bengalis against the autocracy of Pakistani rulers. The date of its commencement is recorded as March 25, 1971. The targets of the operation were the main hubs of East Pakistan, including Dhaka. However, among the common people too, religious intolerance had already raised its ugly head. Unorganized, ill-informed enthusiasts unfortunately created stray riots in remote villages, some of which coincided with the duration of Operation Searchlight.
- According to official records and history, the rebel sepoys of the 34 BNI lost the battle of Latu in 1857, but succeeded in killing Major Byng, the Commander of the confronting force, 11th Sylhet Light Infantry. This has led to the impression that the sepoys of the rebel 34 BNI won the Battle of Latu.

Pippa Rann Books & Media
and Global Resilience Publishing
imprints of
Salt Desert Media Group Ltd., U.K.
Working in collaboration with international distributors from the whole of the English-speaking world.

Salt Desert Media Group Ltd. (est. 2019) is a member of the Independent Publishers Guild. At present, the company has two imprints, **Global Resilience Publishing** and **Pippa Rann Books & Media (PRBM).**

PRBM was launched on August the 17th, 2020, with the first title published in Autumn 2020 – Avay Shukla's *PolyTicks, DeMocKrazy & MumboJumbo: Babus, Mantris and Netas (Un)Making Our Nation.*

Since then, we have published:
- Sudhakar Menon's *Seeking God, Seeking Moksha*;
- Sudeep Sen's *Anthropocene: Climate Change, Contagion, Consolation*;
- Brijraj Singh's *In Arden: A Memoir of Four Years in Shillong, 1974 to 1978*;

- Valson Thampu's *Beyond Religion: Imaging a New Humanity*; and
- *Mantras for Positive Ageing*, edited by Padma Shri Dr V. Mohini Giri and Meera Khanna, with a Foreword by H. H. The Dalai Lama.

If there is no further significant disruption by pandemics and wars, PRBM plans to release, in the near future, Jyoti Guptara's *Business Storytelling From Hype to Hack*, Varghese Mathai's *The Village Maestro and 100 Other Stories*, Rashmi Narzary's *An Unfinished Search*, and Anthony P. Stone's *Hindu Astrology: Myths, Symbols and Realities*.

In addition, there are two books especially commissioned for the 75th anniversary of India's independence: Catherine Ann Jones's *East or West: Stories of India*, and *Converse*, an anthology of Indian poetry in English, especially chosen by the international prize-winning poet, Sudeep Sen.

We are always open to first class ideas for books, provided complete manuscripts can be turned in on time.

Please note that Pippa Rann Books & Media focuses entirely and exclusively on publishing material that nurtures, among Indians as well as among others who love India, the values of democracy, justice, liberty, equality, and fraternity.

That means we publish:
- Books and media by authors of Indian origin, on any subject that broadly serves the purpose mentioned above.
- Books and media by non-Indians on any subject connected with India or with the Indian diaspora, which serves the purpose mentioned above - again, broadly interpreted.

* * *

By contrast with PRBM, Global Resilience Publishing began operations in Autumn 2021, with the first publications being released from Summer 2022. As the name suggests, the imprint focuses on subjects such as:
- Climate Change
- The Global Financial System
- Multilateral Governance (e.g., the United Nations)
- Public-Private Partnership
- Leadership around the World
- International System Change
- International Corporate Governance
- Family Firms around the World
- Global Values
- Global Philanthropy
- Commercial Sponsorship
- New Technologies including Artificial Intelligence

Two things make GRP unique as an imprint:
1. Our books take a global perspective (not the perspective of a particular nation);
2. GRP focuses exclusively on such global challenges.

* * *

Global Resilience Publishing and **Pippa Rann Books & Media** are only two of several imprints that are conceived of, and will be launched, God willing, by Salt Desert Media Group Ltd., U. K. The imprints will cover different regions of the globe, different themes, and so on. And if you have an idea for a new imprint that you would like to establish, please get in touch.

Prabhu Guptara, the Publisher of Salt Desert Media Group, says, "For all our imprints, and for the attainment of our incredibly high vision, we need your support. Whatever your gifts and abilities, you are welcome to support us with the most precious gift of your time. The *seva* you do is not for us but is for the sake of our nation, and for the world as a whole. Please email me with your email, location, and phone contact details on *publisher@pipparannbooks.com*, letting me know what you feel you can do. Could you be an organiser or greeter at our events? Could you ring people on our behalf? Write to people? Write guest blogs or articles? Write a regular column? Do interviews?

Help with electronic media, social media, or general marketing? Connect us with people you know who might be willing to help in some way or other?"

He adds, "I am one man, so I do not and cannot keep up with everything that is happening in India, let alone in the world. There are many challenges and numerous opportunities – help me to understand what these are. Pass information on to me that could be useful to me. Put your ideas to me. Any and all insights from you are most welcome, as they will multiply our joint effectiveness. It is only as we work together that we can contribute effectively to changing our nation and our world for the better".

* * *

Join our mailing list to discover Pippa Rann Books which will inform you on a wide range of topics, and inspire as well as equip you as an individual, as a member of your family, and as someone who loves India.

www.pipparannbooks.com